Daughter of Earth

Regine Haensel

SERIMUSE

Daughter of Earth
Book Four of The Leather Book Takes
©Regine Haensel 2022

Interior design by Regine Haensel
Cover photo by Meshon Cantrill
Cover design by Meshon Cantrill
Printed by Amazon.com

Serimuse Books
Saskatoon, Saskatchewan, Canada
booksserimuse@gmail.com

Haensel, Regine, 1948-, author
Daughter of earth / Regine Haensel

(Book four of The leather book tales)
ISBN 978-0-9939032-3-6 (paperback)

I.Title. II.Series: Haensel, Regine, 1948- , Leather book tales; bk. 4.

THE LEATHER BOOK TALES is a fantasy set in western North America. Four powers – fire, water, air and earth – reveal themselves in four young people, triggered and enhanced by a pair of silver bracelets. The young people's abilities increase as they overcome challenges and collaborate against forces that oppose and threaten them. The Leather Book holds old and tangled tales that connect with what is happening to them, but the stories don't reveal all that is behind the events. The young people face risks, not only for themselves but also for their world and its people.

The Leather Book Tales Series
Queen of Fire
Child of Dragons
Companion of Eagles
Daughter of Earth
Time Dancer (forthcoming)

Other books by the same author
(short stories)
The Other Place
A Rain of Dragonflies

Acknowledgements

A book is a product of many years and many hands. For years I've benefited greatly by being a part of the Saskatchewan writing community and a member of the Saskatchewan Writers' Guild.

Special thanks for this volume go to three people who read the book at various stages and made suggestions that proved useful. Eve Barbeau, a talented visual artist as well as a writer, read the book at an early stage and helped me to see a number of areas that required work. RoseAnne Thorpe, a former work colleague and commercial artist read a draft of the book closer to the end and gave me recommendations to improve it. And Martha Mantikoski did an extensive copy edit very near the end. Much thanks to all three!

I'm dedicating this book to the Book Babes, a book club, social gathering, and group of supportive friends who have been with me since before the first book of the series was published.

Daughter of Earth

For the Book Babes

Chapter I

Ali

I woke just now, not sure why, keeping my eyes closed, still feeling sleepy. Images in my mind – rosy sand dunes at sunset, rippling shadows over sand, a long caravan of camels – fragments of a dream or memories? I've seen all those things at one time or another. Wind touches my face, maybe that's what woke me. I must have left the window open; the nights have been hot lately, almost unbearable at times. I wake often when its like this, drink from the ceramic jug that keeps water cool.

Brightness penetrates. When I finally open my eyes, for a moment I'm not sure where I am. Not in my room, and it's night though a lantern gleams beside me. There's a tree at my back, leaves rustling above. I'm in our courtyard by the fig tree. How did I end up out here under the stars,

dressed in my night shift? I've never walked in my sleep before. There are no lights shining from any of the windows
of our house, no sound of voices; the others must all be
deep in dreams. The air is warm but not as bad as it's been.

I'm sitting tailor-fashion, the way my friend Samel always sits. When I glance down, I see the black stone he
gave me, gleaming in my cupped hands, have no idea how
I ended up holding it. I look at the sky, find the familiar
grouping of stars we call The Chariot, a bond to reality. And
yet, I could be dreaming all this, dreams within dreams.

For some reason I recall night festivals when the gates
of the city are left open, watch fires are built, and people
walk out into the desert. Those times often feel dreamlike,
enchanted. Itinerant costumed performers dance, drum
and sing. Hawkers call out their wares, while the aroma of
cooked meat, pastries and other foods wafts from booths
set up here and there. Samel and I would stroll together
with our families, chatting, and laughing.

Where is Samel now? There was so much I should
have said to him before he left for the mountains, but the
time never seemed right, and I couldn't find the words. We
didn't see much of each other toward the end, and when we
did, we argued. I should have tried harder.

The black stone, smoothed by time, perhaps wind and
water, sits warmly in my hands. Samel gave me this piece
of obsidian just before he left, a quick good-bye. Maybe it
was a sort of apology. I should have found the words then.

I stare into the shiny darkness of the stone, think of
my friend's dark eyes when he smiled, the gold flecks in
the brown irises. Is there a glimmer of fire in the depths of
the stone? Obsidian comes from fire mountains. A shiver
trembles across my shoulders. I blink and look again at the

night sky where stars flicker. We do occasionally have earthquake tremors here, but that didn't feel like one. I do and don't want to believe that the stone has powers. Samel found it in the dungeon of the old sorcerer who held Samel, his father, and sister prisoner for a while last year.

"Think of me when you hold it," Samel said, "and I'll think of you. Maybe just before we go to sleep each night. It will be a way to keep connected while I'm away."

I asked him if he meant that we could see and talk to each other the way he and his sister do using their magical silver bracelets. He said that we could try. He couldn't have been too annoyed with me if he wanted that.

I wish I could see Samel right now, talk to him.

The stone feels heavier in my hands and my eyes are drawn to its darkness. I see no light anywhere; has the lantern gone out, have the stars been covered by clouds? I blink, try to look away from the stone, but nothing changes. What if I can't get away from this? Sweat runs down my face, I'm finding it hard to breath.

Gradually I'm aware of a shimmer, like heat rising in the desert, faint at first, like the beginning of sunrise, and then gradually brighter and brighter. I squint against the light. A dark shape forms, familiar. Samel hovers in front of me, his feet not touching the ground.

"Ali, how did I get here?" he asks. "I went to bed in the tower room of Grandfather Frog's house."

"I think it's the stone," I say. "The piece of obsidian you gave me."

And then his face and body begin to fade, blowing away like mist on a windy morning. I reach out to grab for his hand, but it's too late. The stars disappear.

***

I wake staring into the predawn shadows of my room. It's real this time. Grope under my pillow, pull out the stone. It looks and feels ordinary. No matter how long I stare at it no visions come. I wish I could see the rock collection, be with Samel at the house in Schönspitze. Find out more about Grandfather Frog. If all that was true.

Does Samel know his sister is back from her journey to the east? He didn't mention her. Maybe I should have but there was so little time. I can't help thinking that if Rowan had returned sooner Samel might not have gone away. I know it's not fair to blame her for how things changed after she first came, but they did. Maybe it was because she brought the news that their mother had recently died. It was a shock because Samel's Papa had always told him she died long ago. Then, after Rowan left again, Samel was restless, and his cousin Thea's arrival didn't help. She wanted Rowan to go off to the mountains with her, but of course, Rowan wasn't here anymore. So Samel went instead.

I can't decide if I like Rowan or not. She came back with a boy, well a young man really. Good looking. I think he's a bit older than she is, and she's sixteen or seventeen. Maybe she's thinking of getting wed, like my sister, Magenta. That's just guesswork, so it's good I didn't say anything to Samel. Mère doesn't like us to gossip.

What would Mère or Père think if I told them that I saw Samel in a vision? Probably not much. Père dreams works of art now and then, tries to reproduce them, not always successfully. Making art has its ups and downs. Like life I guess, or friendship. Just now my room has no murals on the walls, no paintings, sketches or other work lying around. Haven't felt like doing much since Samel left.

He and I have been friends since we were tiny daubs of paint on the picture of life. I heard Père say that once about Mère. The person he was talking to looked at him cross-eyed, unsure what he meant. I feel a lot like a tiny smear in an unfinished painting right now. It's so easy for a smudge like that to get painted over or wiped away.

We're not the only artists in this city, of course. Samel and his father are musicians. In the market you can find weavers, potters, people who supply art materials, traders who bring in all kinds of crafts and creations. The variety is one of the things I like about Aquila, and I thought Samel did too. But before he left, he talked a lot about wanting to see more of the world, like his sister. Someday I'd like to travel. I've imagined Samel and me going off together.

A crack of thunder startles me. Rain begins to drum on the roof of my bedroom. We've had an unusual amount of rain the last while. Everyone in Aquila has been talking about our odd weather – searing heat one day and unrelenting downpour the next. It started several days after the caravan Samel joined left for the mountains. Could there be a connection?

So many strange things started happening around the time Samel found out he had a sister. I had weird dreams; Samel found the bracelet. And then Samel and his father were magically transported to that castle. I don't think I'd have wanted to go back to mountains where I'd been held prisoner not so long ago. Schönspitze, where Samel is now, might not be anywhere near the old sorcerer's home though. I've never travelled away from Aquila, so I don't know.

The black stone seems suddenly heavier in my hand. It's cold and doesn't gleam the way it did last night in my dream. Samel said the stone made him think of home when he found it, gave him hope when they were trapped because it was like the obsidian the Lord's Militia use for their arrowheads. My sister Magenta's man serves in the militia, and I've seen some of the arrows that he uses. He has ones with black tips like my stone, though his favourites are the colour of mahogany. One of the stone and gem sellers in the market told me that he's seen blue and grey obsidian as well.

Stones are fascinating: their varied shapes and textures, the surprises inside a few when you split them. Though most of the houses in Aquila are of sundried brick, parts of the palace, its walls and paths are of stone. Père and other artists grind some stones for pigments. It's amazing how many colours stones can hold – black and white, cinnabar, yellow and rose, emerald, terra cotta, variegated and speckled, marble and granite, sandstone and gems. But this piece of obsidian made me uneasy as soon as I saw it. Maybe because it came from the dungeon of the castle. Even before Samel gave it to me I asked if the old man, the sorcerer who held them prisoner, could have put a spell on him. I thought it might explain his restlessness and irritability.

"He's dead," Samel said. "Rowan killed him because he wouldn't let us go."

I knew that, of course. Samel had told me the story soon after they got back to Aquila. It was all mixed up with the magical silver bracelets of ivy leaves which had helped them find each other. Besides using his bracelet to talk to his sister at a distance, Samel can create a breeze with it. I have no idea how that works. He thought there was more to learn about them, but Rowan didn't like using hers much after if helped her kill the old man. Samel said that the silver bands didn't always work as he expected, which I considered worrisome, but he didn't. He said that he'd try more things to figure them out but hadn't learned any more about them by the time he left. At least he didn't tell me if he did.

For a while, I kept the black stone on the table in my room. Still didn't trust it no matter what Samel said. How did we know that remnants of the old sorcerer's magic might not remain in the stone, even though he was supposedly dead now? In stories sorcerers sometimes come back to life.

After Samel left, I kept thinking of what he'd said about us connecting with each other through the stone. I wanted that. One day I tried carrying the stone in my pocket. Nothing weird happened and I didn't feel any different. I even asked Mère if I was acting oddly, just to check, because you might not know yourself if you were.

She frowned at me and put her hand on my forehead. "Have you got a fever?" she asked. "You look a little flushed."

"No, I'm all right," I said. "Just missing Samel."

"Ah," she said, and gave me a hug.

The hug was nice. I guess she expected me to be fine after that because she went back to her weaving and ignored me. Mostly in my family we're used to paying no attention to each other if we're in the middle of an art project. But this time I wanted Mère to notice that I felt sad.

Anyway, that night I had a dream about riding a camel through the desert under the stars and a bright moon. I could see another camel far ahead, but I couldn't catch up to it. When I woke, I didn't want to get out of bed, thinking of Samel getting farther and farther away. But I also thought maybe the obsidian was working to show me Samel, and that was good. I could have been wrong about it being bad. I made a little leather pouch for the stone and wore it around my neck under my tunic. That helped me to feel closer to my friend.

I had no more dreams about Samel after that, so one evening a few days later, after everyone else had gone to bed, I snuck out and sat under the lemon tree by the light of the moon. Moonlight helps Samel's bracelet work, and I thought it might do the same for the stone. I held it in my hands and closed my eyes. Thought of Samel, pictured his face, his red hair. And there he was, right in front of me, smiling at me! I smiled back, and then he was gone. I tried for a while to see him again, but it didn't happen. After that I put the stone under my pillow before going to bed, but nothing happened until last night.

I open my door a crack to check on the rain; it's still sheeting down. Hard to tell exactly what time it is. What if the old man's spells are responsible for our strange weather even if he is dead? Maybe spells can linger after the person who cast them is dead. Should I destroy the stone? Or am I just thinking crazy thoughts? I don't know who I could ask about what's normal for sorcerers. He had a wife and daughter, too, who I think are living in his castle now. What if the two women are involved in the dead sorcerer's plans to take over the city of Aquila? That's what Samel said the old man wanted to do. I know the ruler of Aquila, Lord Davo, has soothsayers and others who protect us, as well as the militia and our guardian eagles, but do they know all the details about the sorcerer? I hope that Samel and his family gave a full report.

My stomach rumbles. Whatever time it is and even if our cook isn't up, there'll be food in the kitchen. Because of the rain, I walk quickly and quietly along the interior halls instead of dashing across the courtyard. I find Père sitting at the table munching a banana. Besides the bowl of fruit, there's a loaf of fresh bread, so I get a knife to cut myself a slice and grab the jug of honey and a spoon.

"Bonjour gloomy face," Père says. "Why do you look like a morose camel?"

"Rain," I respond shortly, chomping a big bite of bread and honey.

"The rain will stop, and besides in this land, rain is a blessing."

"Yah," I mumble.

I want to say that my best friend is gone, mon Père, and I miss him. Why can't you tell me you understand that? But I don't say any of it, because Père has finished his banana and is arranging the peel in different patterns, probably thinking about an art venture he's planning. I hope it's not a collage made of fruit peelings. I keep eating bread and honey. He grabs a fig and chews. I'm thinking of asking him what he knows about sorcerers when he stands.

"Rain or no rain, I need a few things from the market," he says. "Viens avec moi? You could buy pigments or other painting supplies. I'll give you the money."

I shake my head; the thought of wandering the market without Samel doesn't appeal today, even though I love looking at all the art materials. Not long after Père leaves, Mère and my sister Ivoire enter the kitchen.

"We're going to Magenta's," Ivoire says, bouncing to the table to snatch an apricot from the bowl, "and make plans for her baby."

"You want to come?" Mère asks.

I shake my head. "Things to do here. I'll see Magenta another day."

After the two of them have left, I wander through the house, my steps echoing. The cook isn't anywhere; she must have gone out earlier. Now that I'm alone here it doesn't feel that good and I can't settle to anything. The rain and the grey skies make all the rooms seem even smaller. Stupid of me not to realize I need company when I'm missing my friend.

I should have gone with Père, or Mère and Ivoire. I stand for a while at a front window looking across the street at Samel's house. No matter how long I stare at it he's not going to emerge.

I suppose I could cross the street and see if Rowan is home. We did spend time together at the opening of the arts school and she seemed all right then. It wasn't until the river almost flooded and she and her new friend stopped it that I got a bit scared of her. Anyone who could do that might do a lot more, not necessarily good. She did kill a man.

What would I say to Rowan though? Hello, I just talked to your brother in a dream? And I didn't have time to find out very much? Do you have any news of him? I shrug my doubts away because not knowing about what's going on with Samel is worse than anything. And maybe a sister will know about her brother, even if she didn't grow up with him.

It doesn't take long to get to our front door. I open it and stare out. No one is in the street, but no wonder with rain still pouring down. Père probably holed up in an inn or tavern, drinking ale and waiting for the down pour to stop, engrossed in intense discussion with one or more of his cronies. I'd have been bored. It's not far to my sister's house where Mère, Ivoire and Magenta will be talking about the baby, discussing room decorations and what clothes to make. That doesn't appeal to me either. Poor me. Ugh, I hate it when I get like this.

I can't tell from here if anyone's home across the street. Their Papa has been spending a lot of time working at the arts school, just like Mère and Père. Rowan might be out with her young man. No way of knowing unless I check, and I need to do something.

Grabbing a hooded cloak and taking a deep breath, I race the short distance and pound on their door. No answer. I stand there for a while, getting wet. Knock again with no result. Head home, retreat to my room. I've never felt so alone before. I lie on my pallet thinking of Samel until I fall asleep.

**

I've never seen mountains, never travelled in them, but this must be where I am, surrounded by high peaks and evergreen trees. It's raining here, too, just like in Aquila except the rain is white flakes. Wait! This must be snow. I've heard tell of it. Wind whips the snow around and I can't see very well. Anyone or anything could be out there, creeping up on me. Is there a dark shadow hanging over one of the mountains?

I wake to slamming doors and voices. My family have returned. There'll be food and chatter and projects to work on. I might even try a small painting.

**

The next morning a brilliant sun dries up any puddles that remain from our recent storm. Already the air is hot and humid. I feel vaguely worried about Samel, remembering my mountain dream from yesterday.

I'm not hungry yet and the house is quiet. I think about what I could paint on the walls of my room. Before he left Samel asked me why I covered the old murals of him and his sister with white.

"I got tired of sleeping among them," I said.

The truth is, I painted over them one night after Samel and I had another argument. He was so bad tempered those days before he left, and destroying those murals was a kind of revenge. Besides, I'd had enough of looking at pictures of his sister, who he always seemed to be worrying and talking about.

I jump out of bed and start low in one corner with a few charcoal sketches, straight lines and curves to represent buildings. I'll create Samel's journey to the mountains, the way I imagine it, starting with the city of Aquila. I pull out brushes and my pigment kit. I'll mix blue for a wash of the sky. It's best to start with small batches because pigments are expensive. A blob or two of ultramarine and a bit of white. It seems too pale, so I add a lick of black. Before I know it, I've got silver and that's no good for the sky, so I try a small ivy leaf at the edge of the wall, just like the ones on Samel's bracelet. When I stand back, it's hardly visible. Still it's comforting to see it there, so I add another and another, making a row across the wall. Could be a border.

I'm standing back, trying to decide what to do next when I hear footsteps, voices. A sudden thump on my door and my younger sister Ivoire's voice tells me the morning meal is ready.

When I reach the kitchen, Mère exclaims, "You've been painting!"

I look down and notice the spatters on my tunic. "Just doodling."

"We started a mural for Magenta's baby yesterday," Ivoire says. "Too bad you weren't there." She sticks her tongue out at me. "It's going to be a collage, with paint and bits of cloth, shells, and shiny things stuck to the wall."

I ignore her and help myself to chewy bread and a tangy spreadable cheese.

"I hope you washed your hands after painting," Mère says.

I don't say a word and concentrate on eating because I didn't wash my hands. I'm too old to be treated like a little girl. Père munches steadily, probably thinking about his latest artistic endeavour. Mère and Ivoire keep chatting, interrupted now and then by the cook when she brings in more food. I think about ivy leaves and black stones. They are similar because both come from the ground – silver ore was once rock. I have no idea what silver ore looks like. Someone at the market would probably have some. I excuse myself after a while, full of food, and sated with hearing others talk.

My room feels stuffy, so I open my door to the courtyard. A breeze rattles the olive and lemon trees and sun glints on the leaves. What is it like where Samel is now? Is Schönspitze as large a city as Aquila? I hope he'll come home soon. We could sit in our garden together or wander through the city, spend time at the river or the sand shrine while he tells me of his adventures. A huge sigh whooshes out of me.

I bend to gather leaves and bits of bark from our trees. Take them back into my room and use globs of green and brown paint to attach them to the wall. Sketch in a few more trees, but my heart's not in it. My skin prickles and itches. I drop the charcoal stick onto the table, wipe my hands on a damp cloth.

Sitting on my pallet, I pull at the ties that hold the leather pouch under my thin short-sleeved tunic. Fumble out the piece of obsidian. It feels warm today, sticky. I hold the stone in my cupped hands, close my eyes and think of Samel. A sudden flare jerks my eyelids up, but my room is still shady. I stare down at the stone, glimpsing fleeting shadows and sparks. As I bend closer, I feel as if I'm moving forward into darkness, but there is light there too, in the distance. The world shakes and rumbles as ahead of me a dark mountain erupts with smoke and flame. I sense someone beside me and turn.

"Samel."

The earth shudders under our feet. Samel is closer to the mountain and farther from me. "Samel," I call, "Be careful!"

A shadow rises and covers everything.

I realize that my eyes are closed. When I open them, my room looks just the same, though it feels chilly. The stone in my hands is a cool, impenetrable blackness. I tuck it back into its pouch and rub my shivering arms. Pull a blanket from the foot of my pallet and wrap it around my shoulders. I've got to talk to someone about these dreams and visions, about my uneasiness. In the past I would have talked to Mère or Père, but not this time. I'm not sure why; it just doesn't feel right.

Quietly I leave our house and cross the street. Stand in front of the door. She's his sister and I don't like her that much, but she might know more about what he's doing than I do. Or she could find out. I knock softly on the door. If they are sleeping it won't disturb them, but if anyone's up, they'll hear. The door opens.

"Ali," Rowan says.

Chapter II

Rowan

A li clears her throat. "I'm not disturbing you?" Her hair is dishevelled, and her tunic fastened crookedly. I've never seen her quite this messy.

"No," I answer, though I'd prefer to shut the door in her face. I don't want company right now, have been reading some of Mother's old notes about healing herbs. But it's best to be polite, so I step aside and gesture her in. "I've been up for a while. Father's still asleep though, so we'll be quiet as mice. He had a late concert at the palace last night."

I lead her into the kitchen, pull out a chair for her at the table. She looks around and then sits. She must have been here often with Samel, but she seems uncomfortable, as if it's strange to her now that he's not here. I don't know her well at all, though Samel talked about her all the time when we were both here. I've always thought she didn't like me. So why has she come for a visit?

"Would you like some tisane?" I ask, continuing to be polite, as my mother taught me. "I've just made a pot of red leaf. I discovered it this last journey in Vatnborg, and I quite like it. Brought some back, but don't know if I'll be able to buy it in the market here." I realize I'm babbling and stop. Let her tell me in her own time what she wants.

"You can get most things in the market," Ali says. "And yes, I'll try some."

I pour tisane into ceramic beakers for each of us. She's staring at me. Have I got dirt on my face? I was cleaning earlier. Woke and couldn't go back to sleep. Is that sadness in her eyes? How close are she and my brother anyway, and why doesn't she speak?

"Is there something I can do for you?" I ask after we've each taken our first sips.

"Umm, well, I was thinking about when you and Samel see and talk to each other. With the bracelets. You know he told me about that?"

"Yes. Neither of us have told many people. But you are his oldest friend." I'm not particularly happy that she knows about the bracelets. Our parents thought they were dangerous, and though I'm convinced they acted wrongly about them, I'm certain Samel isn't cautious enough with his. And our father doesn't like us using them at all.

"So how does it work? Do you mind telling me? Do you ever get feelings about how he's doing, worry about him?"

I stop with the beaker halfway to my mouth. Set it back on the table and stare at her. I feel suddenly cold.

"What's happened?"

She clears her throat. "Do you remember a black stone? One that Samel pried out of the dungeon when you were held prisoner?"

I half close my eyes thinking back. I don't really like to recall our time as prisoners in the castle and a lot of those memories are hazy. But I do remember being locked in a dungeon room with Samel early on. "Vaguely." I lean toward her. "Has something happened to my brother?"

She shakes her head. "Not as far as I know. I came to find out if you'd heard anything."

"Heard what? What's this really about? Why are you here?" I know I sound cross, but I don't care. Why can't she just say what she means?

"That piece of obsidian. It reminded him of the arrowheads of the Lord's Militia. He gave it to me before he left this time."

"Spit it out, can't you?" One of my knees is jiggling and I stop it by pressing my foot hard against the floor.

She jerks once, then stares across the kitchen as she speaks. "For some reason he thought the stone might work for us, him and me, the same as the bracelets do for the two of you."

There's a roiling in my belly. This is heading in a direction I definitely don't like. "And it has?" If Samel is talking across distance again, I don't want Father to find out.

Ali nods. "I had one real vision, a dream maybe, where he told me that he was in Schönspitze and that he'd sent the eagle that appeared at the arts school opening." She stops and fumbles at her neckline, then drops her hands to the table and looks down at them.

"But that's not all. If it was you wouldn't be here."

She sighs hugely. "I've had fragments of dreams about shadows, and fire spewing out of mountains. You haven't talked to Samel recently?"

All this could be just ordinary nightmares and worries; I want it to be that. Don't want to think about the troubles the bracelets brought us. A magical stone to add to the mix is not something I want to contemplate. Why did my brother have to involve her?

"I did talk to him once," I say, "not long after they got to Schönspitze. I asked him how their travels had gone, whether anything strange happened when they passed near Hrashak's castle. He said everything was fine."

"Hrashak. That's the old sorcerer who held you all prisoner, right?"

"Yes. He's dead, but his wife and daughter are living in the castle now. His wife left him long ago and his daughter didn't know her mother was still alive." I take a sip of tisane to wet my lips and tongue. "Too much like my life and Samel's. Anyway, I don't think we need to worry about them."

"Are you sure? How do you know?"

"The woman, Julina, sort of helped me on my way when I was searching for Samel and our father."

"Sort of helped you?"

"I could never make up my mind about her," I say reluctantly. "And then there's her son from Aquila. Is he helping her in some way?"

"What?" Ali leans forward. "I didn't know she had a son here. You've met him?"

"He was with the caravan when I travelled east. His father, Julina's second husband, is or was a merchant and horse dealer here in Aquila. I didn't know about the connections at first."

"It seems complicated. There are a couple of horse breeders in Aquila that I know of. You say 'was.' Are the father and son not here now?

I get up to fetch the pot and pour us both more tisane. My feet want to walk, but I can't just get out of the house and leave her here. I hope that our father will stay asleep. He's not good about all this, will not be happy if there's more things to worry about. I'm not keen about it myself. Why couldn't Samel have left that stone in the dungeon? Still, I'd better try to get as much information from Ali as I can. Maybe if I tell her some things she'll be more open herself.

I sit back down. "Remember the rainstorm at the arts school opening? The river almost flooded?" She nods. "I think Jernan, the son, might have had something to do with that. But I haven't seen either the son or the father since. They might have been swept away by the flood, or be lying low, or even left the city."

Ali rubs her arms as if she's cold. Which she shouldn't be because the sun is finally shining, and the temperature of this house is comfortable. Strangely, I'm feeling chilled, too.

"None of this sounds good," she says slapping the table. "Does the Lord know? Is anyone doing anything about it? I've been worried. There must be something in the air and I'm sensing it. I had dreams before, you know, when Samel first found the bracelet. They were about you, even before he knew you existed."

"He told me."

Ali grimaces. "We've got to do something. Tell someone at the palace."

I wrap my hands around the cooling beaker, tighten my fingers as I think of the man we consulted who was worse than useless. "There's a soothsayer called Tristicus. My father brought him here after I got back from the east. I told him my worries about Jernan and Julina, son and mother. He said he'd keep an eye on things."

"You didn't think much of him," Ali says. "I can tell by the way you're squeezing that cup."

"He said there was a flock of ravens hanging around Hrashak's former castle. Nothing else strange was going on."

"And you believed him?"

"About the ravens, yes. I'd had the same information from someone I trusted more. Knowing the ravens were there made me feel better. I had a tame raven once and was told he flew to the castle to keep watch."

Ali gets up and walks back and forth. She's got the same restlessness that I feel. "It's all strange, and not enough. I want to know what else is going on, what's being done to protect Samel!"

"As far as I know, Samel isn't in any danger. He's in Schönspitze, which is quite a distance from the castle, and he hasn't had any trouble from that direction."

"But you haven't spoken to him for a while. What about my visions and dreams?"

"From what I saw of Tristicus, he's not going to take those seriously."

Ali stops and sits again, leaning toward me over the table. "What do you know about sorcerers and their spells? Could spells last after death? What if our weird weather is a result of spells?" She shakes her head, sending wisps of hair flying. "There's too much going on."

"I don't know much about sorcerers at all. And I don't understand about the weather. How does that fit in?"

Ali shakes her head. "Never mind. I have to find someone who knows about sorcerers. And quickly." She leaps to her feet and heads for the front door.

"Ali," I say, "wait." But she's already gone.

I put away Ali's cup and refill the pot of tisane leaves with more hot water. The most useful thing to do right now would be to get out my bracelet and try to connect with my brother but I'm reluctant. For one thing, Father won't like it, and he might be getting up any minute. For another, I haven't liked using the bracelet since it helped me kill the old sorcerer. Even though it was useful on my journey back from Vatnborg, I still don't quite trust it. Also, I don't know how much of Ali's ravings to believe. Yes, she apparently had dreams about me before Samel knew he had a sister. But the recent dreams and visions she talked about could just be an overactive imagination.

"Rowan. You're up early." Father smiles at me as he enters the kitchen. He pours himself a cup of tisane and sits across the table from me. It still amazes me that I'm here with him.

"The early morning sun shining in my window woke me."

"We could buy a piece of cloth to make a curtain."

"Hmm. It's a relief to have sunshine, though, after the downpour."

"Yes, we continue to have an unusual amount of rain," he says. "There's a lot of talk about that at the palace. The soothsayers keep going into huddles."

"Oh? Do they have any ideas about the weather?"

"If they do, they don't share them openly. Some of the other musicians and I have been talking about writing several pieces of weather music."

"What's weather music?"

"Just music that would represent weather. You know, thunder drums, rain on the harp and so on."

"What about sunshine? How would you make that sound?"

Papa smiles. "I'm sure I and the other the composers can come up with something. Now, what about breakfast? I think there's still bread, honey, and fruit. After that do you want to come with me to the arts school? I think they want you to pick a space for an herb garden and lay it out."

"I'd like that."

Ali's visit and the worries she raised are at the back of my mind, but I don't know her very well. She could be missing Samel, worrying for nothing, making it up to feel important. The last time I talked to Samel, he said he was all right. I'm certainly not going to worry Father about this.

Chapter III

Ali

Tacitus. No, Tristicus. Tristicus. I repeat the name to myself as I hurry up the cobblestone street to the palace. They may not let me in and the soothsayer might not be there, or he may not agree to see me, but I have to try.

To the right our street leads to the palace where the Lord's soothsayers work. Samel pointed out their red clay-coloured tower to me once when he had an errand to run for his father and took me along. When I reach the walls and turrets rising out of elm, cypress, palms and other trees, I remember that Samel always says it looks as if the trees and walls have been planted and grown all of a piece. I don't get to see the inside of the palace grounds as often as he does. Though my parents are well known artists in Aquila, neither of them is one of the Lord's special artists as Samel's papa is among the favoured musicians. Still, Samel has taken me there now and then on his errands, and I've been to performances inside, so I know which gate to use.

I approach the small side entrance to the left of the larger gate. A single man of the militia in his black leather armour and crimson cloak stands on guard by the pale grey door. He's looking straight ahead, feet spread, hands on his sword belt. Even when I'm standing right in front of him, he says nothing and doesn't look at me. I know that a few women are part of the militia and I wish that one of them guarded this gate today; I'd feel a little less scared. Still, I've got to try.

I cough a couple of times to get his attention. "Um, excuse me, I'm the daughter of Patrice, the artist?"

At my father's name, the guard turns his eyes to my face. "Yes?"

"I um have a message for the soothsayer, Tristicus. Is he here?"

"I'll ask." The guard opens the gate and speaks words I can't hear to someone I can't see.

He's probably assumed the message is from my father. Now I just have to hope the soothsayer is here and will see me. If he isn't, they'll probably ask what the message is. I wipe sweat from my brow. Is it getting hotter or is it just worry?

The guard closes the gate and comes back to stand in front of me. "Tristicus is not here and we're not sure when he'll return. If you leave the message with me, I'll make sure he gets it."

"That's all right," I say. "I'll come back later."

The sound of the fountain in our courtyard soothes my agitation as I enter. It's cooler here. But I'm annoyed that I couldn't see the soothsayer and hope he doesn't come by to see Père to ask about the message. What was I thinking? Maybe I shouldn't even have talked to Rowan since she didn't seem to take me seriously.

Ivoire hunches under the olive tree, rummaging in our small wooden box of odds and ends. Mère said she started the collection when my sister, Magenta, was small. First it was many-coloured buttons and odd bits of cloth, things that little ones could play with and not damage, though Ivoire did swallow a button once. Thankfully, she's long beyond putting odds and ends in her mouth. The collection grew to include valueless jewellery, scraps of leather, broken toys. A rattle and clink of chains along with a sound like fingernails scraping on metal falls on my ears and makes me grit my teeth.

I move forward. "Ivoire! Do you have to be so noisy?"

She sticks her tongue out. "Go inside if you don't like it. Anyway, there's nothing here I can use. I need to go to the market, the street of metal workers. Maybe other vendors, too."

I know that Mère won't let her go alone. "It's too hot in the streets to go out right now. What is it you're looking for?"

"I told you before," she hisses impatiently, "I want to create a musical instrument for our courtyard that the wind can play."

"And you really can't find anything in there? Let me see."

I pull the box toward me. It's been a while since I explored it, and there's things I've forgotten or never seen. Several varicoloured pebbles probably from by the river; Samel and I used to go there often. A few clam and snail shells with sand clinging to them.

I love anything that comes out of the earth, anything you can make paint from like plants or even beetles. I don't kill beetles to make paint, though, just pick up dead ones that are the right variety. My great aunt, Grande 'Tante Rochella, taught me about the things you can gather that are useful in painting. She said that when she was a girl she used to dig in the earth, was dirty all the time. I loved that about her, and I miss her since she died. Most girls think I'm crazy picking up dead insects, but at least my sisters understand, and so does Samel.

The box also holds lots of cloth scraps of varying sizes. Several broken necklaces lie jumbled among small pieces of rough amethyst as well as wooden pegs and discs. I pull out a thin silvery linked chain.

"This might do. You could fasten shells and pebbles to it. Use thin branches or other bits of wood to create tiers."

The links glint in the sunlight, flash into my eyes. I see him sitting on a rock, looking surprised.

"Samel?"

And then he's gone.

"Why are you talking about Samel?" Ivoire asks.

"Hmm?" I shake my head. "It was the chain. I think he might have given it to me." He looked all right, and I didn't get a sense of any danger.

"No, he didn't! That belonged to Magenta. I remember because she got it for one of her birthdays and I wanted one just like it."

"Fine! Your memory is better than mine. Now go away. I want to think."

"No, I was here first. You go."

Without another word I do. I walk through the courtyard, down the hall and out the front door, turning to the left this time. Don't care that Ivoire wants to go to the metal workers' street. Don't care that it's hot. I need to be by myself and think about Samel, why I'm seeing him so often now in dreams or visions. I walk fast, turning into the first right hand street I find, then left, then right again, so that even if Ivoire follows, she will have a hard time finding me.

The obsidian stone hangs in its leather pouch around my neck, hidden under my tunic. I have a strong urge to take it out to see if it can help me see Samel again, to talk to him, but there's too many people around. I head in the direction of the sand shrine. The shrine itself is always guarded now, by two of the Lord's Militia because that's where Samel and his papa were snatched by the sorcerer. I don't want to go there. But not far from the shrine there's an olive grove where Samel and I used to sit to try things with the bracelets. It always seemed a quiet and safe place.

It's been weeks since he left, and I still miss him. I know he wanted so much to see his mother's city, and his mother's cousin was willing to take him. But a part of me wishes I'd had the courage to ask to go along.

I'm brave usually. Climbed my first tree at the age of five – a small one, but it got everyone yelling and Mère crying. When I cut my foot, a few years ago wading in the river and it hurt so bad and bled like anything, I didn't scream or cry. Just wrapped it in a piece of cloth torn from my tunic, hobbled to the nearest house, and waited for a healer.

But I couldn't bring myself to ask Samel if I could go with him to the mountains. Maybe because I feared he or his mother's cousin would say no, or that my parents would refuse to let me go. And then what would I do? Yes, I argue with Mère and Père now and then, but for the really important things I do what they want. I wish now that I had asked though, taken the chance. Everyone might have agreed, and I'd be there with him and know what's going on.

The streets are crowded now with people of all ages and in all sorts of clothes. I love the rich palette of Aquilan life. Samel used to like it, but lately he seemed bored or impatient with it. In a moment I smell baking. I've reached Samel's and my favourite bakery in the market, a small store squeezed between larger buildings. Mmmm, honey cakes with almonds, and cinnamon. It's been a while since breakfast. Luckily, the store isn't busy, so I get to the counter right away.

Lucinda, the baker's sister, smiles at me. "What can I get for you?"

"A couple of almond paste cookies, please."

"I haven't seen you for a while," Lucinda says as she wraps the cookies in a piece of banana leaf. "How are you?"

"Missing Samel. How about you?"

"I'm very well. My brother's giving me more work, so I'm saving for my wedding. But I miss seeing Samel, too. I heard he went to the mountains?" She hands me the cookies.

I pass over the right coins. "Yes, he went to meet some of his mother's relatives. When's your wedding?"

"No idea. I don't even have an intended yet!"

"Oh. Well, good luck."

As I leave the bakery nibbling a cookie, I'm wondering if Lucinda is sweet on Samel. She's too old for him, though, at least two or three years older. Because I'm distracted, I bump into a woman wearing black leather armour. She mumbles a short apology and dashes away into the crowd.

She wasn't wearing the Lord's eagle insignia so she couldn't have been militia. As I rub the shoulder she bashed and brush off cookie crumbs from the front of my tunic, I wonder who she is. Maybe I'll see her again some time and can ask her. Anyway, the other cookie is safe and whole in my belt pouch. I'll eat it later.

Even though I started off to be alone, the market entices me as usual. I can never ignore the stalls that hold art supplies – brushes, paint pots, grinding stones, ground pigments, resins and oils, parchment, reed papers, painting cloths, wood and stone for carving. A few stalls sell a variety of things, but most specialize. Many of the sellers know me and my family. They smile and draw my attention to a brush made of camel hair or a jar of resin for varnishing paintings. I don't see anything really new or unusual today, so finally I tear myself away and leave the market after buying a small skin of water – the day is getting much hotter.

I drink half the water as I walk. There are wells scattered all over Aquila so I can fill the skin again as I need to. I should have brought a jug or waterskin with me from home, but luckily, I had enough coin. I eat my last cookie just as I reach the olive grove. I've got a touch of headache and hope that time in the shade will make it go away.

Goats of all colours and sizes wearing bells wander about among low hummocks and piles of rock scattered throughout the grove. They nibble on leaves, even climbing into low branches to reach more greenery. I settle under a tree, lean against its rough trunk, and watch the goats, listening to the chiming music. Each goat owner has bells with unique shapes and tones so that even if the goats wander far, they can usually find them by the sound. Boys herd the goats together in the evening and take them home to pens for overnight. I might sketch the goats some time, though I haven't the materials with me now.

On the ground nearby lie grey, brown, pink, and white pebbles and larger stones. Some of them are granite, I know, but others I'm not sure about. My Grande Tante would have known them all. A couple of goats draw near and sniff toward my hands. Probably scenting the almond cookies.

"Sorry," I say quietly, "I've nothing for you to eat."

The goats wander off, bleating, and I take the obsidian stone out of its pouch. I press it against my forehead, letting the coolness of the stone penetrate and soothe my headache. There are women who use stones for healing, though I don't have any idea which stones. Grande Tante Rochella used to talk about it, though Mère says it's very chancy. I close my eyes and take deep breaths. The distant tinkle of goat bells fades away, and a breeze ruffles my hair.

After a while I can't feel the tree anymore, nor the ground underneath, though there's still a cool spot in the middle of my forehead. Am I floating on air? That's how the sorcerer transported Samel and his father. I'm tempted to open my eyes, but do I really want to see if I'm up in the sky? Despite my nervousness, coolness and calm spreads from the centre of my forehead through my body. I decide to trust, to not worry about floating or how I might get down. It's not totally dark behind my eyes, so I must still be outside in the sunlight. I keep holding the stone against my forehead, though my fingers are cramping. The breeze around me strengthens, flapping the sleeves of my tunic; I feel as if I'm moving. Gradually the light lessens, and then I settle into darkness. I sense a surface below me harder than the ground under the olive trees.

I take deep breaths, and when it feels right, open my eyes. All is black, not a glimmer of light anywhere. I'm not frightened, though. Whatever has happened, vision or reality, I feel safe. I shift my hand with the stone from my forehead and hold it in front of me in both my cupped hands. Stretch and wriggle my fingers to ease the cramps and breathe in air that holds the scent of damp stone.

Gradually the obsidian begins to gleam, allowing me to see my hands, but nothing beyond that. Am I inside something, a cave? There are no caves in or near Aquila. I could be inside a building with no windows. Am I alone or is there a presence?

"Samel?" I say, though there's no reason he would be here. I just want him to be.

The word echoes, then fades away. There is no other sound. I move the stone to my lips, close my eyes, and whisper, "Be safe, Samel."

"Safe," reverberates around me.

I open my eyes again. The stone still shines in my hands. Around me other points of light begin to glimmer, like tiny stars, bits of crystal, perhaps, in rocks – white, green, red. Something brushes across my shoulders, but when I reach back, there's nothing. Just a breeze probably. It dies away and I strain my eyes to see.

The points of brightness increase. There's a sudden flash and then a brief rainbow dances across the darkness – crimson, indigo, viridian. A painting in light. I laugh and more lights dance – white and silver this time. It makes me think of Samel's bracelet. Magic. What is happening to me?

A breeze rises again, stronger this time and my body is moving once more, without me doing anything to make it happen. Lights flash every which way, making me feel a bit dizzy and like throwing up, so I close my eyes and keep them that way. When I think that I've stopped moving and more light begins to penetrate, I open my eyes.

I'm sitting in the olive grove again; no one is nearby and goats graze in the distance. I take deep breaths, wishing Samel were with me. I want to tell him about this; I'm sure he had no idea of the strange things that could happen with the stone. That must be what's doing this; it's the only thing that's different in my life. I still don't know if I really moved or if I just had a vision. Maybe I should be frightened, worrying about the dead sorcerer's influence, but the more I spend time with the stone and use it, the safer I feel.

It's like painting, trying out different things, making discoveries. I don't remember my first attempts with paint, though Mère has told me how she mixed vegetable pigments and let me and my sisters play with them as we wished. There was no right or wrong about it, just exploration.

I tuck the stone away, stand up and stretch. I have a strong feeling that Samel is all right, even if I couldn't see or talk to him. I'll trust in that for now, wait for the stone to show me what it will.

On the way home I wander through the market again, consider consulting one of the fortune tellers that now and then ply their trade there, ask them what they know of spells and sorcerers. Strangely, I can't find even one. But it's all right. I'll let the stone be my guide.

Chapter IV

Rowan

My back twinges and I pause to stretch, to wipe dirt off my hands onto my father's old breeches. He said I could have them for working in the dirt. I've cleared weeds from about a square of three cubits, a start on the arts school garden. I've also found a couple of useful plants that I recognized and left in the soil – mallow and portulaca. I probably pulled up others that I'm not familiar with; have to ask someone who knows about local herbs. It's late in the year to transplant most plants or sow seeds. Though in this climate, that might not apply. Garlic and onions make for good fall planting. Mother showed me the wild varieties years ago, said besides adding flavour to other foods, they are both good in keeping people healthy. When I mentioned this to Father recently, he told me that the Lord's

Militia like to eat garlic regularly, believing that it improves their strength. I'll have to find out more about that.

There've been a lot of changes in the school's buildings and surroundings since I came back. Father says they'll be ready to start classes soon. My friend Atsu has helped here often, but I haven't seen him in a day or so and want to talk to him about some of the things Ali said. He's good at listening and helping me to figure things out. When Atsu came back with me from Vatnborg I wasn't sure if he'd stay because he has his own problems to sort out about his parents. But he is staying for now. Because he was a teacher in Vatnborg, he's been offered a position here when lessons start. He'd teach about the outdoors, land formations, rivers, rocks and so on, but I'm not sure if he's going to accept or how long he'll remain in Aquila. I hope he will stay but I haven't said anything about that to him.

I'll be teaching about growing and using herbs and other plants for healing. Father was so pleased when I said that I wanted to do that. I know he thought I might not come back from my journey to Vatnborg. Things hadn't been that good for me here before. I didn't realize how hard it would be once I found my father and brother. Not knowing they existed, I felt so many emotions when I found out. Even though I really wanted to see them, it was hard to try to fit into their lives and to fit them into mine. It probably still won't be easy, but now I'm ready to work at it. I guess finding those two orphans and reuniting them with the Grasslands People made me see my own life differently. As did learning about Atsu's difficulties with his parents.

I notice Atsu sitting under a tree overlooking the river, his back to me, motionless. He must have arrived while I was distracted. I don't want to disturb him if he's deep in thought, doing water magic, or about to transform. Though I can usually feel it if he's starting to change into a dragon, and I don't sense that now. I walk slowly toward the river, then stop to search for signs of anything unusual. An oval patch of water shows small ruffles shaped like the bark of an old tree. Atsu could be doing that, or it could be just an errant breeze.

Atsu has done much more elaborate things with water in the past. It's a legacy from his parents who are also shapeshifters and water dragons who can control the tides, rivers and lakes, floods, rain. They live in a land far across the western sea. Atsu's parents left him in an orphanage when he was small, and he had no contact with them until recently. He thought they were dead. I know what it is to have complicated relationships with your parents, to need time to sort through what that means for how you choose to live your life.

Wanting to help, to be a comfort if he needs it, but not to bother him if he wants to be alone, I move forward quietly. A twig turns and snaps under my foot. It's enough to swivel Atsu's head.

"Rowan." His smile is bright in his brass-coloured, moon-shaped face. "Come sit."

"I'm not disturbing you?"

"Not at all. I was just daydreaming."

I sit beside him, not too close, though I'd like to lean into him. To distract myself I glance at the river again. The ruffles I saw earlier are gone, so perhaps he did make them. We sit quietly for a few moments.

"Onoku is leaving soon," Atsu says. "He hasn't decided exactly when yet."

Onoku is the soldier, teacher, wise man who joined the caravan to Vatnborg because he had messages for Atsu. "Is he returning to your parents? Are you thinking of going with him?" I ask. There's a hollow feeling in my chest at the thought.

"I've been trying to imagine what it would be like to see my parents in all their magnificence. I'm not sure I'm ready for it."

"The Obsidian Dragon and the Pearl Princess," I say. "A lot of flesh."

Atsu snorts, and rubs his arms as if he's cold, though the sun shines brightly. "Formidable names, and frightening beings to confront, even in visions." He glances at me. "You remember?"

I nod. "The Pearl Princess, longer than a house and thick as two ancient tree trunks. Eyes as big as plates. I'm glad I didn't have to see her for very long, even in a vision."

"What might the reality be like? I've gathered from Onoku's tales that my father was much larger than my mother, and fiercer."

"Does Onoku expect you to go with him?"

"He hasn't said that. Just told me that he's getting ready to leave, to go back and report to them."

Atsu stares at the river again. I mull over the things I want to talk to him about, things I don't feel like mentioning to my father. But Atsu has his own decisions to make. I shouldn't burden him with mine.

"Tell Onoku I'd like to see him before he leaves, to say good-bye." I stand. "And if you …"

"You're not going already?"

"I … you've got things to think about, to decide. I don't want to …"

"No." Atsu grabs my hand and pulls me down to sit beside him again. His hand is warm, and I'd like to keep holding it, but he lets go. "Talking to you helps." He peers into my face and frowns. "You came looking for me, didn't you? Was there something you needed?"

"Well …"

"Come, I've told you mine, now you tell yours." His wide smile lights up his golden eyes and there's a shimmer of blue green around his face, a hint of fangs in a large square jaw. The shimmer fades, and it's just the human face that I like to look at, that I see at times in dreams.

"I did want to sound you out about some things."

"So?"

"You know that my brother, Samel, left on his own journey before we got back."

"Yes, of course. And sent an eagle with a message. Which means he's as amazing as you are."

I can feel the heat of a blush in my cheeks. "I've spoken to him since with the bracelets."

Atsu nods. "You told me about them. And I remember how you used yours to help me."

"The last time I spoke with Samel he said that all was well."

I stop and stare to the west, squint my eyes as if I might see through the distance and into the mountains. The bracelet should help me to do that, but I'm not wearing it today, because Father doesn't like to see it. It is in my belt pouch though.

"But for some reason you feel uneasy?"

I turn to look at Atsu. "It's my brother's friend, Ali, one of the daughters in the artists' house across the street from us." I grimace. "She's the one who's uneasy, says she's been having dreams of danger."

"If you're worried about your brother that can easily be fixed, right? Just use your bracelet to talk to him again."

"That's the thing. I've tried and I can't raise him. I don't know if it's the distance or the mountains or something or someone who's preventing it. Or maybe it's my own uneasiness with the bracelets that's blocking things."

"Who would prevent you?"

I rub my arms. Now I'm the one who feels a chill. "Julina and her daughter maybe? They're living in her former husband's castle, that's the old sorcerer who kept us prisoner there. But I don't know why she'd be interfering with me reaching Samel. I thought she helped me to find my father and brother, though I never totally trusted her. She did some things I didn't approve of. But the ravens are watching the castle and surely I would have had some kind of message if there's danger. Ali might just be having ordinary dreams or nightmares that reflect her own worries. What do you think?"

"I think that you're getting yourself all worked up. If that was me right now I'd be changing into a dragon."

He touches my hand briefly and I have a sudden urge to throw myself into his arms, but I don't do it. Instead, I take several deep breaths and that helps a little to calm me.

"Do you have the bracelet with you?" Atsu asks.

"In my belt pouch."

Atsu scans the area. "No one is near us right now. Why not try the bracelet again? See if you can talk to your brother or get any kind of vision of him. Maybe whatever dragon powers I have can help."

I hesitate, still not sure if it's good to use that silver wristlet too often. What if it could get a hold on me some how, make me do things I don't want to do? But Atsu is looking at me, and the sun is shining brightly. I do want to know what's happening with my brother. I pull the bracelet out of my pouch, push back my left sleeve, slip on the silver ivy-leaved band, and close my eyes. I breathe deeply and think of Samel, picturing his red hair and his gold flecked eyes, his engaging grin. Atsu's face keeps flashing into my mind instead, and I'm very aware of him sitting beside me. No visions come. My legs are cramping and my back hurts. Finally, I give up.

"Nothing?" Atsu says.

I shake my head. "Maybe I'll try again later. I have to go now 'cause I told my father that I'd eat the mid-day meal with him. But don't forget to tell Onoku I want to say good-bye before he leaves. And you let me know what you decide about going, all right?"

We're both standing now, and Atsu gives me a quick hug. It feels so good but ends too soon. He stands back.

"I promise."

And then he's gone, running toward the city. I wander slowly back in the direction of the school and the various work sites. Father will probably look for me at the garden; and a few people are supposed to come this afternoon to help with digging and removing weeds and grasses. Soon the fence will go up.

Father's sitting on a stump waiting for me, with a woven basket beside him. "Ah there you are! I've brought a picnic. Shall we go sit by the river to eat?"

I nod, pleased that he isn't questioning where I've been. I think he's gotten better about trusting me, isn't so afraid that one day I'll just leave again. We reach a tree overlooking the water. He spreads a blanket and I help him set out the food – bread, cheeses, fruit.

"Looks good," I say.

"Simple, but filling," he smiles.

I'm reaching for a chunk of cheese with my right hand when my left wrist warms suddenly. Oh no, I've forgotten the bracelet, Father will see it and be angry that I'm wearing it again. Before I can push the bracelet under my sleeve, my brother's face appears, floating against the sky. He seems to be in a dimly lit room.

"Samel?" I say. Father turns his head to look at me.

"Rowan!" Samel says. "At last. Can you give a message to Papa?"

"He's right here, tell him yourself." I don't know if this will work. Our father has never talked to either one of us using the bracelets.

But Father stares at the spot where my brother's face hangs. "Samel, are you all right?"

"I'm fine. I just wanted to tell you … I'm sorry we haven't been getting along."

"I'm sorry, too," Father responds, and I think I can see tears in his eyes.

There's a shimmer and flicker around the edges of Samel's head. I'm not sure if we're going to be able to hold the connection.

"Papa, I love you," Samel says, and then he's gone.

Father grabs my left wrist. "Is that it?" he asks. "We don't get to see any more of him?"

"I'm sorry. Sometimes it's like that."

He lets go. "Did I hurt you?"

"No, it's all right. You're not angry? That I've been wearing and using the bracelet? I tried earlier to talk to Samel, but then it didn't work."

"I'm not angry." He sighs. "Maybe this is another thing I've been wrong about. Disapproving of you and Samel using the bracelets." Then he smiles. "It was good to see him. Neither of you has paid much attention to what I think, have you?"

"Well, we've been careful."

"Careful not to flaunt your use of them? And you seem to have gotten over the fear you had of using yours after the old sorcerer's death."

"Hmm. Somewhat. That's partly Samel, and partly the experiences I had on my journey to and from Vatnborg. Samel said it was like learning to play a musical instrument; you get better with practise. And on the journey, I needed the bracelet's power at times."

"So, there's stories I haven't heard." He cuts a slice of bread and a couple of pieces of cheese. "Why don't you tell me some of these tales while we eat."

Chapter V

Ali

My family's chatter washes over me at the first meal of the day; they talk in a bunch as usual, interrupting each other at times, taking turns now and then. I don't try to follow the conversation. The voices weave in and around each other, loud and soft, Père's deep baritone, Ivoire's shrill squeals, Mère's calm and even tones. I'm busy thinking about Samel, haven't had any dreams or visions since I sat in the olive grove, can't decide whether that's good or bad. I decided to let the stone guide me that day, but now I'm thinking that might not have been wise.

I haven't heard anything from the soothsayer Tristicus, but then I didn't leave a message. Perhaps they didn't even tell him I'd come by. Which is probably a good thing because he'd have contacted Père. Haven't done anything more about trying to find someone to talk to about sorcerers and spells, dreams and visions. Has Rowan done anything about it? My thoughts are as useless as the chatter of my family.

A plate of cut fruit sits in front of me and I study the fresh colours – cream banana, green melon, yellow lemon, purple grape. The hues make me realize I haven't felt much like painting for a while, but my spirits always rise when I do. And it's a good way to clear the mind, let thoughts roam, weave new connections.

"Ali!" Mère snaps her fingers under my nose. "You haven't said a word since you sat down. Haven't responded to any questions. What's going on?"

"Just thinking," I mumble, pushing her hand away.

"We've all been talking about our plans," Mère continues. "Père is making a cradle for Magenta's baby. I'm weaving a blanket."

"And I'm creating a moveable sculpture to hang over the crib," Ivoire shouts. "What are you going to do?"

"What about helping us with the mural?" Mère says. "You haven't done one for ages, and we could use your ideas. Things a baby might like to look at. You could start a few sketches."

"Hmm," I say. "I'll think about it." And then I get up and leave the table, walk into the hallway and out the front door.

I know it's rude, but I can't be bothered being polite right now, want to figure out what to do about Samel and the stone. My family seems oblivious to what's going on in my life. Though to be fair – I haven't tried to talk to them about how I feel. Should I talk to other people? In the past I've gone to Mère or Père if I had problems, but this time

I just don't want to. Is it because I think they'd make light of my worries? If Ivoire gets wind of this, she'd tease me about Samel. I stand outside our door and stare across at Samel's house. I could go and see if Rowan's there, though she wasn't very encouraging the other day.

Should I try again to get into the palace, past the guards, ask for the soothsayer's tower? The tops of trees shimmer green around the palace, contrasting with the pale tan and cream walls. My fingers half curl to shape a brush, but I can't go back into the house now because my family will start babbling at me again. I need a quiet place.

"Ali?" Rowan is standing across the street. "Were you coming to see me? I have news about Samel."

I'm beside her before she can say another word. "What?"

"He's fine. My father and I spoke to him briefly yesterday."

"What did he say?"

"Not much. That he loved us. The connection didn't last long."

"Oh."

"Have you had any more upsetting dreams or visions?"

"No."

"So, you can stop worrying, right?"

"Guess so. Thanks. I have to go."

I turn to the left, away from the palace. It seems that my worries have been for nothing. Perhaps the stone's purpose is to confuse me. I wish I could have talked to Samel myself, asked him what he thinks of what's been happening to me, the visions and dreams. I still feel restless.

I've got a few coins, so will go to the market and buy a roll of reed paper and charcoal. Find a spot to do some sketching. The cacophony of the crowds and sellers is more than I can stomach this morning, so I quickly find a stall where I can buy what I need and leave.

Not far from the market, at the end of a narrow side street is a square with a small fountain. A few trees grow around it, scenting the air – a pink-blooming almond, a lemon tree, and a couple of myrtles. The square is deserted and so I settle myself on one of the benches and begin to sketch.

Is Samel really all right? If his sister didn't see him for long, how can she know for certain? Still, what can I do about it?

The coo of a dove and the quiet rustle of leaves along with the trickle of the fountain relaxes me as my fingers fly over the paper. A sprig of myrtle leaves flutters down and I draw it, then across the square a crooked door catches my eye. I wish I had my paints because the wooden door is painted the most brilliant blue. It shines as if it held a light inside, but I suppose it's merely reflecting the sun. One of the cooing doves alights and searches the cobblestones near my feet for crumbs or bugs. My fingers are cramping so I stop drawing for a while, spit on my hands and wipe them on the bottom of my tunic to clean the charcoal off. I lean back against the bench and close my eyes. The sun warms my head and shoulders.

There's a cool spot in the middle of my chest where the obsidian stone hangs in its leather pouch. I see the stone behind my eyelids, as if it rested there, glinting darkly. Deep within the darkness are tiny lights, like stars in the night sky. I'm searching for the moon, but I can't see it. Maybe it's behind a cloud.

And then the stars begin to disappear.

My throat tightens and there's a hot spot at my chest. I grab for it, to pull the stone away, jerk open my eyes. I'm sitting on a bench by the fountain, my drawing materials on the ground.

A young woman in black leather armour stands in front of me. "Sorry to wake you," the woman says. "I'm hoping that you can give me directions."

I release a long breath. "I saw you before. At the bakery. Do you belong to the Lord's Militia?"

She shakes her head. "Sorry, I don't remember that. I'm a stranger to the city and looking for the sand shrine."

"It's some distance away, at the northwest corner of the city."

The woman steps closer. I notice that she's wearing a long sword in a scabbard, and a knife in her belt on the other side. Her hands hang loosely, but her stance feels mildly threatening. I slide along to the far end of the bench.

"I can walk there?" she asks, not moving any nearer. "Or will I need to get a horse?"

"You can walk." I stand and point in the correct direction. "Just follow this street to the market, then take the widest road north. When you come to an open square, larger than this one, take the narrowest street to the left. It will take you directly to the shrine."

I reach down to pick up my drawing materials. When I straighten the woman is standing less than an arm's length away. Her right hand is clenched into a fist. Is she going to hit me? I step back. The woman flicks her fist at me, flinging it open at the end. A puff of fine peppery-smelling dust hits me in the face, making me cough. I bend, blur into fog, thick and soundless …

I'm so tired. My eyelids feel as heavy as stones; can't open my eyes. Is it the middle of the night? I don't seem to be lying in bed. Can feel arms holding me.

"I told you to use it as a last resort! Can't you do anything right?"

"It seemed to me she was going to run away."

"Nonsense!"

Managing to open my eyes a slit, I peer, squinting. See that I'm stumbling along the edge of the market between two women – the leather armour clad one has me by one arm. An older woman in purple robes, a streak of red in her wild black hair is on my left side. I move my lips, trying to talk, ask what is going on, but nothing happens. I can walk, but I can't talk.

A whisper comes in my left ear, "Don't worry, we're going to take very good care of you." Fog swirls again.

Chapter VI

Rowan

Father and I are scraping the last bits of a rosemary chicken fricassee from our plates when a thump rattles the outer door. The noise comes again. Both of us have worked long and hard at the arts school site today so we're tired, reluctant to move. And a knock at this time of night is unusual. Father is the first to stand, but I follow.

He motions me back. "Wait until I see who it is."

By the light that spills from our rooms, I see Père from across the street standing there. "Have you seen my daughter, Ali, today?" he asks. "Is she with you?"

"I haven't seen her," Father says.

I step forward. "I saw her this morning when she left your house."

"Come in Patrice," Father says.

He shakes his head. "I haven't time." He turns to me. "Rowan, isn't it? Did she say where she was going?"

"No, but she was heading in the direction of the market."

"It's rather late for her to be out," Father says. "Perhaps she's at her sister Magenta's house?"

"We've checked there, and looked around the market, asked if anyone has seen her. Nothing so far. Magenta's man and I searched the riverbank, the arts school site, anywhere she might be. Magenta's man is in the Lord's Militia, you know, so he's called a few of them out, and they're combing the city now, but I thought I'd ask you, too."

"I'm sorry we can't tell you more," Father says. "If there's anything else we can do let us know?"

Père is already turning away. "Yes."

Father and I watch Père hunch down the street towards the palace. A movement across the way catches my eye. Mère and Ivoire stand in the doorway of their house looking at us. Father and I shake our heads, and their door closes.

"Can you think of anything, Rowan?"

"No."

"I hope they'll think of the eagles." He's still staring out of our open door.

"The eagles?"

"Yes, the great guardian eagles of Aquila. Their eyes are so much sharper than ours, though they don't hunt at night. If the militia haven't found her by morning, I'll suggest it, though they'll probably think of it themselves."

Father closes our door and heads back to the kitchen. I follow and begin clearing the table. He fetches a flask of wine and a beaker, pours a measure, takes a sip. His fingers drum the table. "I feel so useless. Should we go over and stay with Melisande and Ivoire?"

"Who?"

"Melisande, Ali's mother."

"I don't know. What if it was Samel who was missing? What would you want people to do?"

He jumps to his feet. "I'll go over and ask. You stay here, I won't be long."

I've washed the dishes by the time he gets back and am sitting at the kitchen table thinking of Samel and how worried Ali was about him. What if he's somehow involved in this? But how could he be?

"What did they say?"

"I told them to call on us if they needed anything. Their cook is plying them with tisane and trying to get them to eat a little soup."

Father walks from the kitchen into the hall and I hear him climb the stairs. His steps cross from his room to Samel's, then thump downstairs again. He doesn't appear in the kitchen, has moved into our main room. I follow to see what he's doing – just pacing.

"Has anything like this ever happened before in Aquila?" I ask, leaning against the doorway. "Children going missing?" I think of the two children I found on the lake north of the Vatnborg School. They'd been lost from their family for years. "Are there people here who would kidnap children?"

Father stops his pacing, a hand to his mouth. "Bad things have happened here now and then. Children do get lost sometimes, fall in the river, get run over by a horse. Samel's first friend died when a horse stampeded." He sinks onto the divan. "But Ali's not a little girl anymore. She's nearly grown, should know how to take care of herself in most situations." He stares at me, his face worried.

"So," I say slowly, "you think that means it's not an accident that she's missing."

He shakes his head. "I don't know."

***

I wake, lying on the divan in our living room. In the darkness I can just see Father snoring in a deep chair across from me. It must be the middle of the night. Neither of us wanted to go to bed in case we were needed or there was news. My thoughts and speculations kept me awake for a while. Should I have taken Ali's dreams and worries more seriously? Would she have decided to go after Samel? It seems unlikely, especially since I told her he was fine. I get to my feet and peer out of the window toward the artists' house. A light shows in one of their windows and there's a huddle of figures holding lanterns near their door. Moving as quietly as possible so as not to wake Father, I make my way to our front door and ease it open. One of the figures turns: it's a man with four eagle feathers embroidered on his tunic: The Militia Commander.

I step forward. "Please, is there any news of Ali?"

The Commander doesn't answer, but Père appears and beckons to me. "Yes," he says quietly. The men and women of the militia make way for me. "They've found a few people who saw Ali earlier today. She was with two women."

The Commander nods at me. "You a friend of hers?"

"My brother is, but I know Ali, too."

"Your brother is away? Left the city some time ago?"

"Yes. But does anyone know who the two women were?"

"One looked like a soldier," a woman of the militia says. "Black leather armour, a sword. The other wore robes, had black hair with a streak of red."

A gasp escapes me.

"You know who they are."

"It sounds like a woman called Julina and her daughter, Varonne. They were supposed to be living in a castle in the mountains to the west. I don't know whether you heard about my father, my brother and me being held prisoner there over a year ago?"

The Commander nods. "Something. But I thought the sorcerer who lived there was dead?"

"Varonne is his daughter, and Julina his former wife. This is not good." I turn to Père. "I'm sorry."

"But what would they want with my daughter?" Père asks.

"Julina is a soothsayer, Varonne a free mercenary. I'm not sure what they'd want." I turn to the Militia Commander who is murmuring to his soldiers. "I thought the Lord's soothsayers were keeping an eye on the castle in the mountains."

"You're thinking they should have given warning if the women left the castle," Père says, before the Commander can respond.

"Except that Julina is a mistress of illusion as well. But surely the Lord's soothsayers would know that and …"

The Commander has been listening to our exchange. "We need to go back to the palace," he interrupts. "We'll consult with the soothsayers, widen our search, beyond the city if we have to, alert the eagles." He pats Père on the shoulder. "Wait here with your family." He glares down at me. "Leave this to us, we know what we're doing." He turns back to Père. "We should have more news soon." And then they are gone, marching quickly up the street to the palace.

My father shuffles out of our door and crosses. "What's going on?" he asks.

"Come in," Père says. "I don't want to keep talking out here in the street."

We follow him into the kitchen. The cook is asleep in a chair, her head on the table. Père puts a finger to his lips and leads us into a small room lit by a lantern. He closes the door.

"We can talk here. The rest of the family is asleep," he says. "They're worn out. Magenta's here, too, but her man is still helping with the search." He motions us to chairs. "Now, Rowan, tell me more about these women."

"Which women?" my father asks.

"Julina and Varonne. They seem to be responsible for Ali's abduction. It could have something to do with Samel and me."

Father frowns. "Wasn't Julina the woman who helped you when you were looking for Samel and me? And Varonne was Hrashak's daughter. I remember her in the castle."

"Yes, it seems they have their own plans, perhaps to do with the bracelets."

"I don't understand," Father and Père say together.

"The sorcerer Hrashak had plans to try and take over Aquila," I say for Père's benefit. "He thought he had rights here because of a family connection to the rulers. When he died, that danger was gone. His daughter didn't seem the type to care about such things, though she had been a mercenary soldier. Julina, Hrashak's former wife, had been separated from her daughter for a long time. As far as I know, Julina had no interest in Aquila at all, though she may have lived here at one time."

"You mentioned bracelets," Père says. "What did you mean?"

I sigh, not looking at Father. "It's a long story but in short, my brother Samel and I came into possession of a pair of silver bracelets that have magical powers. Nothing really amazing so far. We can talk to each other at a distance; Samel can make the wind blow; I can make fire. But the old sorcerer thought they could help him with his ambitions. It's possible Julina and Varonne have decided they want the bracelets, too."

"Julina could have taken yours any time when she was helping you," Father says. "Why now?"

"And why take my daughter?" Père adds.

"I'm only guessing. She might have discovered things at the castle that made her realize the bracelets could be useful. And she might have found out that Ali was Samel's friend."

"So, my daughter is a hostage to a pair of bracelets? Let's just give them to this Julina person."

"Except we don't know where the women are," Father says. "We'll have to wait for more news from the milita's search."

I'm glad that Father has said this, even though I'm thinking the women are making for the castle in the mountains, if they're not there already. And this isn't the time for me to go into all my reasons for not wanting to give up my bracelet. No matter my reservations about using it, if Julina is involved, I want all the help I can get. As for Samel, maybe he's in danger, too, right at this moment. I need to try and talk to him.

"We'll go back home," I say, standing. "Wait until the militia needs us."

Père doesn't try to detain us.

I convince Father that I'm exhausted and need to sleep. I close the door to my bedroom and get out the silver bracelet. There's no moon tonight, which will make things more difficult, as the bracelets respond best to moonlight. Still, I try, sitting for some time with the bracelet in my hands. There's nothing from Samel, not a murmur, not a flicker of a vision. I lie on the bed in frustration, waiting for sunrise, thinking I'll try again then. When I need the bracelet to work it won't and when I don't really want it, it gives me visions. I have to know what Julina might be up to. Are my guesses correct? And what can I do if they are? Despite all these questions and worries, I sink into sleep.

It's sunrise, barely beginning to get light. I'm standing on a hill at the edge of the grasslands overlooking a cluster of pale tents. There's a shuddering under my feet and a rumble in the distance behind me. I turn to red flickers in the west, smoke billows. Ahead of the smoke a heaving, thundering mass of wild cattle races toward the hill, toward the village of tents.

I shout, wave my arms, run down the hill into night.

A light flashes in darkness, and then another, a whole cluster of torches. By their flickering I see an open gate in a tall stone wall; it looks like Aquila. I've moved somehow. Weapons glint as a troop of militia marches through the gate. A howl splits the night and then another. There are snarls and shouts as soldiers begin to fight wolves the size of two men.

"Shut the gate!" someone shouts.

I can't tell where I am. It's dark and I hear an odd thumping and fluttering. I open my eyes to sunlight blazing into my room, overlaid by shadows. I squint against the brightness to look at my window. Leap out of bed and fumble with the window catches.

"Morde?"

A raven flaps in, lands on the floor and squawks loudly, ducking his head up and down. It's definitely my raven, the one that was my companion when Mother and I lived in the north. I can tell by the patterns of his feathers, and a nick in one of his claws.

"You should have come before now!" I scold. "Brought warning of what those women were up to."

Morde leaps onto my bed, shakes himself and then hops onto a chair, cocking his head, first to one side and then the other.

"Yes, I know, the Lord's soothsayers should have been paying attention as well. I know it's not all your fault. Besides, who knows what Julina might have done to you?" I move closer to him. "Are you all right?" He hops back to my bed and rubs his head against the blanket. "What's the matter? What are you trying to tell me? I know there's danger, but I can't speak to you and understand, the way my father can with eagles."

Morde squawks again and flutters right at me. I catch him in my arms, and that's when I see the bit of parchment hidden in his feathers, tied around his neck with a black ribbon. My fingers are all thumbs, but finally I get the message untied and unrolled. Morde hops to the floor.

Come to the castle, Rowan, you and Samel with your silver bracelets. Bring your friend Atsu, and Samel can bring the old man who calls himself Grandfather Frog. No one else. If I see any sign of soldiers Ali dies. J

"Rowan, what's going on? I heard noises and then I heard you talking. Who's there with you? Let me in!" Father thumps on my door.

Father has never seen Morde, though he has heard me talk of him, so his surprise changes quickly to concern, as I hand him the note. That turns to anger as he reads. "No! You will not go, not alone or any other way. We'll take this to the Militia Commander immediately and he can make his plans. Besides, how do we know that it really is from Julina?"

I snatch the parchment out of his fingers. "Père should see it first."

"I don't think that's wise."

"As I said once before, what if it was Samel who'd been snatched? You would be acting differently, doing whatever the note said."

Father shakes his head. "I wouldn't put one child in danger for another."

"None of us are children anymore."

I storm from my room, out of our house and across the street to batter at the door of the artists' house. Père opens immediately. I can tell by his draggy face and rumpled clothes that he hasn't slept.

"There's news." I hold out the note. "It came by raven messenger."

I'm aware that Father is standing behind me, in our own doorway, but he doesn't move or say a word. Père glances at him, and then motions me inside, while reading the note. He lifts his head to look at me and then reads the note again.

"You think this is legitimate?"

"Yes. The raven that brought it was once mine."

"And Atsu is the young man who came back with you from Vatnborg?" I nod. "Are you planning on going, and do you think he will, too?"

"Absolutely."

"Then send to your young man, and let's get busy with preparations. Horses, supplies, whatever you need. I know people who can organize all that."

Father is beside us now. "You don't think we should show this to the Militia Commander? Wait for his advice?"

"Could you look after that for me, Yarvan? I want to let my family know about this; there's lots to do." Père hands the parchment to Father, nods at us and closes his door.

Father starts down the street toward the palace.

"Wait," I say. "Could you send a message to Samel by one of the eagles? I haven't been able to speak to him through the bracelets."

"No," Father says. "Samel is well out of this." And he hurries away from me.

I go back into the house. Can't stop shivering, remembering fragments of dream and thinking of Julina's note. I feed Morde scraps of leftover meat, which he gulps, and then he flutters out of my window and away. Is he off to keep an eye on Julina again? I hope so. Maybe he'll come back and find a way to let us know what is happening.

I grab my bracelet to try and talk to Samel. It doesn't work. I write a note to him, just in case I can persuade Father later to use one of the eagles or find some other way to send it. Maybe Magenta's man can ask the Captain of Eagles to send the message for me. Samel has to find out what Julina wrote so he can come as she requested. I'm sure he'll want to do anything he can to help Ali, his long-time friend. Even if I don't like the girl much, I can understand that. And because he's my brother, I'll do all I can. I put the parchment into my belt pouch and set off to find Atsu.

***

At mid-morning, Atsu and I sit under a tree at the riverbank talking things over. I reached his hostel in time to say good-bye to Onoku. When the former mercenary heard what had happened, he wanted to stay and lend a hand, but we both insisted there was nothing he could do, and Atsu's parents would be waiting for news.

Atsu had no hesitation about coming with me. "Of course, Rowan, I'll do whatever I can."

"Do you think Julina knows about me, about my abilities?" Atsu says now, twirling a twig between his fingers. Drops of water spiral from the tips of the twig, sparkling in the sun, some shrink, others expand.

"After you and I stopped the flood during the arts school opening? Defeating her son? Of course, she does." I catch a few drops of water in my hand. "I've never seen you do anything like this before."

He puts the twig down. "This is just a little thing, but I've been practising. Water is like paint or clay to me now. I can find it, shape it, use it."

"I wish I had as much confidence about using the bracelet. I haven't been able to talk to Samel since this happened and he should know. I asked Father to send a message by an eagle, but he wouldn't."

"Send the message yourself."

I stare at him. "I can't talk to eagles! I wouldn't know where to start."

There's a screech from above us. We lift our heads. An eagle is perched on one of the branches peering down at us.

Atsu gestures. "The answer to your problem."

I keep watching the eagle. "Do you really think …?"

The great bird flutters to a lower branch.

"Yes, I do think," Atsu says. "I'll just stay very quiet."

"But how? I mean why did this eagle show up now. Do you think it's coincidence?"

"At least one of the eagles knows you because of that earlier message from Samel. Maybe this is the same one. Why not try?"

Carefully, making no sudden moves, always aware of talons, powerful wings and beak, I fumble the note out of my belt pouch. There's a bit of string in there as well. By the time I have these in my hands, the eagle has reached the ground in front of me. It's as large as a small goat, except more compact. I've never been this close to an Aquilan eagle before. The other time we sent a note, it was Father who did it. The eagle regards me with one golden eye and then tips its head to look at me with the other. Somewhat impatiently, it seems to me.

Tentatively, I hold out the note and the bit of string. "Can you take this to my brother, Samel, in the mountains at Schönspitze?"

The bird sticks out one leg. I lean forward and duck my head, preferring not to look directly into either of those eyes or to face that scimitar-like beak. The talons are fearful enough, black hooks twice as long as one of my fingers. Finally, I get the note tied tightly to the leg, and draw my hand back, accidentally rasping across the point of a talon. The bird leaps into the sky and its wings beat over my head.

Then the bird rises higher, flapping westward.

"You're bleeding," Atsu says.

A line of red oozes across the back of my hand. I lick it off. "Just a scratch." I rip a piece off the bottom of my tunic and Atsu ties it tightly.

We're just sitting there watching the dot of eagle disappear into a cloud when the tramp of feet makes us turn. Father and a couple of soldiers, as well as the Commander march toward us. There's no time to ask Atsu to say nothing of the eagle and my message.

"We've been looking all over for you," Father says. "Thought you'd been kidnapped, too. You should have left me a note. The Commander wants to ask you a few more questions."

"What do you want to know?"

"First, I want to impress on you that you mustn't try to go off on your own to rescue your friend," the Commander says. "It's far too dangerous. The militia will work something out. We'll let you know what, if anything, we want you to do."

I'm about to reply when there's a shudder in the earth and all of us are tossed to the ground. Out of the corner of my eye, I see a green-blue shimmer around Atsu, who is lying next to me. I hope he doesn't go into full-fledged dragon mode here, in front of these people with swords. My next thought is that this is not a normal earthquake. I'm not sure how I know, but I'm certain. And even if it isn't, I can use it.

"That was a warning from Julina," I say.

The soldiers rise to their feet. Father and I get up more slowly. Atsu stays sitting, but at least he's no longer shimmering.

"Nonsense!" Father says.

"What makes you think that?" the Militia Commander asks. "We do occasionally experience earthquakes here."

"Because she made her son create a flood during the arts school opening."

"I remember that flood," one of the women soldiers says. "The river almost overflowed its banks. But there was a storm. That kind of thing can happen naturally."

"She has a son? Living here in Aquila?" the Militia Commander asks.

"Jernan," I say. "I don't know if he's still here. His father raises horses and has a shop with leather workers. I haven't seen either of them since the flood."

"I thought you said before that Julina's husband was the old sorcerer who lived at the castle, and he's dead."

"It's complicated," I say. "She had at least two husbands, a child with each of them."

"Marcus," the Commander says to one of his men, "go see what you can find out about this horse breeder or leather worker, and his son." The man leaves. "Now, Rowan, you think this earth tremor was Julina's creation? Why would she do that? And do you think she has the power to see and hear what we do here?"

"A warning, as I said. To prevent us from disobeying her message, maybe. And she does have ways of seeing what is going on far away. I've seen her do it. I don't know if she does it all the time."

"Don't forget the flood," Atsu adds. "It could have killed a lot of people."

"You say she was responsible for that," the Commander glances from Atsu to me. "Where's the proof?"

"Jernan, her son, was there," I say. "We heard him muttering incantations. Maybe she has other spies in the city here who can get messages to her quickly."

"I need to consult the Lord's soothsayers again," the Commander says. "Don't leave the city."

He and his soldiers march rapidly away. Father stays, frowning. Atsu has gotten up; he's staring at the river. A small whirlpool churns not far from the bank, dragging leaves and bits of twigs down into the vortex.

"Atsu," I say, "are you …?"

"It's not me doing that," he says.

"It's just a whirlpool," Father says. "They happen now and then on the river."

"Believe what you like," I say. "I'm going to see Ali's family, find out what preparations Père has been able to make. Atsu, do you want to come with me?"

He shakes his head. "I have plans to make, too. I'll come see you tomorrow morning at your house."

Father watches him go, then turns to me. "I insist that you leave this to the militia. They are trained for this kind of thing. And you can't head off on a dangerous journey with a young man I hardly know."

"You've forgotten something."

"What."

"I found you and my brother. And then I found two children for the Grasslands People. Even though I haven't been taught how to search and find, I've been able to do it, with the help of the bracelet."

"Those bracelets! I curse the silversmith who made them for your mother and me! I'm sure Hrashak had something to do with that, and now his former wife is trying to carry on his plans! Where are you keeping yours?" He glances at my wrists which are bare, then at my belt pouch. "You should hand it over to the Lord's soothsayers. They might be able to use it to find out where Julina has taken Ali."

I make no motion toward my pouch. "Father, you know the bracelets can't be handed over that easily. Remember how Hrashak couldn't take them from us?"

"What if Julina can? What if she knows things he didn't, is far more devious and powerful than he was? I can't take the chance of losing you, Rowan!"

I take a deep breath. "Father, this is about more than risking the loss of a daughter or a son. About more than the ownership of a pair of magical bracelets. Hrashak wanted to take over Aquila. Perhaps that's what Julina wants, but she could want even more. I have a feeling that there is peril not only for this city and its people, but for our whole land. Before she was kidnapped Ali was having dreams of danger. I had a dream last night of destruction, danger for the Grasslands People as well as for Aquila. I have to pay attention to that, do what I can. Sorry if you don't agree with me. See you later."

Chapter VII

Atsu

Wind presses against my body as I dash along the bank of the grey river past the arts school; it's what I imagine flying is like. I've heard of dragons taking to the air, but my family are water dragons so I don't think we can fly. I've certainly never sprouted wings and didn't think to ask my mother when I met her. Could a dragon fly without wings? There's lots of things I still want to learn about my powers. Maybe I should have gone with Onoku to see my parents. I could have gained much knowledge quickly. But then I wouldn't be here to help Rowan.

The preparations I need to make at my hostel and in the city can all wait; they won't take long. As I told Rowan, I've been practising with water, testing my abilities. If we're going to be facing a sorceress I need to know even more. There's a spot to the east that I found recently, wanted to show Rowan today. It's perfect for practise – a small, se-cluded beach hidden at the bottom of a steep bank over-hung by bushes.

When I reach the area, I search all around; see no one nearby. Carefully, I clamber down to the strip of pale sand, take off my sandals and dabble my feet in the clear water. A few tiny fish flick away. It's chilly at first but I soon get used to it. Half closing my eyes I concentrate on seeing green webbed claws instead of toes. I've never done any-thing like this before, don't know if it will work. When I've transformed into a dragon in the past it's been when I'm angry or upset or feel in danger. Are my toes lengthening? Turning green? Or is it just the ripples of the water making me think my feet are changing? A fish the size of my hand darts by and a green claw extends and grasps it. I've done it! The fish struggles and I release it.

"Sorry, instinct, I guess."

The fish flicks its tail as if in forgiveness. Fish and drag-ons are similar in some ways. We both have scales and a tail. My family are water dragons so we must be familiar with fish if we spend time in rivers, lakes and seas. I wonder if I played in water as a child, had fish friends. It's the kind of thing my parents could tell me. Someday maybe. Right now my focus has to be on helping Rowan, which means thinking about the lost girl, Ali her name is, and about the two women who kidnapped her – Varonne, the mercenary, and Julina, the sorceress.

What if Julina's watching and seeing? Could she tell what I'm trying to do, find some way to stop me or think of ways to thwart me in the future? I need to protect myself, be able to guard Rowan as we travel.

I bend forward and blow hard onto the water raising a spray of silvery droplets. I think of grey mist rising from the river and enfolding me, thickening. I concentrate hard on feeling dampness around me, the taste of fog on my tongue. As I imagine, so it happens. I'm hidden now, hopefully from Julina, too.

Quickly I strip off the rest of my clothes, drop them beside my sandals, and plunge into the water. Sink into it, cold, then cool, then warming against my skin. Hands turn into webbed claws, an undulating tail grows. A sinuous and scaled blue-green body expands around me. My head feels strange, heavy. I open my mouth and it keeps opening, larger and larger. I swallow water, breathe it in, taste the scent of fishes, small crabs, pebbles and mud, sand and weeds.

I sport in the water – rolling, leaping out and in, splashing, making waves. The fog keeps me hidden, safe, but it's not good to be too obvious. The sound of my body slapping the water will be heard despite the fog; hopefully anyone who hears it will think a large fish is jumping. At last I stop, lie quiet in the shallows and let myself become a man again.

After dressing I sit on a rock and stare at the pewter coloured river as the last of the fog dissipates and I think about shaping water without changing myself. I've done a little of this before. Can I do even more? A ridge of water rises, a fin emerges, the back of a large fish. It sinks, then two more rise. Soon a whole gathering of fishes twists and turns through the water. I concentrate harder, think of my mother rising from the sea as Onoku described her, a woman with dark hair, pale skin, wearing green robes. And for a moment a small figure stands half in and half out of the water, a little girl who looks like Rowan. But I can't hold her, and she fades away. I lie back, exhausted, and hungry. I can't do any more of this today. I'm about to leave the river, have climbed the bank when Rowan's father arrives. How did he find me?

"Atsu," he says, "I need to talk to you."

"Anything I can do?"

"Yes. I want you to promise me not to go off on this journey with Rowan."

I stand there staring at him, not knowing what to say. Of course, I'll do anything Rowan wants me to do. She is my friend and she's helped me a lot. But this is her father in front of me and I have an inkling of how he is feeling.

"I understand that you don't know me, but Rowan and I got to be good friends on the journey back from Vatnborg. I'd never do anything to harm her."

"Then we're agreed." He smiles.

I clear my throat. "Umm, not exactly."

"What then? What are your intentions?"

"I'll help Rowan do whatever she needs or wants to do. It's as simple as that."

"My daughter is barely seventeen years old. I don't think you're a good judge of what she might need to do."

"Sir, I'm sorry, but I got to know your daughter quite well on the journey we took with Onoku and the two children. We faced dangers together; we helped each other."

"Is there an understanding between the two of you?"

"Umm, do you mean life partnering?" He nods. "No, of course not!" I can feel the heat of a blush in my face. "We're good friends."

"Well, then I'd like you to think about a father's concerns and a father's rights." And he turns and hurries away before I can say anything more.

I follow slowly, letting him get ahead and out of sight. What is he expecting? If Rowan wants my help of course I'll give it, no matter what her father says. As far as anything else goes, well, I like Rowan. Maybe more than like. But I don't think about that much if I can help it. There's too much else going on to think about life partnerships, especially for one who's part dragon. When I reach the market, I stop to buy a couple of bananas and an apple, then a hunk of cheese. Munching as I walk, think about buying supplies for the journey if we decide to make it.

Not far from the market is the stable where my horse is kept. I feed him the apple, stroke his neck. I haven't ridden much since I got here from Vatnborg, left his exercising to the stable owner. The horse looks in good health, prancing a little in his stall.

"Soon," I whisper, "you may get all the exercise you can handle."

I check my saddle and bags, the horse's tack stored in a cupboard next to the stall. All in good order. I find the stable owner in his office next door.

"I could be taking a trip in a day or two," I say. "Let me pay you for the board this week and can you let me have a bag of feed?"

The transaction is soon finished, and I head to my hostel. Tell the hostel keeper I might be leaving soon. Ask if he'll store those of my things I don't want to take. I pay him to hold my room for a couple of moons. By that time, I hope, we'll have rescued Ali. Or not.

In my small room I sit and think for a while. Should I pack whatever clothes and odds and ends I'll need now, or wait? I might as well be prepared, so I put my things into one sack that I can sling behind my saddle. Once that's done, I go out again to a nearby inn and eat a huge meal of fowl, tubers, bread, and fruit. After that all I feel like doing is sleeping.

I'm awake shortly after sunrise, but it's far too early to disturb Rowan and her father, or Ali's father. I'm itching to be on the move even though I know Rowan's father doesn't approve. I wander into the streets. People, donkeys, and carts are already out, heading toward the market or toward other shops and workshops all over the city. I find a bakery open and buy a couple of honey cakes. As I step back outside the door, Rowan nearly runs into me.

"Atsu! I'm glad I met you. I think we might be able to leave today." She grabs my free hand and tugs me along. Her fingers are warm and strong entwinned in mine.

"The militia and your father won't try to stop us?"

"No. The Lord's soothsayers did some kind of spell craft last night apparently, and it convinced them that Julina means business, though they didn't say what they thought that business might be. The soothsayers impressed on the Militia Commander that thwarting Julina would not be wise. And the militia haven't been able to find Jernan or his father."

"What about your father?"

"He's still not happy, but there's not much he can do. I'm seventeen, which makes me of adult age. Father's been insisting that he should go with us, but no one will agree to that because of Julina's threat. Apparently one of the Lord's soothsayers was scalded by a spilled cauldron last night and he thinks it's a sign we should listen to Julina."

"Hold on a moment, I need to catch my breath. Running, talking and eating is hard to do at the same time."

Rowan stops and to my regret, lets go of my hand. "There's lots to do though if we want to leave quickly," she says. "Which I think we should."

"Has Ali's father been able to help?"

"He got us a pack horse. I told him you and I had our own riding horses. I'll pick up Lady from the stable at the Arts School. Ali's father has given us food, a tent, pots and pans, everything we might need for our journey to the mountains. Money to buy supplies for the way back."

"Why don't I return to my hostel and get my bag, then? After that I can pick up my horse and meet you at your house. We can leave directly from there?"

"That sounds good! See you soon."

Chapter VIII

Samel

The earth shakes and mountains crumble. I'm alone in a valley watching the land disintegrate around me and there is nowhere to run. Slabs of rock and boulders thunder down slopes, bounce, roll, smash trees, leap streams. A torrent of stone rushes inexorably toward me. Soon I will be smashed, buried. The rumble of stone grows louder and louder.

Heart pounding, I gasp for breath, and find myself sitting in a tent, blankets sliding from my upper body. I shake off the dream; Grandfather snores peacefully beside me. A flash of light, a crack of thunder, a distant rumble. Just a storm coming on.

I edge carefully to the tent opening, hoping not to disturb the old man. He needs as much sleep as possible.

Peering past the tent flap, I see that our horses are still securely tied at the other end of this overhang where I pitched our tent last evening. Izmeer continues in horse shape, though for all I know, he might change back to being a camel at night. I never did get around to asking my cousin Thea whether her spell to change Izmeer from a camel to a horse would wear off eventually. Occasionally Izmeer has changed briefly on his own, but I haven't seen that for a while. Since we're in the mountains it's just as well he continues as a horse.

A few drops of rain spatter against rocks, but none hit the tent. Another flash of lightning. Luckily, we found this sheltered spot. I shiver and crawl back to my blankets.

It's our first night since we left Schönspitze, but it seems forever since the eagle came with Rowan's message. I hope Ali is safe. Surely Julina and Varonne won't harm her if they expect our cooperation. Bits of my dream come back to me. Julina's doing I bet. She's trying to scare me, wear down my courage before I even reach Ali so that I will not be fit to oppose her.

"It won't work," I mutter, but I don't know what we will have to do to get Ali back and it worries me.

Grandfather moans a little and I hold very still. He sighs and turns over but stays asleep. He shouldn't be on this journey. My cousin Thea was right about that, but he wanted to come, and Julina's note said that he should. I'm glad of his company, have grown used to having a great grandfather, even though not so long ago I didn't know that I had one living. Why does Julina want him? I hope he's not going to be in danger from her; this journey through the mountains will be hard enough on him. Grandfather said that he thought Julina had plans for him. What might those plans be, and why didn't I think about that before? Maybe she wants to threaten him in order to get me to do what she wants, whatever that is.

All these thoughts and worries, as well as thunder, lightning and rain, keep me awake, even though I know that I need sleep. Tomorrow will be another long hard day riding south through the mountains.

I roll over, trying to get comfortable. The bracelet that I started wearing in a leather pouch around my neck yesterday, presses into my chest. I turn again. I wanted it closer than my belt pouch, easier to get if I needed it, but there's no reason why I shouldn't wear it around my wrist. Grandfather knows all about it, and no one else is with us.

It takes only a moment to sit up, open the pouch and slip the silver circlet of ivy leaves onto my left wrist. It's always felt most comfortable there. As soon as it touches my bare skin a tingle moves up my arm. That's never happened before. I close my eyes to concentrate on the feeling. All is dark behind my eyelids, then gradually pinpoints of light appear, like tiny stars. I feel a warm breeze on my face.

"Samel?" a familiar voice whispers. "Are you there?"

"Ali?" I whisper back, not wanting to wake Grandfather.

"Yes, it's me."

"Where are you? Do you know?"

"I think I must be in the old sorcerer's castle. They put me on the flat roof of a crenellated tower. I'm locked in, high up. Are you in Schönspitze?"

"No. On our way to rescue you."

And then I see her, sitting with her back against a stone wall, night sky above, stars twinkling. "I can see you now!" she says. "Are you in a tent? What if Julina is watching?"

"It doesn't matter if she is. She sent a note saying she's got you and telling us to come."

"You and who else?"

"My great grandfather – I just call him Grandfather - is with me, and I think Rowan and her friend Atsu are coming as well."

"I should have been more careful and not let myself get captured."

"I doubt that you could have prevented it unless you had militia guards with you all the time." I smile. "What's really amazing is that we are having such a long talk. With Rowan, I've done that only occasionally."

Ali shakes her head. "It's making me nervous. What if this is part of Julina's plan? I think we should say good-bye now."

"All right. How do we do it?"

Before I can say another word, Ali is gone. "I hope we can talk again soon," I whisper.

I snuggle back into my blankets, feeling very sleepy now. I try to think about what just happened, to figure out how it could have happened. Ali was afraid that maybe Julina had planned our connection and our talk. From my encounter with Julina during the fire near Schönspitze I know what it feels like to have Julina in my head, and this time I didn't sense her at all. It's possible that she can shield herself from me, but for some reason I doubt that. I touch the bracelet and it warms to my fingers. Ali is safe for now; that's the most important thing.

Chapter IX

Ali

So stupid. In all the years I've known Samel I never thought that his friendship could be dangerous. And then the times he talked about the old sorcerer and being held prisoner in his castle it never crossed my mind that any of it had much to do with me. The things he knew about Julina seemed rather vague. I don't remember him ever describing her or her daughter to me.

I have to admit, Samel's gone through a lot in the last couple of years. First, he found that silver bracelet that helps him call wind and his father didn't want him to use it. Then he discovered he had an older sister, and that their mother drowned recently. Samel had always thought his mother died long ago, so for a while he was furious at his father for not telling him the truth.

Maybe all that turmoil is why Samel didn't think to warn me about Julina and Varonne. Still, the rage that rises in me makes me reach for the stones of this tower, wanting to tear it down with my bare hands! Ouch! All that gets me is broken nails and scraped fingers. When I think about it, I realize that of course my friend had no idea the women would take me, how could he?

Samel, his father and sister were imprisoned in this very castle by Hrashak. Maybe I should have tried to talk to Samel longer tonight, asked him what he knew about the castle that might help me. Secret passages? Weaknesses?

Varonne put me in some kind of trance when she threw that dust into my eyes in Aquila. I remember coming back to myself once when we were walking through the market. Then later it was dark, and I lay on sand. Once I sat at a table and Julina urged me to eat. Was I in a trance for more than a day? How many days have I been gone from home? I should have asked Samel, but he wouldn't know because he wasn't in Aquila. Unless Rowan mentioned it to him.

Rowan killed the old sorcerer by magic, using her silver wristlet. I have nothing like that, only the piece of obsidian that Samel gave me. It's still hanging in the small leather pouch around my neck. Neither Julina nor Varonne tried to take it away from me. I don't know if they searched me, so it could be that they don't know I have the stone. Or they don't think it's important.

You'd think that Rowan killing the old man was a good thing: he was keeping them prisoner and had caused her mother's death. But Samel said it made Rowan sad for a long time. Before Hrashak's death she'd been brave and angry and determined. When they got back to Aquila, Samel kept trying to think of things to make his sister feel better – showing her the city, introducing her to people – but nothing seemed to work. I don't think I've ever been as sad as Rowan looked. It must have been terrible when she found out that her parents had lied to her and Samel, separated them when they were too small to remember. Maybe all those things made her like she is, kind of abrupt sometimes, closed to others, hard to like. How awful if I'd never known my sisters, not grown up with them. I'd be a different person.

Suddenly I want them terribly: my sisters, Mère and Père. I want to be in my room, in our house, among all the familiar things – my paints and drawing materials, the courtyard. Tears gather at the corners of my eyes, flow down my cheeks. I brush them away angrily. Have to keep up my courage, not let sadness and sorrow keep me from making plans.

A yawn nearly splits my face. They left me a couple of scratchy blankets, though it's not cold up here. I could make a sort of mattress with them, then sleep, maybe think more clearly in the morning. I need to figure out if there's a way I can help Samel and the others to rescue me. My thoughts keep running on, through the conversation I had with my friend, speculating about the two women who captured me, wondering what might happen next and what I could possibly do about it. The stars twinkle above me in a friendly way, though there's no moon. I yawn, close my eyes.

***

"Wake up!"

A groan escapes me. I stretch arms and legs, unwrapping from the tight ball I've been as I slept curled against the warm wall of stone. I squint against brightness, see the shadow of a person above me.

"What's the matter now? Can't you let me sleep?"

"My mother wants to see you. And there's food."

I sit up, realizing that it's brighter up here on the tower; it's morning. "Where?"

"Downstairs. Hurry up. Bring the blankets."

I bundle the blankets under my arm and follow Varonne through a trap door and down a steep grey stone stairway. She's wearing her black leather armour already this early in the morning. Maybe she never takes it off. Does she sleep in it? It could be that she didn't sleep last night, stayed on guard.

"Were you awake all night?" I ask.

"What business is it of yours?" she flings back over her shoulder and speeds up.

"Only trying to be friendly," I mutter, but either Varonne doesn't hear or she's ignoring me.

I move much more slowly and carefully than Varonne. The stairs are lumpy in places, cracked here and there. I don't intend to stumble, fall and batter myself, so I take my time. Where are we going? I think about asking, but Varonne will likely not answer. Finally, she waits for me beside a small plain wooden door, tapping one foot, impatient with my slow pace.

"I'd think you'd be hungry," she says, "after not eating much for a couple of days."

I don't answer, just follow her through the door. She's given me useful information: it has been at least a couple of days since they took me away from Aquila. Which means that they probably used magic to get me here, because from what I remember Samel saying, it took them several days by horse and cart to return from the castle to our city.

We enter a wider hallway decorated here and there with rusty bits of armour and weapons. There's dust along the base of the walls and spider webs scattered here and there over the weapons. No one's been taking care of this place.

Varonne stops at the first door we reach, to our right. This one is larger than the door to the tower, and carved with leaves and curlicues, but stained and darkened in spots.

Varonne knocks. The door creaks open. Varonne motions me to enter ahead of her. I step forward into dimness, a single candle on a small table lighting the way. The room feels airless and a slight tightness in my temples signals a headache coming on. A shadow moves beyond the candle to my right.

"Come." Julina gestures and another candle lights in her hand. "Sit here."

I follow her to a heap of dark pillows around a low rectangular table. It's laden with platters of bread, cheese, and fruit, jars and small dishes, a couple of goblets and a flask. I put down my blankets and sink into a pillow. Julina sets the candle on the table and sits opposite me. My head is thumping like one of Samel's small drums.

"We could use more light," Julina says, as if she's just thought of it. Her hands clap and lanterns spring to light all over the room. Maybe she's showing off, trying to scare me with her powers. Her long robe is the colour of dried blood.

It's not a large room. Dark tapestries hang on the walls; I smell the dustiness of them but can't make out details of their design. A couple of wooden chests sit in a corner, along with a smaller table. Heaps of multi-coloured pillows lie scattered about. When I turn back to look at Julina I can tell she's waiting for a reaction to her magic. And to the room perhaps; she probably chose it deliberately to set me off balance. Or maybe there's just not much furniture in the castle. I keep my face as blank as I can. But even that will give her some idea of me, how I'm likely to act in the future. I'm going to stay as calm as I can, try not to show my feelings.

"So," she says, "pretending to be a brave one."

I don't answer, ignoring the attempt to belittle me. Instead, I reach toward the nearest platter and snag a slice of bread, tear off a bite. My stomach has suddenly let me know how empty it is. As I chew my forehead begins to itch. I rub it and stop chewing. Is there something wrong with the food? Should I spit it out? Julina chuckles. She isn't eating anything herself. What if the food is poisoned?

"It's perfectly safe," Julina says. She picks up a knob of cheese and nibbles at a corner.

I hesitate for only a few moments before swallowing and taking another bite. After all I have to eat some time, keep up my strength for whatever is to come. If she wanted to kill me she'd have done it at the beginning, wouldn't she? Of course, she could have put something in the food that will make me sick, a sort of torture to weaken me, but I'm too hungry to let that thought deter me. The headache isn't any worse and the itch on my forehead fades.

After pouring from the flask into one of the goblets, Julina watches me in silence. She sips now and then but doesn't offer me anything to drink. It doesn't matter; I'm not thirsty yet. Finally, my hunger somewhat appeased, I sit back and wait.

"Well, what do you think?" Julina asks.

"About what?" There's an odd feeling inside my head, as if sticky fingers are trying to snag my thoughts. Some of the candles have gone out and Julina's face is harder to see, but her eyes catch the gleam from one of the remaining flames.

"Anything at all. The reasons why we took you. What's going to happen next."

My throat tightens, tickles; I cough to clear it. "You're the one who knows the answers to that. You tell me."

I feel more than fingers in my head; pressure, squeezing, that reminds me of someone juicing a lemon. Is she trying to pry into my mind? Will all my thoughts be laid bare, including my talk with Samel in the tower? That can't happen! Then all goes dark. I can't feel any part of my body and I can't see a thing. I try to speak but that doesn't work either. Help! I think very strongly, not sure who I am addressing. In that instant, I feel warmth at my chest, a spot under my tunic. It must be the piece of obsidian that Samel gave me, letting me know that it's there, giving comfort. The pressure in my head fades. I can see again, am in the same dim room, Julina sitting across from me.

"I'm tired," I say, and yawn as widely as I can.

Julina leans forward. "What do you know about the silver bracelets?"

My teeth snap together. I don't say a word.

Julina stares into my face. Her eyes are dark and deep as wells. I could fall into them and drown. Black water rising from my feet, over my legs, up to my waist. I can't move. She wants me to think of the bracelets. To thwart her I think of the black stone hanging secretly under my tunic. Feel its warmth and its friendlier darkness, a rock to stand on. The images of water recede.

"You've done nothing but sleep for days!" Julina exclaims.

Have I been here that long? Or maybe she's just trying to confuse me. "Could be the mountain air." I yawn again. "Or it's this room. I can hardly breathe here." I'm babbling and it doesn't make sense. The two things cancel each other. All I want to do is get out of here, back to the tower.

Julina stands. "Fine. Varonne will take you. You and I will talk again later."

It's both a threat and a promise, but I'm not going to worry about that now. I step into the hall and take a deep breath. Varonne is there to lead me upwards.

Chapter X

Atsu

Near the western gate out of Aquila I watch Rowan say good-bye to her Father. I expect another argument, but though Yarvan's face looks as if it could crumble at any moment, he says only a few low words to Rowan. She responds with a quick hug.

Yarvan moves closer to me and I hear him say, "Take care of yourself, daughter."

"I'll let you know how we're doing," Rowan says. "I think I can do it, using the bracelet."

Yarvan's eyes light up. Then he frowns and shakes his head. "But I don't have a bracelet so how will you do it? Besides would it be wise even if you could?"

"I'll be careful, Father. Won't you want to know how we're getting on? And find out if we meet Samel?"

He sighs and finally bobs his head. Then he touches my shoulder. "Take care of each other."

I nod, and he grasps my hand. Rowan is already mounting her horse, Lady. Yarvan steps back. I give him another nod and mount my own horse. A group of soldiers clusters by the gate to watch us leave – all looking grim. One man comes forward to speak to Rowan – he wears a wide leather baldric over one shoulder down to his hip, but it holds no sword though it looks scratched and worn. Rowan leans down to him; I can't hear what he says.

I grab the lead of our pack horse and we ride away from the city with the light of the sunrise behind us, darkness still ahead. The sun will be climbing higher soon, brightening the west eventually. Rowan doesn't look back but stares forward and spurs her horse. I follow a little more slowly and do look back. The group still stands watching, Rowan's father among them. The man with the baldric is the only one who turns and leaves.

I nudge my horse to catch up with Rowan. "Who was that man?" I call to her. "And what did he say to you?"

Rowan slows her horse so that we're riding side by side, the pack horse behind. She gives me a small smile that makes my throat tight. "The Captain of Eagles. He told me that though no people could come along to help us, the eagles of Aquila will be watching. If we need them, they will come down, and we can send a message."

"Do you believe him? And what about Julina? She will surely know the eagles are with us."

Rowan sighs. "Yes, she has ways of seeing into distance, but it involves using water and candles. At least that was the method she used when she helped me. Not simple, and not something she can do constantly."

"You don't know that for sure, though."

"No, I don't, but eagles can fly very high and still see what's going on below them. Julina may not notice the eagles if she's concentrating on us."

"She could have other ways of keeping track of us. Can she hear us talking do you think?"

Rowan shrugs. "We can't worry about all that. No matter what, we're going to the mountains."

Should I tell her about what I discovered at the river? I felt confident then but now I'm not certain mist can keep Julina from seeing us. My shoulders are tight. I loosen them. Why not tell Rowan anyway? I say quietly, "I think I have a way to keep her from seeing what we're doing."

Rowan whispers, "Really? What is it?"

Just like Rowan I have a small water skin hanging around my neck so we can drink as we ride. Larger water sacks hang on the pack horse; you have to be well prepared in the desert. I twist off the stopper of my skin and squeeze water into my cupped left hand. Breathe gently across that water, dispersing drops into the air, creating a ragged patch of mist. As I blow the mist continues to grow and thicken until it gradually surrounds us. I cork the water skin and grin at Rowan.

She shakes her head gently. "Julina will see the moving mist and know that we're coming."

"Yes, of course. She knows we're coming anyway, but she might not know what we're doing or saying inside the fog. Do you think that's possible?"

Rowan doesn't speak as we ride side by side along the clearly marked Traders' Road, inside my mist. Is she angry at me for some reason or just thinking? As we move further into the desert and as the sun rises, the air warms. Arid dust rises and tickles my nose. Soon I'll want to take off my cloak.

Finally, Rowan reaches over to touch my arm briefly. "Thank you Atsu, for trying. It does make me feel safer to be riding with fog around us."

"We still don't know if it makes any difference to Julina. Um, what if you used your bracelet? Can you try to find out if Julina's presence is near?"

"I've never done anything like that, but I'll try."

Rowan ties the ends of her horse's reins around her saddle horn. I'm impressed how easily she rides, though I do remember that she was good on a horse when we rode back from Vatnborg. I'm feeling out of practise. Rowan has the bracelet out now on her left wrist. Even though hardly any of the sun's light filters through the mist, the silver bracelet glimmers. She lifts her arm and moves it in a circle above her head, something I've never seen her do before. Sparkles trail from her arm, falling around her, floating through the haze along with us. Rowan laughs and I catch her joy, letting my own chuckles out.

"I don't think Julina's with us," Rowan says. "At least, I don't feel her presence, nothing that reminds me of her as I knew her in Timberton." She lowers the bracelet toward her lips and blows as I did with the water. More sparks fly. "You've inspired me, Atsu! And you've made me feel more hopeful. Who knows what we can do if we try?"

I barely feel the horse under me. I've inspired Rowan! I'm suddenly filled with joy and hope lightens my heart. We will do this. "Let's go then! I want to move faster."

We spur our horses on. Periodically as the fog thins, I pour more water into my hand and blow it into the air. We stop briefly at two oases along the way to top up water, eat, and rest the horses. As the sky darkens toward evening, I let the fog fade away. By nightfall, we reach the village with the hostelry that Rowan has told me about. This is the only such place before the desert ends. According to the map I saw, it will take several days from here to reach the castle in the mountains. I rode further north when I journeyed to Vatnborg; seems a long time ago. I was alone then and thought myself an orphan. Now I have friends and know at least something more about my parents and why they left me. Life can change.

The yard of the hostelry holds a couple of wagons, as well as a few horses, camels, and oxen in the stables. One of the stable boys directs us to three adjoining empty stalls. They are clean enough, with fresh sand on the floor, buckets for water, and mangers for feed. One of the stalls has a wide shelf up high on the outer wall with a ladder to it.

"Some puple sleep wid anmals an tack," the stable lad mumbles.

I hand him a copper coin. "Thank you. We'll look after our own water and feed."

"Watersina yard," the boy says as he leaves.

"I'd prefer to sleep here, too," Rowan says.

"You'll be more comfortable in the inn," I say. Though I'd be glad to have her stay close to me, I know what her father would want.

"I'd rather not share a room with anyone."

"Ask for a small room with a lock."

She shrugs and we set to unloading and caring for our horses. I haul water, while Rowan measures out grain for each animal. It doesn't take long, but I'm very hungry by the time we finish, and my body is stiff and aching.

"I could do with a dish of something hot," I say.

"I'll go see what I can find and get a room."

While Rowan is away, I arrange the shelf to make a comfortable bed. Put a saddle with tack at each end, a couple of blankets in the middle. I take the time to bend and stretch to work out a few kinks from the ride. It's some time before Rowan returns, and I'm thinking of going in search of her when she finally appears, carrying two bowls on a wooden tray, along with spoons and a round loaf of bread.

"Roast rabbit with tubers," she says. "It would have been chicken except they've had trouble with foxes, lost some hens."

I take one of the bowls and we sit on a rickety bench near our horses' stalls. I poke at the meat in the dish. "Are you sure it's rabbit and not snake or something worse?"

Rowan snorts out a laugh. "The kitchen maid let me taste it. It seems fine."

I take a mouthful and nod. "Good."

"She's also letting me share her room. There's an extra cot."

"The kitchen maid?" I say between bites. "Why is she being so helpful?"

"I gave her a couple of copper coins."

"Hmm."

"I also asked if there'd been any women travelling through here recently, and she said not."

I finish chewing a tough bit, swallow. "Was that wise? What if someone finds out you've been asking questions?"

"Don't worry. I said they were friends of ours, and we were hoping to catch up with them. When she said she hadn't seen any women, I shrugged as if it didn't matter, said maybe they'd gone a different way."

Rowan tucks into her meal. I wipe the last of the sauce out of my bowl with a wedge of bread. Wash it down with the last of the water from the bag around my neck.

"I'm going to fill my water skin at the well. Then, if you like I can take the tray and dishes back to the kitchen."

"I guess you want to see the kitchen maid. She's pretty."

I smile and shake my head. "Just going to have an ale and listen for anything useful. Wait for me here; I won't be long."

The kitchen is quiet, with only two women in it. One clears a table of leftover food, the other washes dishes. The elder must be the cook.

"I've brought our dishes," I say.

The plump older woman, smiles and takes the tray from me. "That is kindly done," she says. "Most often we find pottery lying all over the inn yard, and it's easily broken there."

"I also wanted to thank your maid for sharing her room with my charge. I need to stay with our horses, but I didn't want her to be left unguarded."

The girl washing the dishes, ducks her head and whispers, "I'll take care of her."

"Mina's room has a stout bar inside the door, so the two of them will be quite safe while sleeping," the cook adds.

"Thank you again."

I make for the other door which I assume leads to the common room of the inn. If Rowan had heard me talking to the servants, she'd be annoyed that I represented things in the light I did. But I didn't want to go into long explanations, and I couldn't say Rowan was a relative, since I don't look like her. It seems to me that in this case a simple explanation was best.

The common room holds only a few people, not a busy night. Most heads turn as I enter. In a far corner someone gets up and leaves by the front door. There's something familiar about the way he moves, but I didn't see his face. Before I can do anything, one large man bustles forward.

"You'll be the new arrival," he says. "I'm the innkeeper. Can I be of service?"

"A half of ale, please."

I scan the room again, seeing no one else that seems familiar. I settle at one end of a table where two grizzled long-haired men hunch over tankards. They wear half armour with swords belted about their waists. Soldiers or guards of some sort probably. I nod at them; they nod back. The faces that turned to me when I entered the room have returned to their own affairs.

"Travelling far?" one of the men at my table asks.

"To the mountains. Supposed to meet up with a couple of friends. Have either of you seen a young soldier in black leather armour accompanying an older woman?"

The man who spoke shakes his head. The other stares at me for a moment as if thinking, then he, too, shakes his head. The innkeeper arrives with my ale and I hand him a coin, then down a swallow. The innkeeper heads back to the kitchen; the two men turn to their own drinks. I'd like to ask more questions, but I don't want to rouse any suspicions or draw too much attention to myself, so I finish my drink quickly and return to Rowan.

She's curled up with a blanket on the rickety bench where we sat to eat. Her eyes are closed. I hate to disturb her, but she'll be more comfortable in a room. When I touch her shoulder, she sits up quickly.

"Is it late? I had a strange dream. We were at the river and it rose up and flooded the land. The horses were foundering. Then you woke me. Do you think Julina might try creating a flood again? To drown us?"

"What would be the point of that? She wouldn't have your bracelet then."

"You never know. If she's desperate enough she might hope to recover our bodies."

I shake my head. "Too chancy. From everything I've heard Julina's not a stupid woman."

Rowan sighs. "Guess you're right. Probably it was just a dream, not an omen." She frowns. "You've been a while. What have you been doing?"

"Just having an ale, taking a look at the company. I thought I saw someone familiar, but he left before I had time to be sure. Could have been someone from Aquila travelling in the area. Anything interesting you've noticed out here?"

"No. Before I dozed off, I tried to contact my father with the bracelet, but he was asleep, so I sent a message in a dream that we've reached this inn. I hope it worked." She yawns. "Guess I'll go join the kitchen maid."

***

I wake suddenly, confused for a moment by the smell of horses. Then I remember where I am and look down to check that the horse in the stall below me is all right. It's moving restlessly. Over the stall half door, I catch a low shadow moving. The stable cat? A shaft of moonlight pierces the gloom and I discern the long low body of a fox. It turns its head, eyes glinting, and looks directly at me. I remember that the hostelry has been having trouble with foxes killing chickens.

"Hey!" I say, swinging my legs down over the edge of my shelf bed.

The fox continues to stare at me. It opens its jaws a little, tongue protruding. Looking as if it's smiling at me.

By the time I get to the ladder and climb down, ease past the horse and look over the half door, the fox is gone. I step out, making sure to close the door behind me. Even though I search the whole stable, there is no sign of the fox.

In the yard the moon shines brightly. Again, no sign of any fox, and no sound of restless chickens. I don't know where the chickens are kept anyway, and there's no point waking the innkeeper.

A figure detaches from the deep shadow of the side of the inn, a man wearing a short sword. "Anything wrong?"

"I thought I saw a fox," I say. "I was sleeping in the stable with my horses."

"No worries," he says. "I'll take a look out here."

As I go back to settle myself for a few more hours of sleep, I think about that fox. In my country, across the western sea, we have stories about women who entice men into the forest with their beauty. Once they have the men alone and in their power, the women shift shape, become foxes and tear the men's throats out.

Chapter XI

Samel

"With a hey and a ho, and a jolly so and so we'll travel along while singing a song!" Grandfather croaks this tune while riding beside me on a trail through a green valley, snow-capped mountains on all sides. He's seated safely in the special saddle that we borrowed from the Schönspitze guards, which is a bit like a bucket and a bit like an armchair. Anyway, it holds him securely and gives more support than a regular saddle. Grandfather's voice is no better than a frog's but I don't complain because he's happy.

He stops singing. "I can't remember any more words. Do you know this tune?"

"No, sorry."

"Do we have much farther to go? How many days?"

"Several more days as long as the weather holds."

Grandfather claps his hands. "More adventures!"

He hums to himself, sounding like a swarm of bees. The sun warms and a light breeze ruffles the horses' manes. I pet Izmeer and he turns his head and nickers. A perfect day. We've done well so far, and I've had little to worry about except the occasional bad dream. Of course, I'm always worried about Ali, concerned about how she is being treated, but since we talked, I'm feeling more confident that Julina and Varonne will take care of Ali so that she will be in good shape when we arrive. It's after that things will get more difficult. I touch the silver bracelet on my left wrist to give myself courage, and it warms to my touch.

"Hungry," says Grandfather.

"Didn't you eat enough breakfast? It's not time to stop yet. We can't dawdle on this journey."

"I didn't feel like eating much, we got up so early. Haven't you got a handful of dried fruit or a bit of soft cheese in your belt pouch?" Grandfather asks rather plaintively.

"What about your own pouch," I say.

"Forgot to fill it," he says. "Please?"

I sigh and pull Izmeer up close beside Grandfather. Share a handful of dried apples with him. He nods his thanks.

"Can you chew these all right?" I ask. He doesn't have all his teeth anymore.

"I'll suck on them till they're soft enough for my gums to masticate."

We trot along contentedly for a time, the horses' hooves thumping in rhythm. As we climb out of the valley and onto a narrower track we must ride single file.

Leading the pack horse behind me, I let Grandfather's horse go ahead. Not far above on the mountainside lie a few patches of snow. There's a chill in the air, too. I notice Grandfather shivering.

As soon as we reach a wider section of the trail, I call to the old man. "Let's stop and put on extra layers."

The horses drop their heads as soon as we stop, searching for clumps of grass to nibble. I dismount, reaching into the bag strapped over Izmeer's rump. My warm cloak is in there. As I pull it out, a large feather flutters to the ground. It's the eagle feather that fell as a gift to me on my previous journey with Grandfather and the two soldiers from Schönspitze. I reach down to pick it up; it floats against my bracelet, sending a sudden tingle up my left arm. I grab the feather in my right hand, and that hand tingles, too. What is this? Nothing like it has ever happened. I stroke the feather along the silver ivy leaves and a chime of tiny bells rises into the air.

"What's that noise?" Grandfather asks. He's still sitting on his horse.

I start to answer and then my throat closes, because I'm high in the air looking down on Grandfather on his horse, with me standing alongside, and the pack horse ripping up grass. Everything seems brighter and clearer than normal. My head swivels to the left and I see a great wing, discern the details of feathers. There's another wing to the right. How can I be down there and up here at the same time?

"Samel?" Grandfather's voice is faint.

I'm standing beside my horse holding the eagle feather in my right hand. "I … I just saw … through … um, the eyes of an eagle, I think," I stutter.

"What did you see?"

"Just us, down here."

"Why didn't you look around? How far can an eagle see?"

Hesitantly I reach out with the eagle feather and gently touch the bracelet with the tip. Again, I'm sharing the vision of an eagle. This time I look ahead over mountains, valleys, streams, and trees. Far to the south lies a patch of mist and faintly through that I make out the ramparts and towers of a castle. To the east the mountains gradually sink into hills, and I can discern the outline of a large river. Near the river I spy a thin trail of something in the grass; the eagle knows it's urine, a hare. I am aware of hunger and need drives the eagle as it plunges.

"It's the river from Aquila," I say, standing beside my horse again. "The eagle is going after a hare."

"What?" says Grandfather, and he's shivering a great deal.

"An eagle can see a long way." I tuck the eagle feather carefully into my belt pouch, wrapping it in the bit of cloth that usually holds the bracelet. "Hang on, Grandfather, I'm going to take out your cloak." I get the old man wrapped up, then help him to a drink of water.

"If you can see through the eyes of an eagle …" Grandfather starts.

"It will be very useful," I finish.

"Yes, but it also means that we may have at least one eagle watching over us."

"And ready to help, perhaps." Eagles helped us when we were surrounded by fire on a previous journey into the mountains.

The old man nods and smiles. I remount Izmeer and we set off again. How much of what has just happened does Julina know? Can she see us all the time? Is she following our progress, listening to us talk? If she's keeping an eye on us, she likely can't watch Rowan and her friend at the same time. And whenever she's paying attention to Ali, she probably can't observe the rest of us.

I hope that I'm right about all of this. If so, it means that Julina's attention is split and we might be able to make plans, find ways to defeat her. When Grandfather and I left Schönspitze all I was thinking about was getting to Ali as soon as possible. Now that I've had time to reflect, I realize that it's not going to be easy. But I do have the bracelet and now the eagle feather, weapons against Julina. I can raise winds with the bracelet and see a long distance using the feather. Surely these will give me an advantage.

By the time the sun lies directly overhead we've reached another valley, this one with a stream running through it. We find an open spot surrounded by scrubby evergreen trees. It looks as if others have stopped or camped there; stones in a circle mark a fire pit. A couple of stumps and a log are places to sit. Grandfather groans as I help him off his horse.

"I'm not sure I can get back on again," he says as I help him to a seat.

"Let me start a fire to warm the outside of your body, and then I'll make a tisane for the inside. That ought to help."

"While you're doing that, can we talk?" Grandfather asks. "I think we should make plans about what we might do when we reach the castle."

Chapter XII

Ali

They've put me in an actual room this time, with a wooden bed, a round table holding a jug of water, a stool, and an unlit brazier filled with charcoal. A storage chest stands at the foot of the bed. From the one small window I can see that I'm in a tower looking down at a steep cliff. No way to escape since I don't have any rope and even if I could tear up my blankets and knot them together, they wouldn't be long enough. I asked Varonne why they didn't put me in this room last night, and she mumbled something about it not being ready. It makes me wonder if they have only a few servants here.

I'm glad that Varonne offered a bath; I've barely been able to wash since they kidnapped me and even a horse might hesitate coming close to me.

Certainly, Varonne has kept her distance. Maybe Julina found me too strong smelling in that room where we ate, despite the scents of candles and food. Hah, I hope so. Her own fault. Anyway, Varonne said she'd come to get me when the bath is ready.

They obviously did some preparation for my capture because the chest holds clothes too small for Varonne, unless they're castoffs from when she was younger. They smell clean and are close to my size, so I choose underclothes, a long-sleeved cinnamon-coloured tunic, and a pair of loose viridian pants. Fold them into a pile to take to the bath.

The door opens. "Ready?" Varonne asks.

I'm tempted to ask her a bunch of questions, but she hasn't been forthcoming with answers in the past, so I follow her silently down several sets of stairs to a small room without any windows. A fire crackles in a small fireplace and there's an oval copper tub filled with steaming water. A stool holds a brown towel and pale soap. There's also a large brass ewer holding more water.

"I'll be back in a while," Varonne says, and a key clicks in the lock.

I wish there was a way for me to fasten the door from the inside as I'd rather not have anyone walk in on me when I'm in the bath. I push the stool up against it so at least someone coming in unexpectedly will make a noise. Then I strip and test the water. It's a bit hot, so I splash in cold water from the ewer. I don't think I've ever appreciated how wonderful a tub full of hot water can be because I always had it whenever I wanted it. I soak and scrub, enjoying the lavender scent of the soap.

So Julina wants to know about the bracelets. Not surprising. Maybe she thinks I know more than I do. Samel told me when he found his under his father's bed, but I don't know how Rowan came by hers. I have no idea where the bracelets came from originally. I've seen Samel summon wind with his, and I know that he and his sister can talk together using them. Even if I told Julina all this, which I have no intention of doing, what good could any of that do her? Besides, she may already know some of it.

While lying back and staring at the ceiling festooned with dusty spider webs, I think I hear crunching and creaking noises. I sit up, splashing a bit of water onto the floor. Could there be rats in the room? It wouldn't surprise me. Better get out of the tub; the water has cooled anyway.

I dress in the clean clothes, not forgetting to put the black stone in its leather pouch around my neck. Then I wash my own clothes, wring, and hang them over the stool near the fire, keeping an eye out all the time for furry creatures. I don't see any and the crunching and creaking noises have stopped.

Not long after that the door opens and Varonne waves me out.

"What about my wet clothes? Shall I leave them here to dry?"

"No, bring them back to your room."

As we return up the stairs, I'm thinking that I haven't seen anyone except Julina and Varonne since we came to the castle. I remember Samel telling me that there were guards. Have they all left? And what about a cook, or maids to bring the water for my bath? Surely Varonne and her mother aren't alone in this huge stronghold.

"Umm, who does the cooking?" I ask, just before we reach the door of my room.

"Why?" Varonne says, sneering. "Do you have a request?"

"I'm not hungry right now, but a hot dish would be good later. Stew or a roast chicken with vegetables."

"This isn't an inn!" Varonne exclaims. "You'll eat what you're given!"

She slams the door and locks me in. I drape my wet clothes here and there around the room, wishing someone had lit the brazier. If Rowan were here, she could probably do it with her bracelet. I still feel nicely warm from my bath, but there's no shutter for the window and the room holds a chill. My clothes won't dry very fast. The blanket from the bed will make a good wrap if I get too cold, I guess or I could hang it over the window. At least the bed is on the opposite wall from the window, a bit of shelter when night comes. On impulse, I get out the obsidian stone and place it in the brazier. Close my eyes and think of flames. When I open them, nothing has changed. Either I don't have the right skills, or the stone doesn't work like that. I put the stone away.

I've never been locked in a small room with nothing to do before – no parchment or reed paper, no paints or drawing materials, though I suppose I could take some charcoal from the unlit brazier and sketch on the stone walls. As soon as that idea occurs, I smile and put it into action. If it annoys my captors, so much the better. They'll see that they can't have it all their own way. From now on I intend to resist in whatever way I can, cause whatever trouble that crosses my mind.

There's a particularly smooth part on the wall beside the bed, so I start my drawing there. A few lines and I've got Julina's face. I will need more space for a sketch of Varonne, but all the stones nearby are too rough to take a good image. I walk around the room searching for more flat surfaces to draw on. I could use the floor, but charcoal would be scuffed and worn away quickly by my feet. Movement helps keep me cosy, and I notice a particularly warm spot in the middle of my chest. When I draw out the piece of obsidian from the leather pouch again, it heats my hands. I keep holding it and the warmth spreads to my arms and the rest of my body. I don't need a brazier at all.

Did Samel discover that the black stone could warm like this? If so, why didn't he mention it? He couldn't have known. Probably spent time focusing on the magic of his bracelet. I hope Julina and Varonne don't learn of the comfort of the stone and take it away from me. Quickly I tuck the leather pouch back beneath my tunic. The stone continues to warm me from there.

The sill of the window is wide and smooth enough for a drawing. I brush away the dust with my hand, which is still quite warm. The sill turns oddly slick under my palm and my hand cools. It seems to me that the stone of the window ledge is more even than before. Strange things have been happening. Why not this?

I take the piece of obsidian out of its pouch, hold it in my cupped hands until it feels as if I've wrapped my fingers around a hot beaker of tisane. Lay my left palm against a rough projection at the side of the window. My hand sinks slightly into the stone and I'm scared that I'll be stuck there, but I lift my palm easily, though it leaves a permanent impression. I can't help grinning; I'm tempted to make handprints all over the room but stop myself. The fewer signs of this power, whatever it is, the better. I mustn't give Julina and Varonne any sign of what seems to be developing.

I make a sketch of Varonne on the windowsill, all the while thinking of possibilities. If the stone is powerful enough, it might be the key to helping me escape. How deep a hole could it help me make? It's too soon to try that. I need to wait until my rescuers are closer so that I'll have some place to run. After all, I don't know these mountains, and have no equipment to sleep outdoors or even tools to get food. Though perhaps I could find recognizable berries.

As I draw, I'm aware of odd sounds, as if stones are shifting somewhere. I study floor, walls and ceiling. Is the castle so old that it's no longer stable or safe? But I see no cracks anywhere.

Chapter XIII

Rowan

Sun behind, a few clouds overhead, crisp dry air and a cross breeze – I can't think of a more perfect day for riding through the desert. It can be unbearably hot at times, but right now it's lovely. My body feels light on my horse, Lady as we skim over Traders' Road. I'm thinking of the other horse I had, Angel. He found his way back to the Grasslands People after Varonne took me to Hrashak's castle. I saw him later and decided to leave him there since I had Lady by then. I glance sideways at Atsu riding close; he smiles at me and I grin back. He hasn't cast a mist this morning to hide us. Like me, he probably wants to enjoy the sunshine.

Aquila, the City of Eagles, the arts school, my father, and the hostelry are all left behind. With some regrets I realize in that moment. I'd been wondering ever since I first came to Aquila whether I was meant to stay in one place or not. Yes, I lived for most of fifteen years in a northern cottage with my mother until she died, but I'd been feeling restless there for moons. I don't miss that place, though I think of my mother often and wish she could still be with me. At times, my body aches with missing her. I can go back to see Father whenever I like, but that isn't possible with Mother, harder because our lives were so intertwined. I didn't remember Father and Samel at all, and though I'd wanted so much to find them, life with them turned out not to be easy. However, Aquila has grown on me lately. I liked being involved with the arts school and was looking forward to teaching there.

"Do you miss your parents?" I call over to Atsu.

He moves closer. "I miss never having had parents; they left me in the orphanage when I was so young that I haven't any memories of them. A few visions and stories about them haven't made them feel real to me. I do want to meet them eventually, but who knows whether we'll like each other?"

The Pearl Princess and the Obsidian Dragon are Atsu's parents. They were involved in some huge conflict long ago, so left him with a group of monks to keep him safe. He didn't even know his parents were alive, much less that they were shape-shifting dragons until recently. Families can be difficult. But the sun continues to shine, and the sky is blue.

"I've just been thinking how much I enjoy travelling," I say. "I don't think I'm finished with that, even though I'd been getting used to Aquila and I may make it my home in time."

"Then it's a good thing we have this rescue to take care of, isn't it?"

"It seems wrong to be glad when the journey is about saving a kidnapped girl. I hope Samel got my message, and that they're on their way, too. We'll need to figure out what to do."

"Why don't you try talking to him with your bracelet?"

"It hasn't been easy to contact him, and I worry about Julina overhearing us. I'd rather not use the bracelet too much. Anyway, I don't want to take the time. We should be moving as fast as we can. I'll try to talk to him later."

"Rather than dawdling and enjoying the day?" Atsu slaps the rump of his horse, and gallops off, tugging the pack horse behind.

I urge Lady after them and for a while we make good time. Eventually, though, the horses tire and slow. We let them walk for a while and then Atsu points to a large rock ahead that casts a bit of shade.

"Let's stop there."

We give the horses some of our precious water and a bit of grain. Then wipe them down without taking off saddles and packs. Atsu and I munch on handfuls of dried fruit and nuts. I try not to stare at Atsu too much – his brass-tinged face, his silky black hair. I don't want to make him uncomfortable, but I'm so glad to be with him.

"Are you going to cast a mist at all today?" I ask.

Atsu shrugs. "Julina knows we're coming. Unless there's something specific you want to conceal from her, I think we should ride in the open."

"Fine with me."

We set off again, holding the horses to a trot on the gritty road. Around us, small shrubs and thorny growths dot the sand. I haven't had a chance to learn much about desert plants yet, their uses and dangers. Perhaps I will when we return to Aquila. In the distance to the north rise flat topped hills of stone. After a while, more clouds gather in the sky, particularly to the west and they are tan coloured. I remember that on my first journey to Aquila I ran into a storm of sand. If that's what's massing ahead of us, we should think about what to do.

I pull close to Atsu. "See those clouds? A sandstorm might be stirring. We should stop and shelter beside the horses."

"A sandstorm? Are you sure?"

"Didn't you encounter any in your own travels to Vatnborg?"

"I guess I was lucky."

"It's not uncommon to have such storms in the desert," I point out.

"How long might it delay us? Wouldn't Julina want us to reach her as quickly as possible?"

"You're thinking she might be causing the sand to attack us?

"Maybe. Because if it's natural, why wouldn't she stop the storm or send it in another direction?" Atsu asks. "To get us to her sooner."

"Could be she doesn't have that kind of power. Unless she wants to see what we do, test us in some way." A gust of wind whips grit around the horses' feet. "None of what you say really matters. If that is a storm, we've got to deal with it, no matter what or who may have caused it. I think we should stop now."

Atsu reins in his horse. "There's no shelter. Should we stay in the middle of the road or move off to the side?"

"On the road. At least here we'll have a hard surface under us."

We huddle among the horses and wait. The clouds aren't moving very fast, but the wind is increasing. Atsu and I wrap the ends of our headscarves around our mouths and noses.

"This feels ridiculous," Atsu says.

"What else can we do?"

"If I had experienced such a storm, I guess I'd have done exactly what we're doing now, but I've learned things about my abilities that might help." He taps my shoulder. "You have abilities, too. Let's use what we have."

And then the tempest is upon us, wind swirling sand, tossing it into our faces. We close eyes and mouths, tuck our scarves and hoods tightly around us. I hope that we can breathe well enough. Sand whispers across my shoulders.

"Die, die, die."

Is it a real voice or merely my imagination? Is it a prediction of what awaits us now or at the end of this? I haven't thought about the worst that could happen, and I don't want to. I squint to protect my eyes, still able to see a little, but there's nothing much to discern except tan sand swirling. The wind roars. Is there a dark shape standing in front of me? No, it must just be one of the horses' heads. A brief flash of light, quickly gone.

Atsu leans against me and shouts into my ear. "Did you see that?"

"Flash of light," I shout back.

"Remember our powers," he yells. "Let's use them."

I touch the bracelet on my left wrist. It warms slightly, but nothing else happens. "What do you suggest?"

"Water against sand?"

I see him struggle, then Atsu opens the water skin hanging around his neck and manages to empty some into a palm. He hands the skin to me and I close it. Watch as he stares at the liquid. Nothing happens.

"It's not working," I say.

"Give me time. I'm still thinking what to do."

I stay quiet, barely open eyes watching sand drift over my ankles. My bracelet stays warm and I think about how in the past I've been able to help Atsu with whatever he does. I hope that once he figures out something to do, I'll be able to join in a useful way. The wind dies slightly, and I think that I hear the hooting of an owl. But it can't be. I think of Grandmother Wisdom who died and the owl who came after. Maybe she's watching over me. I grasp the bracelet with my other hand.

Atsu takes a deep breath and blows hard over the water in his hand, scattering drops into the air around us. Is my bracelet getting warmer? I glance at Atsu; he has his eyes closed and is frowning, maybe in concentration. I don't say anything to distract him.

A drop of water hits my nose. Then one lands on my hands. Atsu blows air loudly and opens his eyes. A smattering of raindrops slants across us and I can see the horses more clearly.

"Rain against sand?" I ask. "Do you think it will work?"

"I don't know. Maybe you can get your bracelet to help."

How though? I look at the circlet of ivy leaves around my left wrist. It gleams slightly. I can make fire with it and combined with Atsu's water, have created steam in the past, but that won't help us here. Samel can summon wind, which might blow the sand away, but I've never been able to do that.

"I think the wind is dying," Atsu says. "I can see more clearly."

I look in the direction he's pointing. A new cloud, grey in colour, has appeared to the west, close to us and moving in the direction of the larger sand-coloured clouds.

A ray of sunlight penetrates the clouds and glances off the edges of the silver leaves on my bracelet, hits me in the eyes and I tear up. Drops fall on the bracelet and glitter like tiny jewels; they seem to be growing slightly. I think of a vine of real ivy climbing along a fence, dusty in the sun and then I imagine rain falling on the leaves to wash them clean and green. The wind throws rain and mud into my face.

"Yes!" Atsu shouts.

"No, ugh!" I respond, wiping mud from my lips. I look up and see the intermingling of tan and grey clouds, shapes like two fists. Are there fingers amongst the clouds struggling with each other? Another blast of wind sends sand swirling, then a scatter of rain. The horses huddle closer. Rain, then sand eddies around us, and soon we are in the middle of a warm mud shower. Atsu shakes his head, dirt trickles down his face, his teeth flash white as he grins. I keep my mouth closed and my eyes slitted.

I'd rather have either rain or sand but not this slimy goo. Several more blasts of wind shake us, and then it's mostly over. The wind dies gradually, clouds scatter, and the sand settles. Rain falls for a little longer, which is good, because it washes most of the grime off us and the horses.

"That was weird!" I say.

"Yes, working together isn't always a good thing, I guess."

"Let's head out of here. We must be close to the river by now. I think we should reach it by evening at the latest. I'd like a wash."

"Is that the same river that runs through Aquila?" Atsu asks.

"Yes. It starts in the mountains near Hrashak's castle."

"We just follow it to get to our destination?"

"Right," I say. I think about mentioning the fears that rose in me during the storm when the wind seemed to say, "Die," but I decide not to. I don't want to think about that and there's no point worrying Atsu.

Chapter XIV

Samel

My eyes are filled with blue sky as I soar, circling among white clouds. I see the currents of wind beneath and above, all around me.

"Samel! Samel!"

"What? Why are you shouting? I'm right here at the fire next to you."

Grandfather glowers at me. "No, you were far away. Behind the eyes of an eagle again. I hope you don't try to do that too much while we're riding. You could fall and tumble off a mountainside."

I sigh. It's true, I am holding the eagle feather and I did let my mind wander off. I could see so far, nearly to Aquila. The sun shone over the desert and a couple of riders with a pack horse looked as tiny as ants. At the same time, I was aware of an eagle's mind, one that searched for food and for currents of air to dive into and soar on. The eagle's shriek lingers in my mind, like an eerie melody.

"I might have seen Rowan and that young man she's travelling with."

Grandfather sits straighter. "Really? That's remarkable."

"I'm not sure. I was up so high, and they were too small for me to see their faces."

"Why didn't you fly lower?"

"Because you called me back! And anyway, it wasn't really me flying. I'm not in control. The eagle had its own concerns."

We've been travelling for several days without meeting any major obstacles. There's been wind and rain sometimes, streams to ford, a near miss with a rockslide. A couple of times Izmeer has shimmered and changed back to camel shape, but not for long. Otherwise the journey so far has been uneventful. Perhaps Julina has arranged it that way so that we'll reach her sooner. I don't know what exactly her powers are. I wish I'd listened more closely when my sister told of meeting that woman.

"You still haven't been able to see the castle where Julina is supposedly holding Ali?" Grandfather says.

"No, the eagle's eyes haven't taken me there. It's been only a few days since I learned I could do this. I don't even know if the eagle is actively helping me or just letting me in. On the other hand, I did talk to Ali at the castle using my bracelet, but the only thing I saw that time was the top of the tower where they were keeping her."

"Yes, yes. I just wish we could make more definite plans about what we'll do when we get there. I told you we should do that."

"You're not satisfied with my suggestion that we try to meet my sister and her friend before we get to the castle?" I ask. "Make our plans when we're all together?"

"That's fine as far as it goes," the old man says, "but I'd like some ideas for strategies beyond that. I had great hopes that you'd be able to see exactly what's going on at the castle and we could plot accordingly. And I'd like to know where that cave is that the old sorcerer supposedly found."

"Make up your mind! First, you're annoyed because I'm spending time seeing through the eyes of an eagle, and then you're not happy because I don't see enough. What about your powers? Can you connect with water, underground streams? Find some that flow close to the castle?"

"I'm tired," Grandfather mumbles, "and my butt hurts. My legs keep cramping, and my guts are upset. Is there more mint tisane?"

I take his metal cup and fill it from the kettle sitting at the edge of the fire. It's hard, but I clamp my lips and manage not to shout that he did want to come on this journey. He might be able to help if he put his mind to it. Still, he's an extremely old man, and I have my own aches and pains. I haven't had a grandfather in my life before, or spent long periods with an old person, so I don't know if this is what they're generally like. Maybe I'm expecting too much.

"We're both doing our best," I say as I hand the cup to him.

"Why don't you try talking to your sister using your bracelet? I really would feel better if we knew what she was planning."

"I'd rather not for now. If Julina is watching either of us, she might know whatever we say."

Grandfather sighs. "All right. Maybe a good night's sleep will help me feel livelier."

Unfortunately, he snores particularly loudly this night and not even tunefully; I could excuse musical snoring. Finally, I take my blankets and go sit by the dying fire. I add a few logs and lean against a stump. I'm wide awake. It occurs to me that I haven't looked in the Leather Book for quite some time. Packed it at the last minute and it must be at the bottom of one of my saddle bags. I drag them close to the fire to see clearly; the book comes to hand almost immediately. For a few moments I just hold it. Often in the past a story has illuminated events – will it do that again?

***

Long ago a young girl named Amalthea lived in a small village at the foot of a mountain. None of the people in the village were rich, but they always had enough to eat, growing their own food, and keeping goats. They drank goats' milk, made cheese from it, and spun goat hair into blankets and cloaks. They managed the flock carefully, killing and eating a goat periodically, so that the numbers didn't grow too large for the amount of forage available. Like all the children, Amalthea took her turn herding the goats on the lower slopes of the mountain. She loved the work so much that she continued to do it as she grew into a young woman. The goats seemed to like her more than other herders, too, because they obeyed her more readily.

Her parents wanted her to marry and brought one young man after another to their cottage to eat with them, but Amalthea preferred to spend her time with the goats. Her father argued and thumped the table but couldn't change his daughter's mind. Her mother made sacrifices to the goddess of marriage and childbirth, for she very much wanted a grandchild. Still, Amalthea wandered off to be with the goats.

One day when the young woman had taken the flock much higher up the slopes than usual, looking for the best grasses, a rainstorm came suddenly. Goats are hardy and can stand rain and wind, but still Amalthea looked for shelter as the first drops began to fall. Just a little higher up the mountain she spied a dark patch that she thought might be a cave. She grabbed the oldest nanny by one horn and pulled her along. The others followed and quite quickly they reached the cave.

As they waited out the storm, many of the goats lay down to nap, and Amalthea, too, became sleepy. In a half waking, half dreaming state the young woman saw a tall figure standing in the mouth of the cave. The figure bent forward, and Amalthea had an impression of long dark hair, piercing blue eyes, a gleaming face, but she drifted in a haze, so couldn't be sure if she dreamt, or saw a real person.

"Amalthea," said a musical voice, "I need your help. A special baby needs sheltering and safe keeping. It's in danger from a wizard father. I can't stay with the child but have placed it in another cave much higher up this mountain. I've seen how well you take care of the goat babies. If you will agree to perform this task faithfully, I will transport you to the cave."

"I would like to help, but a baby?" said Amalthea. "How can I take care of a baby? Won't it need milk? I'm not a mother."

"I can remedy that."

"Will the wizard come after the baby? Be angry with me, and change me into a toad or some other creature? I don't think I'm the right person for this."

"You are right because the goats love you. And I've hidden my movements so the wizard can't find the child. In addtion, I'll block this mountain from his sight so he can't find you. I've already started a rumour that the child drowned. Will you agree?" The blue eyes looked deep into hers.

"All right, as long as you take care of my goats."

Amalthea felt her body change. She looked down and saw four legs with hooves instead of two arms and two legs. She tried to speak but only a bleat came out of her mouth. Then raindrops whirled about her and darkness came. She woke in anothter cave with a baby beside her, suckling on her goat teat.

"Don't worry," the tall figure standing over them said. "I've given you the gift of transformation. You'll be able to change back and forth between woman and goat as need requires. Please stay here with the child until I come back to tell you that it's safe. I'll make sure most of your goats get home. You may need some of them here. There's olive oil and flour in the cave, and berries and herbs grow outside. You should be all right for a while."

***

I stroke the book's leather cover thinking of what our cousin Thea said to me once. "I was named after a legend. Amalthea, a goat who saved a child from being killed by concealing him in a mountain cave." When I asked her who the child was, she responded, "The son of a wizard who feared the child's power. There'd been prophecies. I don't remember all the details now. In the end it was the wizard who died."

Why has the book shown me this story? I wish I'd asked Thea more about what she knew. I ruffle through the pages of the book but can't find any other tales related to this, at least not today.

The night is clear, the sky full of stars. It would be amazing to be up there now. Perhaps I could find a secret cave somewhere in the mountains. Would it help us to overcome Julina? I pull out my eagle feather and stroke it against the bracelet on my left wrist, but nothing happens. Maybe the eagle is asleep or off on its own business. Do eagles fly at night? I don't even know if I see through the same eagle's eyes each time. As I put the feather away, the bracelet warms.

"Samel?" a voice whispers.

I look all around, but there's no one to see; Grandfather's snores come softly from the tent. One of the horses moves restlessly.

"I can see you sitting by a fire," the voice continues. "Can you see me?"

"Ali?" And then I do see her, sitting on a cot with a candle nearby. She seems to be in a small stone room. "Are you in the castle?"

"Yes. They've given me a room inside a tower."

"It looks smaller than the one Hrashak kept us in. Are you all right? Are they feeding you?"

"I'm fine. They haven't hurt me, and I've been eating well. Do you remember how you told me that you and your sister cast a silver bubble around you using the bracelets?"

"Yes."

"Would a bubble like that keep Julina from seeing and hearing us? Do you think you could make one like that?"

"Why?" I ask. "Are you worried that Julina or Varonne are watching and listening now?"

"I think they're probably asleep, but I don't want to take any chances. I have something very important to tell you. Do the bubble now."

"I can try, but even if I make one for me, how could it possibly cover you so far away?"

Ali shrugs. "Worth a try."

I touch the bracelet on my left wrist with my right hand. It's glinting in the light of the fire and warm against my skin. Touching it feels like the right thing to do. At times, the bracelets find ways to let us know what they want. Rowan was scared by that, but I've found it useful.

It's like playing music, in a way. You have to find the right approach, the correct fingering, depending on the instrument. It took me a long time to learn to play a wooden flute, to place my fingers just so over the tone holes, to blow the proper amount of air into the mouthpiece.

I close my eyes and imagine a bubble of silver rising from the wristlet, a bubble that grows and expands to surround me. It was Rowan who did this before so I'm not exactly sure how to make it happen. My body begins to tingle and when I open my eyes, a sphere of transparent silver is all around me. Ali isn't inside it though.

I can still see her sitting on the cot. Her hands are cupped around something that shimmers darkly and her eyes are closed. I try to will my silver globe to expand to include Ali, but I'm also trying to see what she holds in her hands. It looks like a black stone, perhaps it's the piece of obsidian I gave her. She's carried it with her to the castle. And Julina has let her keep it. Is it helping me and Ali talk to and see each other? I hope Julina doesn't know about that.

"Ali," I say quietly, "I can't seem to expand the bubble to cover you."

She opens her eyes. "Hang on, I'm doing my best to help. Let's try together. Imagine again the bubble spreading to cover both of us. Ready? Now!"

We close our eyes at the same instant. I take a deep breath and let it out slowly, willing the silver globe to grow toward Ali. As I continue to breathe out, it's as if a part of my body expands. I extend my hands and arms as if I am going to hug my friend. When I open my eyes, we are together, encased in swirling silver and black walls.

Ali grins widely. "That black stone you gave me is amazing! Who would have thought? I think it's helping make this bubble. And you'll never guess what else it can help me do. It can make my hands sink into stone. Not a lot, but enough to leave a mark. I'm going to keep working on it and see if it can help me escape."

"That's what you wanted to tell me!" She nods. "Be careful!" I say. "You don't know how much Julina sees and senses."

"Yes, I know. We should probably stop now. Does magic leave traces sorcerers can sense? Can you imagine the trail this could be leaving? Best let go, Samel."

"Wait! This is good, but don't try to escape until we're closer to the castle. You could get lost in the mountains."

"I know," Ali says. "Good-bye."

And she is gone just like that. The silver bubble remains around me for moments, fading gradually. By the time it's gone completely, a faint light is glowing in the east. Sunrise isn't far away, and I haven't slept. I still feel wide awake, thoughts whirling in my head. It's as if I've suddenly been catapulted into a totally different world. Yes, I'm used to the way the bracelets work, but now I can see through the eyes of an eagle, and my best friend has found extraordinary powers in a piece of obsidian. I suppose it's not so strange that the stone holds the ability for spell craft. It came from the dungeon of the sorcerer, Hrashak, after all. What other powers might that castle hold, and how much of that has Julina harnessed? I really need to talk to my sister.

I reach for the silver bangle again to try to connect with Rowan, but suddenly I'm so exhausted that I can't even stay sitting. I curl into my blankets, lie near the fire and fall into sleep.

Chapter XV

Ali

After talking to Samel I'm exhausted, as if I've been walking for hours. It's probably because I was so worried about Julina catching us. And maybe it takes a lot out of a person to do this kind of magical work. Samel never said anything about that, but maybe that's partly why his sister doesn't like using the bracelets. I lie flat on the cot to rest, slip back into sleep. And into comforting dreams.

Grande Tante Rochella sits with me by the outer walls of Aquila, not far from the main gate. Her long grey-streaked black hair in a single braid, trails over her left shoulder as she bends forward to show me bits of shiny stuff among the gravel and dirt. Some pieces are white, others clear.

"Quartz," she says. "It comes in other colours too." She turns to point at the wall beside us, which is speckled black and grey. "Granite."

"How do you know so much about stones, Tante?" I ask.

She smiles. "My mother and father. They were stone cutters and taught me a lot about the earth and its bones."

"The earth has bones?"

"That's what I call the rocks and mountains. Dirt and plants are rather like skin on the bones."

"But people's bones don't poke out of them like rocks do out of earth."

"You're right. I'm glad you pay attention. Now put your hand on this wall, close your eyes, and try to feel into the stone, its structure and composition. Granite came out of fire mountains, cooled long in the earth."

I spring awake as the door to my tower room slams open. This time it's Julina standing there, glowering at me. I sit up and swing my legs over the side of the bed. Calm. Whatever she's about to say or do, I need to stay calm. If she doesn't know what I did in the night, I can't show any signs of it.

Julina takes several steps toward me. "There's a scent of magic in this room. Samel's been seeing you with his bracelet, hasn't he? What did he say?"

I just stare at her, concentrate on the streak of red in her hair, how it twists over her shoulder, falls onto her midnight blue robe. Her hair is coarser than my Grande Tante Rochella's was. There's a greasy stain on Julina's robe. Who does her laundry? How many different colours of robes does she have?

A sneer twists her face. "Don't want me to know? If I really push, your mind won't be able to hold out against mine."

An itch begins in my head, one I can't scratch. My head starts to ache, as if someone is thumping it with their fist. I know it's Julina battering my mind. A picture comes of Samel and me near the sand shrine; he wears his bracelet and plays the wooden flute, raising a breeze that makes dried leaves dance. I close my eyes to shut Julina out, but it doesn't work. Phantom fingers twiddle and prod, tease out another memory: Samel stands in front of me and yet his feet don't touch the ground. "How did I get here?" he asks.

"No," I whisper. This is too close to recent events.

Julina laughs, but I don't open my eyes. I try to think of darkness, the night sky over the desert, stars twinkling, a bright moon. Someone is humming, beginning to chant.

"Let them come, the memories. Let go, yield to me."

Samel sits by a fire holding his bracelet. This can't go on, mustn't. I hear Grande Tante Rochella's voice in my head. "Try to feel into the stone. Granite came out of fire mountains, cooled long under the earth." I realize that my feet are cold, bare and touching the stone floor of the room. It supports me, gives me strength.

I move my thoughts from Samel to the fire near him, concentrate on the flames, try to think only of them rising, crackling loudly, the smell of smoke. A shriek breaks my concentration, and my eyes fly open. Julina has turned away from me and is looking toward the window. There are more shrieks and then sounds like laughter.

"What is the matter with those birds!" Julina says, moving forward and leaning out of the opening.

As I take a step forward, a flutter of black wings at Julina's shoulder makes her leap back. Now I can see several ravens wheeling and darting about just outside the tower window. One dives down out of sight while another jumps onto the window ledge and perches there. It opens its beak wide, makes a sound like a rusty door hinge and closes its beak with a click. Perhaps this means something to Julina, for she turns, leaves the room and slams the door.

I rush over and check the door first, but it's locked. Next, I run to the window. The raven has left, though several still fly about not far away. I look down and see a lone horseman beating off another raven. Varonne dashes out waving her sword. That raven flaps away and the others follow. Then Julina is there, too and the two women and the man talk, but I can't distinguish any words. Soon all of them enter the castle gate.

What was all that about? Did the ravens distract Julina on purpose as she tried to find out what I'd been doing? Perhaps the messenger or soldier arrived right then coincidentally, and the ravens set up a fuss. Whatever, it helped to save me from Julina's attack on my mind. I can't expect that to happen every time. Have to think of ways to thwart her, to get stronger at holding her off. I could ask her questions or think of my family in Aquila. What are they doing, feeling? They'll be worried about me, missing me, as I miss them. No, can't go there. I will not break down now.

I'm curious about the man who arrived. Maybe he was bringing news about Samel or Rowan. He's the first person other than Julina and Varonne that I've seen around the castle. But there could be others. I wish I could find out more about what is going on here, what exactly Julina wants. Right now, I should concentrate on finding more ways to fight her.

Thinking of things other than Samel helped a little, but not for long. Asking questions, lots of them is probably better. Just throw them at her one after another. That might make her angry, but at least it would be a distraction. Like, who does your laundry? How many servants are there in the castle? Were you really married to the old sorcerer who lived here before? Why did you leave him?

That dream of Grande Tante helped. She loved stones and did teach me a lot about them, but I don't remember her telling me to feel the walls of Aquila. She's dead now, but perhaps her spirit sent me a message? I've never thought about things like that before.

I shake my head, lean on the windowsill and look around. Beyond the castle all I see are rocks and mountain peaks. Some are blanketed with snow, others bare. Dark trees creep up the slope of many, a few are exposed sheets of rock. A faint path leads from the castle into the mountains, but I can't see very far along as it turns past a cliff and disappears. Are these mountains made of granite? What other types of stones? Might that be important for me to know as I deal with Julina?

I can't see any signs of the ravens now. Samel told me once that his sister had a tame raven that lived with her and her mother. They used him sometimes to send messages. If I could send to anyone it would be to my family to let them know that I'm all right. They must know who took me and where I am because Samel said that Julina had sent a message. I'm surprised Père hasn't set off with Magenta's man and a group of the Lord's Militia to rescue me. Maybe they are on their way and no one else knows about it. Might it help if I suggested as much to Julina? I pound on the windowsill. Where is Julina and what is she doing? Now that she's gone, I want to see her, to try out my ideas of keeping her out of my mind.

As if in answer to my wish the door opens. It's Varonne with a cloth-covered tray. She sets it on the floor just by the door. Starts to leave.

"Wait! I want to talk to your mother."

"She's busy." The door clicks shut.

"I have questions for her!" I shout at the wooden surface. No one answers me.

The tray holds half a loaf of bread, a small yellow cheese, a heap of nuts and dried grapes, and a beaker of water. I am hungry. I take the tray over to the window, pull the chair over so I can look out while I eat. I crumble a bit of bread onto the sill in hopes that it will attract one of the ravens. This is a lonely tower. I like spending time alone, but not when I'm a prisoner. Maybe after breakfast I'll do more drawing. I could try a raven or two, a fitting decoration for these walls.

Are those black dots I see in the sky? I swallow a final bite of cheese and lean out of the window, scrunching my eyes. Yes, two dots, moving closer. Soon I can discern the flap of wings. A faint croaking call comes to my ears. Then I realize that I've knocked the breadcrumbs off the sill. The ravens flutter and skim as they come closer. I never noticed before that ravens aren't solidly black – their feathers hold shades of charcoal, dark blue, and even purple. One of these has a few traces of white near its neck; perhaps it's older. Do raven's feathers lose colour as they age?

Quickly I place a few morsels of cheese and more bread on the sill and move back. One of the birds lands immediately and looks at me, making a chuckling noise. Then it swallows a piece of cheese and leaps off the sill. The other bird approaches and does the same but stays.

"Hello," I say quietly, holding out a piece of bread.

The raven on the sill leans forward and takes the bread, swallows it down. The other bird joins the first and I feed them alternately, the last of my bread and cheese. One of the birds leans against the other, rubbing head-to-head. Perhaps they are a mating pair. What thoughts and memories might they have?

"I wish I could talk to you, and you could talk back," I say. "I'd enjoy your company."

One of the ravens makes a clicking sound with its beak. The other says, "Kraa" very softly.

"Do you know Samel? He's a friend of mine. I wish I had parchment so I could try to send him a message."

The ravens hop around on the window ledge, turning their backs on me.

"Hmm, does that mean no?"

Their heads bob up and down.

"Well, what about Rowan?" I ask. "She's Samel's sister. I heard she was friends with a raven once."

The birds turn as soon as I say Rowan's name. They regard me out of their dark eyes. The one on the right opens its beak, then snaps it shut.

"Taller than me, has black hair and grey eyes?"

More bobbing of heads.

"I guess you can see colours?"

The heads of both ravens nod twice. I can't quite believe that they understand me. Probably head nodding is just something that birds do for no particular reason, though these are doing a lot of it. Still, I like them.

"Thank you for distracting Julina earlier. She's the older woman with the red streak in her black hair. She was trying to ask me questions that I didn't want to answer. I hope that you'll keep watch over me, help me again if you can."

The ravens nod their heads once more and then they fly off. I finish the last of the nuts and dried grapes and put the tray by the door, set the beaker of water near my bed. Get a piece of charcoal from the brazier and begin to draw ravens wherever I find a smooth enough spot on the walls. I become so absorbed that it takes a while for me to realize that I haven't had a midday meal, and the sun is moving toward setting. Have Julina and Varonne forgotten about me or decided to starve me into submission?

As I'm cleaning my hands with a bit of the water, a knock comes on the door. This is unusual.

"Yes?" I respond.

The door opens and a helmeted guard steps in carrying a tray. He's wearing metal plated armour and has a sword on a belt at his side. He's taller and wider than Varonne. Do they fear me now for some reason?

"Are you the one who rode in earlier?" I ask.

He doesn't say anything, merely sets the tray down, picks up the empty one, and leaves, locking the door as he goes. It's a hot meat and vegetable stew and I'm so hungry that I can barely wait for it to cool. There's a half loaf of bread, a beaker of water and a few figs. I guess they don't intend to starve me after all. Perhaps they were so busy that they forgot about feeding me until now. But doing what? If I'm going to be of any help to my rescue party, I need to know more about what goes on here and how many people there are.

After I've finished eating, I lie on the cot. I don't even consider trying to talk to Samel. I've avoided trying to use the stone all day, too. I don't want to leave any more traces of magic for Julina to sniff out if she comes back. But if no one comes, how will I find out what I want to know?

Chapter XVI

Atsu

In the flicker of the firelight Rowan's face glows as if lit from within. She's stirring a pot of what she calls cassoulet and adding pinches of herbs. As she lifts the wooden spoon to sample the latest addition, her eyes meet mine.

"Want a taste?" she asks, holding the spoon out to me. "Someone in Ali's family is a good cook, considering the herbs they included in our supplies."

I feel my face heat with a sudden wish to lean forward and kiss the taste of meat, beans, and herbs on her lips. Luckily, the nearness of the fire can explain my sudden ruddiness.

"I'll wait," I manage and turn to grasp a piece of wood to add to the fire.

"I'm glad we've finally reached the river," Rowan says as she goes back to stirring. "We should be able to see the mountains once it's daylight."

"A long ride today. When do you think we might meet your brother and the grandfather?"

"It depends on when they left and what route they decide to take. The cassoulet is ready, can you get out bowls?"

I have them and our spoons near at hand. Rowan removes the pot, sets it on a flat stone and puts a kettle of water on the fire. I set the bowls beside the pot and begin to ladle out food.

"Hrashak's castle," says Rowan, turning back to me, "is closer to Schönspitze than to us. So Samel and Grandfather could reach Julina before we do."

"But?"

"I'm hoping that they will decide to take a slightly longer route and meet us first, so that the four of us can talk, plan, and then go to the castle together." She blows on her first spoonful of beans and begins to eat.

I leave my bowl to cool. "But we don't know their plans. Couldn't you try to talk to Samel with the bracelet and suggest the meeting?"

"I will have to try that eventually, but I'm not sure how to decide when the right time is. I wish there were some way of knowing if and when Julina watches us."

We both dig into our cassoulet. I find a piece of rabbit and chew it, while looking at Rowan. Her hair flows over her shoulder like a black river. I imagine how soft that hair would feel to my fingers. No. I have to stop these kinds of thoughts. I remember what her father said. I'd like you to think about a father's concerns and a father's rights. As long as I don't do anything, though, I should be able to think what I like.

A sudden screech startles me so that I drop my bowl and spoon. At least it's empty and doesn't spatter food all over me. A flutter of black wings signals a raven landing on the other side of the fire. A second one settles nearby. Onoku didn't like ravens; thought they were spying. Could these be from Julina?

Rowan puts her bowl down slowly, leans forward.

"Careful," I say. "Don't get too close to the fire. Your hair could catch or your clothes."

"Hello," she says softly. "You two look familiar. Could it be …?"

"How can you tell one raven from another," I interrupt. "They're all black and bigger than crows."

"You can if you've spent enough time with them or observed them closely. For instance, I'd know my Morde anywhere by a certain nick in his claw, by the arrangement of feathers, and shades of colour. But neither of these is Morde." She moves slightly away from the fire and slides around the side, closer to the birds. "Thought and Memory?" Rowan says hesitantly.

One of the birds squawks while the other appears to nod its head. It must be just the fire flickering. Then I remember the two ravens that sat on the roof of the school in Vatnborg; Thought and Memory was what the head of the school named them. I hardly noticed the birds, but Rowan watched them all the time.

"You think these are the ravens from the school? What would they be doing so far from home?"

Rowan picks up her spoon and digs into the pot of cassoulet. She puts a couple of pieces of meat on a nearby rock. The ravens hop awkwardly forward. I notice that they each have something grasped in a claw. They gobble the meat.

"They probably haven't just come from Vatnborg," Rowan says. "Don't you remember the ravens that followed us, the ones Onoku didn't like? And later I told you ravens had gathered at Hrashak's castle after Julina moved there with her daughter? I believe these are Thought and Memory, but from that castle."

"They could be Julina's spies."

"I don't think so."

The birds are acting very oddly. Each has put a flat stone that it was carrying onto the rock that just held their meat. They nudge them about with their beaks, creating a peak roof and then changing that by piling one of the stones atop the other to make a very short tower.

"See?" says Rowan. "They're showing us that they've come from the castle. I wonder what they could tell us about Ali?"

"You're not telling me that these ravens can talk?"

Rowan shakes her head. "I very much doubt it. But they might be able to communicate something." She feeds them more meat and studies them.

I'm about to express my disbelief, but before I can say more than, "Well," Rowan holds up a hand to stop me.

She leans toward the ravens. "Is Ali all right?"

Both birds nod, and this time I can't blame it on the flickering flames. The nods are very distinct.

"I wonder if you could take a message to her secretly," Rowan says.

The ravens nod again.

"No, no!" I burst out. "Get them to take a message to your brother. That's more important at the moment, and safer. We don't want Julina to get hold of any messages. Do you really trust them?"

Rowan leans back. "Hmm. That's a good idea."

While she writes the note, I feed the ravens more of the cassoulet, laying it on a rock so they can't nip my fingers. They gobble down meat, beans, and vegetables. It's a wonder they don't choke.

"I'm telling Samel to come down out of the mountains and meet us along the river road." Rowan ties the scrap of parchment securely around one of the raven's necks with a piece of leather thong. "Thought and Memory, I'm depending on you. Find my brother Samel, who is riding with an old man. Samel has red hair and gold-flecked eyes. Make sure they get this message."

The birds screech and then they're off, disappearing into the dark night.

"What if Samel doesn't trust the birds? Does he have your experience with ravens?"

"I told him who the ravens are, and I also wrote something only he and I would know. So as long as Thought and Memory reach him and get him to see the note, all should be well."

I ladle myself another bowl of cassoulet without responding. I have plenty of doubts, but there's no sense airing them now. What's done is done.

"We might as well finish the pot," Rowan says.

Later, after we've washed dishes and banked the fire, we get out our bedrolls. It's a fine night so we decide not to bother pitching the tent. The horses are content, tied to a nearby tree, with plenty of grass to munch. This is the best camping spot we've had since leaving Aquila. Despite wanting to be as close to Rowan as possible, I lay my blankets out on the opposite side of the fire.

Maybe the dream comes because, as I drift off to sleep, I'm thinking of Ali in that castle with a sorceress and a young mercenary soldier. For all I know, there are other soldiers as well, and servants, but none of them are her friends. If there are other soldiers, we could really use Onoku's knowledge. He knows about fighting and strategy, getting through defences. But he's on his way to see my parents.

The main thing I'm aware of is that it's gotten very cold. I can see my breath. I reach for my blankets, but they seem to be gone, and instead of lying on soft ground, I'm stretched out on hard stone. I can't see any sign of our fire either, but it's not totally dark. I sit up, looking for Rowan.

She's crouched a couple of arms lengths away from me and I can see the glint of her bracelet; it's giving off as much light as a dim lantern. I discern the shape of another person opposite Rowan. It's probably a girl because I can see long hair. The illumination around the two of them brightens significantly so that I realize it's Ali sitting there. She's shivering. At the same time, I notice that her hands are cupped in front of her and she's looking down. To see what she's concentrating on, I creep closer.

Ali holds a shiny black stone with silvery swirls, in her hands. The swirls appear to be moving, and it's hard for me to look away from them. "So cold," Ali whispers. "We need to make it warmer."

"Don't look at the stone, Atsu," comes Rowan's voice from beside me. "Only Ali should see into it. And don't look directly at my bracelet either. I feel a lot of power around us, and I think it's from both these objects. It could be dangerous."

I close my eyes. It's the only way I can think to avoid looking at either object. But then I want to see what they're doing, what's happening. When I open my eyes, we are surrounded by a golden light and I'm feeling warmer.

"It's enough," Rowan says.

The next thing I know, my eyes are open for real, and I'm looking at the embers of our fire. A skiff of white lies over everything, including our blankets, but I feel quite warm. I hear the stamp and whinny of a horse and sit up. Rowan is bringing an armload of branches to the fire.

"Snow in the night," she says. "I guess we should have pitched the tent after all."

"I dreamt of you and Ali," I say, "using your bracelet and a stone to keep us warm."

Rowan sets down her armload of wood and crouches beside me. "You dreamt that, too? I thought it was my dream."

"I wonder if Ali dreamt it, as well?"

"It's odd if we shared dreams with Ali. I don't know her well at all and you know her even less. At times, I've not been sure that I liked her. We seemed to rub each other the wrong way."

"If that's true, why did she send the ravens to us instead of to Samel?"

Rowan shrugs. "We don't know that she did. The ravens may have come on their own." She starts putting wood on the fire. "I want some hot gruel and tisane and then I want to get moving."

"Aren't you curious about why we had the dream and why the ravens came to us? What if Julina's behind it all?"

Rowan sighs. "We don't know anything for sure." Then she smiles at me. "I have a feeling neither of these things is anything to do with Julina."

"And you're not worried?"

"Yes and no. We'll just have to see what happens next."

Chapter XVII

Samel

It's harder than usual for me to get Grandfather up this morning. He groans, and moans that he's stiff and it's too cold. Then he has trouble getting his arms into the thicker tunic. I help him and start talking about leaving the mountains.

"Wha? You mean?" he grumbles from inside his tunic. I pull it down over his head. "How can we leave? The castle is in the mountains."

"Yes, but we talked about going to meet my sister before we reach the castle."

"So? Won't we do that anyway?"

I sigh. "Maybe you've never looked at a map. Rowan and Atsu are coming from Aquila, across the desert to the western branch of the great river and then north. If we keep going you and I will reach the castle long before them. So, we have to leave this trail to meet them along River Road."

"Shouldn't we try to get to your friend as soon as possible? Try to rescue her?"

"I think we'd have a better chance if there were more of us," I say.

"I want breakfast," Grandfather says. "Gruel and hot tisane. My bones are cold."

The fire is nearly out but I seat the old man, well wrapped in blankets, beside it. I left a pile of dry wood nearby last night, so it doesn't take long to get a good blaze going. Just after I've put a pot of water on there's a loud screech like a rusty door hinge. A couple of large black birds thump to the ground nearby.

"Ravens!" Grandfather says.

The birds hop over to him; one cocks its head and regards Grandfather out of one eye then the other. Grandfather glowers at it. "I'm not a frog today," he says. "Not your breakfast."

The bird ruffles its feathers and hops toward me. The other one flutters to a stump nearby. A bit of leather lacing shows in the feathers around its neck. This raven opens its beak wide and chuckles at me. That's the only word I can think of which describes the odd sound.

"Rowan," I whisper. She had a raven. "Morde?"

"What are you muttering about?" Grandfather says.

The bird on the stump shakes itself, fluffing its feathers. I notice a bit of parchment tied to the leather. A message?

"Do you come from Rowan?"

The raven nods its head. The other one is circling around Grandfather, giving short squawks. Grandfather continues to glower. "I think he's hungry."

"There's bread in that bag by your feet." I kneel down beside the raven near me and hold out my hand. "Will you let me have the message?"

Out of the corner of my eye, I see that Grandfather is breaking off chunks of bread and throwing them to the other bird. The one in front of me hops off the stump and comes within touching distance. Cautiously I reach for its neck. These birds aren't anywhere near as large as Aquilan eagles, but they could still give me a good bite.

"Save some bread for us," I say, as I touch the leather lacing and fumble with the parchment. The knots are tight, and it takes time to loosen them. The raven hunkers quietly in front of me until I'm done. Then it hops over to get a share of the bread.

"It's a note from my sister, tiny writing."

I squint and read out loud: *Samel, these ravens are to be trusted. Originally from Vatnborg, their names are Thought and Memory. Hope you're, on your way. We've reached the western branch of the great river. Come out of the mountains, meet us along River Road. In the dungeon you said it seemed as if we'd come in during the middle of a piece of music. See you soon. Rowan.*

The ravens squabble over the last of the bread. Grandfather wasn't paying attention when I told him to save some for us. Ah well, we've still got dried fruits, vegetables, meat, and gruel.

"The water's hot," Grandfather says. "Half for gruel, half for tisane."

"Thought and Memory," I say. The ravens raise their heads. "Thanks for bringing the message from Rowan. Would you be kind enough to take a short one back to her?

Both birds bob up and down. I rummage in my belt pouch and find a scrap of parchment. Scribble.

Will do what you ask. Samel.

One of the birds hops forward and I tie the message to its neck. As soon as that's done, the birds leap into the air and are off.

"Well," Grandfather says, "can we have breakfast now? Or are there more birds to feed? An eagle perhaps?"

I ignore the old man and pour hot water into beakers, add dried tisane leaves. Put a couple of handfuls of dried grains into the rest of the water. Stir to try and get the lumps out.

It's mid-morning by the time we finally leave our camp. Grandfather is in livelier spirits, cheered by the food, and probably by the ravens – a change to the monotony of our days. I actually haven't minded the dullness. There'll be enough excitement soon.

I'm hoping that I'll recognize the spot where the caravan I took to Schönspitze turned from River Road toward the mountains. There have been a lot of trails going in all sorts of directions, so I've always followed the widest and headed south, using the sun to orient us. Grandfather has been helpful, too, in offering his opinion on the correct direction. I've trusted his knowledge of the mountains, but soon we'll be leaving them, and Grandfather isn't familiar with the lands beyond. I have to remember the correct landmarks, but one pile of rocks looks much like another. We stop once after the sun has climbed past its zenith, to eat, water the horses, and fill our water skins at a brook. We're still in the midst of a mountain valley. I'm just considering using the eagle feather to get a bird's eye when Grandfather speaks.

"Look," he says, as we reach the end of the valley. There are several trails; I think he's pointing to one we should take, but it doesn't look familiar. "There's a glacier on that mountainside. I haven't seen one as large as that in a long time."

"Well spotted! That's our direction."

Not more than a couple of hours later we pass through an area where there's been a forest fire. Now I know for certain that we are on the right road. I remember how smoky it smelled then, and how we had to clear fallen trees. The scent has faded and the trail is open.

I start to hum, not any real tune, but just improvising whatever comes into my head. Grandfather joins in, singing words. I don't know if it's a real song or if he's making up the words as I'm doing with the melody.

"I love to go a-wandering along the mountain track. And as I go, I love to sing, my knapsack on my back. Tra la la, tra la la! My knapsack on my back. I love to wander by the stream that dances in the sun. So joyously it calls to me, come join my happy song. Tra la la, tra la la! Come join my happy song. Oh, may I go a-wandering until the day I die. Oh, may I always laugh and sing beneath the clear blue sky. Tra la la, tra la la! Beneath the clear blue sky."

Grandfather doesn't seem to know any more words than that for he keeps repeating them. Eventually I join in singing the words and we trot happily along, singing now and then until late afternoon, when we reach a place where the mountain drops away suddenly on our right. It's another reminder that we're on the correct path, but it's also a place where the trail narrows so that we must ride in single file. This will take all our concentration, so I stop singing.

"You go ahead, Grandfather," I say. "I'll follow with the pack horse. Or do you want me to lead your horse?"

"No, I'll be fine."

My hands are clenched on the reins as I watch Grandfather start off. I hope that his horse is calm and sure footed enough to negotiate this part of the trail. It has seemed fine so far, but this is the most difficult section. I'm not as nervous about Izmeer because I know he did all right on this once before. I look straight ahead, keeping my eyes fastened on the back of Grandfather's horse. I remember the empty space on one side of the trail, and I don't want to look at it again. What would I do if Grandfather fell off and tumbled down the mountain? I'm not strong enough to carry him back up and if he hurt himself, I wouldn't know what to do. I guess I'd have to call an eagle and send a message for help. It seems to take forever, but finally we're past this part and I can ride beside Grandfather again.

Soon I recognize the place where I freed the eagle from the trap. There's a scream above us and when I look there is an eagle soaring. That gives an extra lift to my spirits. If I weren't sitting on a horse on a mountain track, I'd get out the feather and try to see through the eagle's eyes. Snow begins to drift down.

"We should camp," Grandfather says. "I don't like riding in snow."

"Maybe it will stop soon. I think we might be almost out of the mountains."

"I don't think so," the old man says.

And he's right. The snow actually grows thicker, and I worry that we might lose our way. So as soon as I spy a flat area with some trees and an overhanging cliff, we pull in and I hurry to set up the tent. Grandfather crawls inside right away, but I have to unload the horses, give them water and grain. Then I make a fire to cook a quick pot of soup from dried ingredients. Grandfather is dozing by the time I take a bowlful into the tent for him, but he's happy to wake and eat. When I go back out to check on the horses, the snow has stopped, but it's getting dark. Just as well that we made camp. Hopefully, tomorrow we'll get out of the mountains.

Chapter XVIII

Ali

Such a strange dream last night! I felt shiveringly cold, and then Rowan and Atsu showed up. It had snowed where they'd camped. Rowan with her bracelet and I with the black stone created a bubble of warmth for all of us. Rowan seemed so friendly and nice, more than I'd ever thought her before. And she is coming to help rescue me, so I have to be grateful for that. Maybe I just never really got a chance to appreciate her before. I'm still feeling quite cozy under my blankets.

The stone is in its pouch around my neck. When I pull it out, I'm surprised to see that it's now got highlights of silver and gold. The stone looked like that in the dream, so maybe that was real. Will Julina sense that something magical happened?

A knock on the door; I hide the stone quickly.

Varonne sticks her head in. "Hurry up and get dressed. My mother wants to see you for the morning meal."

"Fine. Close the door and wait for me outside."

This time we walk down several more flights of stairs until we reach a hallway with windows where I can see that we are on the ground floor. What can be the purpose of this different location? Then I catch a glimpse of half a dozen soldiers practising sword fighting and shooting arrows at targets. Ah, they want me to see that the castle is well protected. I wonder when the soldiers arrived or if they were sequestered in another part of the castle before.

The room where Julina waits is bright with sunlight from the windows. A wooden table is laid with plates, goblets, and cutlery. Pitchers filled with water, fruit juice, and wine, bowls heaped with breads and fruit, plates holding meats and cheeses. There is also butter and honey, as well as a steaming pot holding gruel. Someone has certainly been busy, and I doubt that it was Julina or Varonne. There must be servants as well as soldiers here. Have they been here all along or only arrived recently? It doesn't matter. Julina wants me to know that any attempts at escape or rescue will be impossible. And she's probably also trying to show me that she can be generous and kind.

It's up to me to reveal as little as possible about my friends and their abilities. Nothing about the black stone. So immediately I concentrate on the food, think about what I want to eat first, how it might taste. Is there any sharp cheese or is it all mild?

"Sit, both of you," Julina says. "Eat first, then we talk."

I put gruel into a bowl, add butter and honey. Pour myself a goblet of apple cider. Eat and drink slowly, savouring every bite and sip. Varonne bolts her food as if she hasn't had enough to eat in several days, which could be the case. Julina picks at a slice of meat, nibbles at a wedge of bread with butter. She casts quick glances at me now and then; her interest is in me, not the food.

I decide to think about the scene as if it's a painting I'm planning. Yellow ochre for the cheese, wood brown for the meat. Azurite blue for Julina's robes, perhaps a touch of terre verte for grey-green shadows under the eyes, and hues of cinnamon for the rest of her skin. Lamp black with highlights of white for Varonne's armour. I'll need to mix colours and experiment to get just the right shade of pale grey for the walls.

"So, Alizarine, tell me about your family. You must miss them."

My spoon clatters against my bowl. I realize that my mouth is half open and I shut it. Feel the press of tears behind my eyes as I stare into my nearly empty bowl. She's taken me by surprise after all. But I will not cry in front of this woman! The remnants of gruel in my bowl make a swirling pattern of creamy lines. When our cook makes gruel at home, she often adds bananas or dried grapes, sometimes apples and cinnamon. But I don't want to think about home.

"Alizarine? No response?"

"I have nothing to say about my family." I reach for a slice of bread, pull the butter dish close. "Do you have many servants here?"

Julina chuckles, but I don't look at her. "I'll do the asking," she says. "Perhaps you've nothing to say about your family, but I'm sure you've been thinking about them. They're all artists, are they not? What kind of work do they do? Your father for instance. Does he paint, draw, do sculpture? I might be interested in purchasing some of his work."

If he were here, he'd smash you against the floor I think, but don't say. He's a big strong man. Then I concentrate on buttering my bread, spreading as evenly as I can and making small swirls here and there. Should I add honey or not?

"Come now, my dear, I'm sure your parents have taught you better manners than this."

I still say nothing while taking a small bite of buttered bread. It tastes stale and dry. I put the slice down and scan the table for something more palatable.

"Have you lived all your life in Aquila? It's such a large and diverse city, isn't it? Though I didn't much enjoy my time there. I found the rule of the Lord and his Militia a trifle onerous. Laws for this and that. Don't you get tired of rules, Alizarine? You and Samel must have bent them just a little now and then."

Silence for several heartbeats. No, I don't find the ways of Aquila onerous. They are for the safety of our people. But I've been trapped into thinking about what Julina wants me to think. And I won't think about Samel. Quickly I snag a fresh fig and nibble at it, not raising my eyes at all. I love the crunch of fig seeds.

It's Varonne who speaks next. "She's not going to answer you."

"Quiet!"

The sudden shout makes both Varonne and me jump. Varonne knocks over her empty goblet, shattering it to shards that skitter across the table. I manage not to choke on the remnants of my fig.

More quietly, almost in a whisper, Julina says, "Leave us daughter. Never mind the broken crockery. Go now."

Varonne lurches to her feet. Out of the corner of my eye I see that she has opened her mouth as if she is about to speak. Thinking better of it, she presses her lips together and turns. I hear several steps thump and then the door closes, not quite a slam, but a solid thunk. Silence again. I take a sip of my cider, thinking about Varonne, how she might be feeling at her mother's meanness.

The room darkens. Clouds must be covering the sun, but I'm too far from the windows to see. The darkness feels like a thick woollen blanket pressing down on me. For a few moments it's hard to breathe. Then the room lightens a little.

"Now that we're alone, my dear, perhaps you will be more forthcoming. Did my daughter's presence inhibit you? Never mind, now that she's gone, we can talk freely." I hear a sigh. "Both my children have been disappointments. Did you meet my son, Jernan? He's lived all his life in Aquila as have you. I'm not sure that living in one place is good for a person. It makes some narrow-minded, unable to imagine living differently. Still, both my children have travelled. I had high hopes for them. Do your parents have high hopes for you?"

I shoot a glance at Julina. She's looking directly at me and when our eyes meet, as quick as a scorpion striking, I feel that pressure in my head that I've felt before. I try to drop my eyes, but I can't. A picture of Père comes into my mind. The way he looks when he's sitting at the table early in the morning, slightly rumpled, his hair standing up in tufts.

"Looks worried, wouldn't you say?" Julina asks. "I could send a message to him that you're all right. In fact, I can even make it so that the two of you can talk to each other."

I manage to shake my head but can't move any other part of my body. The pressure inside my head increases, and as before, I feel as if fingers are attempting to riffle through my thoughts as if they were written on pieces of parchment. I try to evade those fingers, but they are sticky and begin to weave webs to ensnare me, like a spider tangling a fly.

"You don't believe me? It's not only people with magical bracelets who can talk to people far away. I have other methods."

It's the mention of the bracelets that frees me. A memory of silver flares across my eyes, and then the gold of sunlight flashing on water. I close my eyes and at the same time I imagine a large and heavy door slamming shut in my head. It's so real that I actually hear the sound, a reverberating boom.

Julina leaps to her feet. "What by thunder and rain are they doing now!" she shouts and rushes to the windows. "Nothing to see." She dashes to the door. Flings it open. "Varonne!"

Her daughter comes running, has obviously not been far away. "Someone shot off a cannon," she says. "Shall I go see why?"

"Yes," Julina says. "No, wait. Take the girl back to her room and lock her in. I'll go see what's happened."

Varonne grabs and shoves me down the hall, nearly making me stumble. I pull away and she nudges me up the long stairway. I try to look out of windows that we pass, but see nothing except blue sky, and once a black fluttering shape that might be a raven. Have they done something to save me from Julina's probing again? I hope they haven't gotten in the way of a cannon.

Back in my room I lean out of the window but can see no people or birds. They must be on one of the other sides, or perhaps in the inner court. I can hear faint shouting; no words come clear.

Finally, I stretch out on my bed, going over everything that has happened today. Was Julina just trying to soften me up so she could read my thoughts or were there other reasons why she talked about families and children, and about Aquila? Perhaps she has plans for the city. Her former husband, the sorcerer Hrashak, wanted to conquer us, Samel said. Is that Julina's wish as well? I have to find ways to get more information from her. Just getting away from her won't be enough if she has nasty plans for my home. If I could respond to her questions without getting totally under her control, I might find out more. I don't have the skills she does, though. It could be too dangerous to talk much to her. What if she gains complete control of me and makes me do things I don't want? Like hurt Samel or the others when they arrive.

Chapter XIX

Samel

We wake to a skiff of snow outside the tent, and the pale light of sunrise. My cheeks are chilly, but I breathe in the crisp air and smile. Grandfather grumbles, moving slowly as a snail, though I've never seen one in the snow so maybe they don't move at all when it's this cold. I put on several layers of clothes and help Grandfather do the same. I tell him to stay in the tent wrapped in blankets until I get a fire going. I'm an experienced camper now, so last night I put an armful of wood inside our tent. This helps me to get a fire going quickly. I set a pot of water to heat.

The three horses are stamping about and finding clumps of grass, their breath leaving small clouds around their heads. I get out a measure of oats for each. They are close enough to a nearby stream so that they can get water when they like, though the water feels icy to my fingers. I give Izmeer several extra pats on his neck.

"I'm sorry it's so cold," I whisper to him. "We'll get back to the desert eventually and you can be yourself again."

Izmeer nickers softly. When I leave him, I hear Grandfather mumbling and grumbling inside the tent, but I ignore him for now. By this time, I've learned that he needs a certain amount of complaining time in the morning. It seems to warm and loosen him so that he's ready for the day.

It's a quiet morning; no sign of any eagles in the sky. I scan the slopes of the mountains around us. So far, I haven't seen any sign of rockfolk, which is just as well. Though we had no trouble with the one we did see on our previous journey, who knows what the creatures might do if they took a notion to bother a couple of travellers on their own. I don't see any other animals either, but then I'm not a tracker or hunter.

"Samel!" Grandfather calls. "Any hot tisane yet?"

The water is steaming so I make a couple of mugs full. Set mine on a flat stone near the fire and hand the other into the tent to Grandfather. Then I add grains to the rest of the water to make our morning gruel. By the time it's cooked Grandfather has crawled out and hunches on a stump as close to the flame as he can get without scorching himself.

"We should get moving soon," I say. "The sun and riding will warm us. See, the snow is already starting to melt."

"More could fall any time. We're getting closer and closer to winter. Why did I come on this journey? I could be warm and snug in my house in Schönspitze."

I don't bother to answer. There's no point in reminding him that it was his decision to come, that he was determined to join me. He'll be less grumpy as the day progresses.

Not long after we pack up and leave our camping spot, the day warms significantly, and the trail takes us downhill. The mountains are smaller as well and have less snow on them. I don't bother pointing this out to Grandfather. I notice that he's got his eyes closed; maybe he's napping. I keep a watch on him in case he slips out of the saddle, but this doesn't happen. By the time the sun nears its zenith I'm hot enough that I have to stop and remove a layer of clothes. Grandfather's eyes are open, but he doesn't say anything.

"Hungry?" I ask. "There's a bit of cheese left, along with a few dried apples."

The old man shakes his head, but he does reach down for his water skin and takes a long drink. I do the same. The horses are chewing at low bushes that hold a few leaves. We set off again, at a trot for the trail is relatively smooth. Soon I see rounded hills ahead.

"We're nearly out of the mountains!" I say.

Grandfather grunts, but his horse raises its head and neighs, then starts galloping down the trail. The old man jounces in the saddle, doesn't appear to have much control over his horse. I urge Izmeer forward faster, pulling the packhorse behind. We clomp along, finally catching up to Grandfather, whose horse has stopped. There's a spring by the side of the road and the horses make for the water.

"I need to get down," Grandfather groans.

Quickly I slide off Izmeer and help the old man. It takes a while for him to be able to stand straight. There's a fallen tree close by.

"Do you want to sit?" I ask.

"No!" the old man nearly shouts. "I need to walk a little."

I prop him up as we walk back and forth along the trail. The horses are happy enough to forage without wandering far. Soon Grandfather stops.

"Tired?" I ask.

"No." He points ahead. "See that dark line in the rock? It may be a cave. I want to take a look."

"We don't really have time to go exploring."

Just then there's a crack of thunder. I haven't noticed that clouds have been building. A few drops of rain patter on my head.

"I guess we'll have to explore after all." Grandfather grins at me. "I can walk to the cave. You get the horses."

"You might get wet."

"A little rain never hurt anyone. But I don't want to get soaked. Hurry up with the horses. We'll need to get a fire going in there."

I gather all three horses together and lead them into the cave. A quick inspection shows me that it's shallow, but uninhabited. There are even a few scattered branches that probably blew in during a previous storm. I leave the horses and run back to help Grandfather. He's puffing a bit, but grinning.

"Go drag in more wood," he says as we reach the shelter. "I'll be fine here."

I'm able to find a few more sticks and a couple of medium logs. By the time I get all that into the cave, rain beats down, turning the trail to mud. I arrange wood well back and to one side of the entrance. The horses are gathered near the back opposite us. Grandfather has hauled out a blanket and folded it and his cloak to sit on, near where I'm building the fire. Rain has become torrential outside, completely obscuring our view from the cave opening. Flames curl up and Grandfather holds out his hands to the blaze.

"Lucky I spied this place," he says. "I'm ready for a hot meal. What have we got?"

"Let me give the horses some oats to keep them happy," I say, "then I'll rummage in our packs."

Dried meat and vegetables with water are soon simmering over our little fire. I notice that Grandfather is dozing, head hanging down. I hope this rain will not last too long. I'm anxious to catch up with Rowan and Atsu. I'd intended to leave the mountains today. We are close, I think, but still have at least half a day's ride to reach the river. Once again, I speculate about Julina and whether she might be causing this weather to delay or to test us. I'm sure she'd rather confront the group separately than together, though of course I'm only guessing. Who knows what Julina's real intentions are?

The stew is ready, so I wake the old man. The warmth of food comforts, but the continuous rumble of thunder and the rush of rain don't. I get up now and then to lean out of the cave opening, but can't see much from there.

"I'm worried," I say. "This cave isn't far up from the trail. What if the stream floods? We could get really wet as well as being seriously delayed."

Grandfather lurches to his feet. I rush over to help him so that he won't stumble and fall. "I'm fine," he snaps. "Let me take a look at the rain, use my frog senses to figure out what is going on."

I help him to the cave entrance, even though I'm still skeptical about what he calls his frog senses. Yes, he spent a lot of time looking at and playing with water at his house in Schönspitze, but I've always doubted his claim that he was reborn for a while as a frog.

He stands looking out, with me close behind in case he falls or tires. The sound of rain drones, making me sleepy. I yawn.

Grandfather sways. "One raindrop has little power; a mass of them eventually wears away stone." He sighs. "I haven't the stamina I used to. I need to sit down."

Chapter XX

Medley

It's a relief to be out of the desert. As we ride along the river under the shade of trees cool air envelops us. That's one of the things I appreciate about the city of Aquila – they saved what trees grew there when people first arrived and planted more as they built the palace, houses and shops. Found ways to conserve and use water to the best advantage in an arid land.

Rowan and I slept well past sunrise this morning. I guess both of us were exhausted. It's been hard riding and I know she's worried about her brother, even though we got the message by raven that Samel and the old man will come out of the mountains to meet us on River Road. I'm curious about the old man that Samel is travelling with. Julina asked for him to come and I gather he's a relative of

Samel's and Rowan's.

But why him? Rowan doesn't seem to know anything either. She told me that Samel called him Grandfather Frog. Odd. Well, hopefully we'll all meet soon and then I'll find out more.

A slight breeze ruffles Rowan's hair as her horse trots just ahead of me. Instead of her usual braid, she's left it loose today. She said that since she hasn't been able to wash it for a while, she wanted to let sunlight brighten and freshen it. Her hair ripples down her back like a dark river at night, glints of light reflecting here and there. Just as I'm thinking about what it would feel like to touch, she turns and smiles at me.

"Am I riding too fast?" she says. "I'm anxious to see my brother."

"His message sounded all right. He'd have said if anything was wrong."

Her smile fades. "There are so many unknowns. What exactly does Julina want? Is it just our bracelets? And if so, what does she plan to use them for? How can we stop her and still rescue Ali? Why couldn't Ali have been more careful? If she hadn't gotten herself kidnapped, we wouldn't have to be doing this!"

I trot my horse closer to hers. "I thought you were going to save all those questions until we met your brother and the old man."

"I can't help mulling it over, wondering if there's a way to prepare, whatever happens. Should I be practising with the bracelet, for example?"

"You said you were worried about Julina knowing when you use the bracelet."

"I've been having second and third thoughts about everything. Maybe I've been wrong not to use the bracelet more." She reaches out a hand as if to grasp my arm but doesn't quite touch me. "Can you make a mist again, to hide us?"

"Of course. Right now? Are you going to try to reach your brother?"

She nods and touches the silver circle on her left wrist. It flashes in the sun.

I slow my horse, squeeze a little liquid from my water skin into the palm of one hand. Put the skin away again and blow gently on the water. As droplets float into the air making a small cloud of vapour, I sense rain, can smell the dampness of it. I've never had this feeling before, a sense of water hanging in the air, ready to gush down. I look all around but see not a single cloud in the sky.

"What's the matter?" Rowan asks.

"I don't know. Something odd." Faintly, I hear a rumble as of thunder, but there is no sign of lightning in the sky. My eyes darken as if twilight has come on suddenly, and I see the entrance to a cave, vague shapes inside it. Then a downpour of rain hides everything. I jerk and find myself on my horse, Rowan gripping my arm.

"You nearly fell off!" she exclaims. "Let's stop over there under those trees."

***

I'm really worried about Atsu; his face is quite pale. After we tether the horses, I make him sit on a stump and sip water, eat a handful of nuts. The hazy cloud that he created while riding still hangs about near his head. It's rather like an odd pet bird that doesn't want to leave. I suppress a smile as I kneel beside him. He closes his eyes and slumps but doesn't slip off the stump.

"What is it?" I whisper, but he doesn't respond. "Atsu!" I grab his shoulder.

Slowly his eyes open. "A vision," he whispers. "I'm seeing a rainstorm and there's a cave. Nothing like this has ever happened before."

"But why? Are there any people? Anyone you recognize?"

"I can see only vague shapes in the darkness because it's raining too hard. Can you help me? Use your bracelet?"

"I'll try."

I close my eyes and imagine rain pouring down. Try to see a cave. Is it in the mountains? Atsu didn't say. Could it be the cave that Hrashak mentioned, where he found his power? I open my eyes to ask. The sun blazes down on us here by the river. As I open my mouth to speak, the silver bangle on my wrist flares brightly, dazzling my eyes.

When my eyes clear again, I'm standing under a tree near a path in the mountains with rain pouring down. Across the way I notice a dark gap in a rock face. A sound behind me makes me turn. Atsu is slumped against the tree trunk, but at least his eyes are open.

"Are we really here? Or is this just a vision. And why are we having it?" he asks. "I felt this rain, this storm from far away. Have I brought you here, too, or did you do it?"

Thunder crackles and I wait for the sounds to die away. "Remember how my bracelet and your powers over water caused us to work together before?" I say. "Something similar could be happening."

"There's need in that cave. We have to get there."

I hold him back. "Look at the road! It's awash. We might be swept away if we try to cross. Could that affect us if this is just a vision?"

"Maybe I can divert the water," Atsu says. "Or I could try to stop the rain, though I've never done that before."

"You made a bubble to keep rain off us before. Is that what you're doing now?"

"I guess so because neither of us is wet. Maybe we are just seeing this and not really here."

"So, you think we can't affect any of it? Then why are we seeing it? What purpose or need brought us here?"

Atsu stamps a foot in frustration. "I don't know!"

I take a deep breath to calm myself. "Let's close our eyes. Try to look into the cave, see through the rain. I'll concentrate on my silver wristlet, attempt to make it give us light."

Nothing comes to me except darkness and scatters of brightness behind my eyelids. A clap of thunder startles me and I open my eyes. More water rushes by on the road, bits of wood and leaves swept along. I don't want to see this; it reminds me of the night my mother drowned in that northern river. I grit my teeth and turn to Atsu. He has his eyes tightly closed.

As I shut my own eyes again, I feel the warmth of the bracelet on my wrist. Imagine it sparkling, taking light from a fire, glowing silver gold, lighting up a pool of water. From somewhere on the edge of night a frog jumps into the water, disappearing, and sending ripples outward. In the darkness behind my eyelids there are two circles of silver moving closer together.

***

"Rowan? Is it really you?"

My sister opens her eyes and stares at me, her mouth slightly open. I reach out my left hand and our two bracelets are drawn together, chiming as they touch. Brightness flares in the cave, outshining the small fire that I built earlier.

"Who is that with you?"

"My friend Atsu," Rowan says. "Somehow he was pulled to you. He heard the rain from the edge of the desert."

"How is that possible?" Samel asks.

"Water," Atsu says. "I'm attracted to water. It's a long story. You're in danger here, did you know? It looks like a flood out there."

"I know. Grandfather has been trying to do something about that, but so far he hasn't had success."

I point to the old man who is slumped on a blanket to one side of the cave entrance. His eyes are closed, and he seems to be asleep. But the rain that has been blowing in and wetting the open edge of the entrance has not touched him.

"What could he do?" Atsu says. "It looks like he's sleeping."

"Grandfather Frog?" Rowan asks quietly.

"Yes," I answer. "He's our great grandfather from Schönspitze. He says that he drowned as a man, came back and lived as a frog, and then was resurrected as a man. He's shown power with water before, has spent a long time studying it."

"Another shape shifter?" Atsu whispers.

"I don't know. I've never seen him change. Did Rowan tell you about our cousin Thea who can become a goat?"

"Yes," Rowan says. "But Atsu is a shapeshifter, too." She clears her throat. "You may not believe this, but he can become a dragon. I've seen it."

"A dragon, a frog, and two people with magical silver bracelets? Surely the four of us can do something about this storm and the flood."

"Let's try," Atsu says. "Concentrate on stopping the rain, on the flood waters draining away. Close your eyes if you have to."

The rush and roar of water surrounds me. I feel it lapping at my toes, creeping toward my ankles. This is not what I want. I must think of the water receding. And then there's a loud plop as a green frog the size of a small dog pops out of the stream and begins sucking up water. Is this Grandfather? But there's way too much water. The frog begins to swell and I'm afraid he's going to burst. The next moment there's a huge, blue-green shape undulating behind the frog. Long neck, a large feathered head, golden eyes – is this what a dragon looks like? It doesn't resemble any pictures I've seen in books. Except … wait a minute! The dragon I'm seeing does resemble the one in the Leather Book, though that one was black. Water sprays as the dragon splashes forward on massive webbed and clawed feet. Rain continues to gush down, water churns past the mouth of the cave, getting ever deeper.

"It's not working!" my sister's voice wails.

My eyes fly open and there's only Grandfather and me in the cave with the horses. Grandfather's eyes are open and he's staring at me. Although I can't see them, I can still feel Rowan and Atsu in my mind. And on my wrist the bracelet continues to shine.

"Keep contact," Rowan's voice calls. "Imagine us all holding hands."

Grandfather lifts an arm and points it toward me. I walk forward, sit beside him and take his left hand with my right. Then I raise my left and extend it in the direction where I think Rowan and Atsu might be. I close my eyes again to concentrate and feel my sister's fingers clutch mine. Will we have enough power to do this?

***

Julina and Varonne have left me alone since yesterday's disturbance. A solider brought food – breakfast and lunch – but I couldn't get him to answer any questions. I've paced this small tower room until it's surprising that I haven't worn ruts in the floor. Probably could if I used the obsidian stone. What would be the point? It would take a very long time to wear a hole through which I could escape. And in the meantime, someone might come in and discover what I'm doing, stop me and take the stone away. At all costs, I must hang onto my small magic. So far it seems to protect itself and me from discovery.

At last, tired of pacing, I look out of the window for a while. But there's nothing much to see – no birds, no people moving about. The sky is blue with a few white clouds high up.

I lie on the cot and think about Samel. Where might he be by now? Still in the mountains or close to the castle? And Rowan and Atsu. Have they left the desert yet? I try to picture the three of them together, smiling and waving at me. It's a comforting thought. What does the old man who is travelling with Samel look like? I yawn. My eyes droop. The smell of rain rises but when I open my eyes all

I see is darkness.

Then a fire flickers, showing Samel and a stooped, grey-haired and wrinkled man crouching in the opening of a cave. Rain pours down outside. They clasp hands and have their eyes closed for some reason. I notice the shapes of two other people crouching under a tree outside. At first, they're faint as ghosts, then come clear, Rowan and Atsu the way I remember them from Aquila. They're actually sitting by a river and they're holding each other's hands, too. I'm seeing two sets of people in two different places.

"Imagine us all holding hands," Rowan says.

"Will we have enough power to do this?" Samel asks.

"We have to stop the rain," the old man murmurs, "stop the flood, so we can get moving again."

There's a warm spot at the centre of my chest. I reach into my tunic with my left hand and pull out the silver and gold swirled black stone. This stone came from a mountain of fire; maybe it can help to dry up rain and a flood. I extend both arms out to my sides, one hand clasping the stone.

"It's Ali," I whisper. "Make room for me."

And somehow, they know that I'm there with them. Samel lets go of Rowan's hand and clasps the one of mine that holds the stone. Rowan takes my right hand with her left. Colours swirl in the night: the glint of silver, the green shimmer of a frog, the blue green undulations of a huge dragon, the sparkle of golden eyes. We breathe together, in and out. I imagine the stone opening a chasm in earth outside the cave and letting water swirl down.

And then, in the centre of our circle a rainbow begins to form, small as a stone at first, then the size of a silver bracelet, but growing rapidly so that eventually it fills the whole sky. The rain has stopped, and the rest of the water gurgles away down a ditch outside the cave.

After a long time, I realize that I'm awake and lying on my cot. I'm exhausted and hungry. It's night but there's the faint glow of moonlight coming in through the window and it shows a tray of food sitting just inside the door. Someone brought supper while I was in a trance or asleep.

My left hand is sore and cramped. I sit up and open my fist. The piece of obsidian lies there, glowing and swirling with all the colours of the rainbow.

Chapter XXI

Samel

The others have disappeared and it's quiet and dark beyond the cave mouth. No rain, no water pouring in. A shape crouches on the ground near the entrance.

"The storm is over, Grandfather. Are you all right?"

The old man raises his head slowly. He's himself again, not a frog. "Tired."

"It's too late to travel now. I'll get you settled with blankets near the fire. You're probably hungry, too."

He doesn't resist as I move and wrap him, lean him in a sitting position against a convenient rock, well padded by another blanket. As I heat water for tisane and get out dried fruit and grain for gruel, his head nods and his eyes close. I leave him like that until the water heats and then until the gruel with fruit is cool enough to eat. He wakes sufficiently to take a few spoons full and some sips of tisane. When he's finished I let him go back to sleep.

The horses stand quietly in their corner, dozing; I unloaded them earlier and wiped them down. Night wraps us in its blanket, safe and comfortable. How close are Rowan and Atsu? Is Ali sleeping? It amazes me that I felt no hint of Julina at any time. Not like when fire threatened Grandfather and me along with the two guards from Schönspitze. Julina invaded my mind then and tried to control things. She seemed not involved during the storm this time. Did she know nothing of what the weather was doing to us? The power of our working together must have caused ripples somewhere. If she felt it, I hope she is frightened. If we can all work together like this, we can surely save Ali. I'm tempted to try to speak with her, to talk about what's just happened, but decide to leave things be – let Ali rest if she is sleeping, don't cause any more disturbance. Besides, I can hardly keep my eyes open. I place the last of our wood on the fire, wind myself in a blanket and let go.

***

The tramping of restless horses wakes me as the sun slants into the cave mouth. They want food and water. Grandfather still sleeps, but soon he'll want sustenance, too. The fire is ashes and there's no more wood. I stretch my stiff body, feed the horses, then leave the cave to gather what I can find of dry firewood. There isn't any.

We're going to have to eat the last of our dried fruit, and a few crumbles of cheese. Only cold water to drink. When I rouse him and explain, Grandfather merely mumbles his disapproval. He deigns to accept some of each, however, soaking the dried fruit in water and then chewing, and chewing it to soften. The way he eats reminds me a little of a goat. But it's Thea who can become a goat; Grandfather turns into a frog. Maybe I should find him some flies to eat! I yawn and stretch again, stop these silly thoughts.

Finally, we're on the trail, making our way down a valley into lower mountains until we can see foothills in the distance. I'm about to call out to Grandfather who is lagging, to point out a glint of water that means the river is near, when pain sears through my head. It's like flame on skin when you put your hand too close to the fire.

Everything goes dark. A weight drops onto my shoulders, bowing me down. The world is a sunless place; it will always be thus and there is no way out. I try to open my eyes, but nothing happens. Next, I try to call out, to speak, to whisper, but no sound comes though a distant chuckle echoes. My chest feels squeezed and I can barely breathe. I see myself collapsing, shrinking, crumbling to dust and blowing away, nothing left of me except the silver bracelet. I clutch for anything to hold onto to keep this from happening. My hands tauten. Both my hands sting, pinched at the palms. I remember reins. I'm holding onto them, must still be sitting on my horse.

"You won't get away from me so easily," a voice whispers.

Breath hisses out of my mouth and a thread of air enters. A slight breeze blows across my face, and then my nose is tickled by strands, horse's hair, the mane. I smell horse strongly. A wild, loud scream echoes around me. I am alive and there are other beings with me.

"No!" the voice shouts.

Again, heaviness and darkness press, but the smell of horse remains. A filament of brightness wriggles into the darkness. The light dances, circles, turns silver and takes the shape of leaves entwined around a wrist. Shadowy fingers reach for the light, for the silver bracelet, but the leaves whirl away and the fingers flutter uselessly. Faint chimes, like tiny silver bells ring in my ears. My left wrist warms and the bracelet blazes behind my eyelids. At the same time, my chest loosens. I take a huge breath and blow as hard as I can, and my breath turns into wind, scattering darkness into fragments. The weight leaves my shoulders.

Slowly I open my eyes to find that the horses have stopped in the middle of the trail. Grandfather slumps; at least he hasn't tumbled off. The sun shines brightly, though there are towering dark clouds to the west of us. An eagle soars above. I think about using the eagle feather to see what the bird sees, but just the thought makes me shudder; what if I fell out of the sky? Anyway, I still feel sluggish. I'm sure we must be near to Hrashak's castle, close to Julina and her power. I remember when I was with the caravan how we reached a place where all the oxen and horses slowed, and I felt for a while as if I carried a heavy pack. Nothing like what just happened, though. I urge my horse to move close to Grandfather. Take the reins of his horse and pull. We have to get away from here.

Slowly the horses walk down the trail toward the bend where the river sparkles in the sun. Grandfather stirs. As we draw closer to the river, the horses begin to trot.

Grandfather raises his head. "What happened?"

"I think Julina just tried to stop us. Or else there's a blackness that hangs around the castle that tries to pull in anything that passes near it."

"Maybe both," Grandfather says. "There are places in the world that hold evil; all who come near are affected.

Perhaps that's what's happened to Julina. Didn't you tell me that she helped your sister? And now she's trying to harm us?"

"You think if she'd never gone to live in the castle none of this would have happened? That Ali wouldn't be a prisoner?"

Grandfather shrugs. "Only a speculation. When are we going to eat? I need something hot. Breakfast, if you can call it that, is sitting in my belly like a lump of clay."

"It's not been that long since we ate! Take a drink of water. I'm not stopping until we're well away from here."

"Where there's a river there ought to be fish. Did you bring any kind of fishing gear?"

"No," I say shortly.

The old man grins. "We'll figure something out. A nice fresh fish roasted over a fire, skin crisping, flesh hot and falling off the bones. Hmmm."

My mouth begins to water. I'm tired of bread, cheese and dried fruit, and anyway, we haven't any more of that. Even stew made from dried meat and dried vegetables doesn't appeal right now. My sister would know what roots to dig for roasting, what fresh plants to pick for greens.

"How soon do you think we'll meet your sister and her friend?" Grandfather asks.

"I don't know." I wish the old man would stop asking questions. I'd like to ride quietly for a while.

"They must be close if they could come to us and help with the rainstorm last night."

"But they didn't help with the darkness just now," I say. "So who knows?"

Finally, Grandfather is quiet. Maybe he's thinking, like I am, that Rowan and Atsu might be having problems as well. Otherwise, why didn't they sense that we were in trouble again and help us?

Chapter XXII

Ali

Two soldiers enter my tower room soon after I'm awake and dressed. I've been expecting breakfast, but they don't carry any food, nor do they speak even when I ask over and over what's happening. One takes me by an arm while the other gathers up my clothes and blankets. Obviously, they are moving me, but where and why? Samel and the rest can't have arrived yet.

Down and down several flights of stairs; maybe we'll reach the ground floor. I see no other soldiers or servants. They could all have been warned to stay away. The empty feeling in my belly is not just about being hungry. If Julina found out about what the four of us did during the rainstorm she'll be furious and wanting to punish someone. Is that what this is about?

The stairways get narrower and darker as we descend, though here and there torches burn in wall brackets, lighting our way. I feel the weight of walls and floors above. The only sounds are the tramp of the guards' feet and the shuffle of mine. My heart pounds, increasing until it sounds in my head like the drums of Lord's Militia as they set off on manoeuvres. We come to the end of stairs and enter a narrow hallway. Chilliness seeps from the floor, penetrating the soles of my sandals and numbing my toes. I smell damp stones and keep expecting to hear the trickle of water. A faint whispering begins, like people talking at a distance. Am I about to meet more soldiers or servants?

The guards stop in front of a barred gate. One of them extracts a key from a belt pouch and pushes me through. They follow and lock the gate again. To either side there are closed metal doors. Dungeon cells? But there are no sounds from behind the metal. Finally, we stop in front of one of the doors.

I have time to notice etchings of rust and then I'm inside a dim room. I can't tell how large it is. One guard puts my possessions on the stone floor just inside the door. The other pulls out a candle and lights it from a torch in the hall, hands it to me. I start to ask a question and the door thumps shut, leaving me inside and the guards outside. Faintly, I hear their footsteps fade away.

The candle illuminates very little of the room. "Hello?" I say, just in case I'm not alone here. There is no response to my voice. I shiver and think about putting on the rest of the clothes they left me.

A few stones beside the door begin to sparkle, reflecting the flame of the candle. At the middle of my chest a tiny spot of warmth grows, and I remember that the obsidian stone came from a dungeon. Perhaps Samel and Rowan were imprisoned in this very room. I drip wax to fasten the candle on the floor, pull out my pouch and take the stone to cradle in my hands. It is still swirled with rainbow colours and its warmth radiates like a well-built fire.

The candle gutters and goes out. But instead of darkness, I'm surrounded by sparkles of light, all the stones in the walls, floor, and ceiling glinting as if they contain tiny stars. There's enough brightness that I can walk about without stumbling. That faint whispering starts up again. I can't yet tell how big this room is, so there could be others here, reluctant to speak to me.

I explore my prison. Find a covered pail that smells faintly of excrement. Further along a different pail holds water that smells clean; I taste a handful and it seems fine. Nearby sits a closed wooden box. When I lift the lid, I find a loaf of bread, a round of cheese the size of my fist, and a handful of dried apples. So, they're not going to starve me for now. I make a meal, then continue my survey. No other people, and the whispering has stopped. The last thing I find is a heap of blankets. I'm meant to stay here overnight, perhaps for many days. But why?

I sink onto the blankets and lean against the wall, close my eyes. I could take a nap since there's nothing to do but wait. I'm still clasping the stone; its warmth is a comfort in this drear and lonely place.

"I don't understand."

I sit up and open my eyes. "Who said that?" The stone walls around me continue to sparkle and no one responds to my question. No others are in this cell with me.

The voice has faded. I lean against the stone wall again and hear, "I wish you'd pay attention. I've tried to explain it all to you before, but you don't seem to grasp what I'm trying to do." That's Julina's voice, I'm sure of it.

"I know it has to do with magic." That sounds like Varonne. "But how do the ravens fit in? Why did some of the soldiers shoot a cannon at them?"

"Stupidity!" exclaims Julina. "I'd warned them to beware of the ravens. One or two of the birds have a connection with Rowan and I thought they might be spying on us. The soldiers took it to extremes and fired the cannon. Scattered the ravens and blew a hole in one of the castle walls."

"And have you moved Ali to the dungeons because Rowan and her brother are getting close?"

"Of course. And because I think Ali has made a magical connection with the others, though I haven't been able to pin down exactly what that is. Those bracelets have more power than anyone realizes. They protect themselves and anyone who wears them. I wish I could have found the smith who made them."

"Do you think he could have explained their powers?"

"Perhaps. I got an inkling, a flash, the first time I met Rowan. It was all about pairs – a pair of bracelets, a pair of people to wield them – that would increase the power. Later it occurred to me that four is a magical number too, a square is sometimes considered part of the sacred geometry that makes up the world."

"I've not heard any of this before."

"That stupid girl and her brother haven't scratched the surface of what those wristlets of ivy leaves can do. They should go to someone who can appreciate and use them to the fullest."

"What will you do when you get them?"

"That is none of your business."

"It's just that if you expect me to help you, to be of the most use I have to know more of your plans."

"All will come clear in time. For now, keep checking up on our troops, make sure they get the castle wall repaired, make sure the girl gets fed; we don't want her to die yet. And keep track of the ravens."

"There's only half a dozen men. I thought you'd have more."

"Just do as I say!"

"What will you be doing?"

"I have to keep an eye on the four travellers," Julina says, "and that's not easy. I can't watch all of them at once."

"Won't it be easier when they meet?"

"Yes and no. They might be easier to see, but they'll also have more power together, which means they could learn even more about how to keep me from seeing them. I've tested them, but the results have been unsatisfactory."

The voices fade and I'm left with much to think about. For one thing, I have a great deal of hope. Julina is not all powerful and is fumbling about, trying to get the bracelets. She doesn't appear to know anything about the piece of obsidian that I have, which holds powers that no one had an inkling of. Wherever this stone came from, it's certainly absorbed magic and it's gifting some of that to me. Unfortunately, Julina also said, "We don't want her to die yet." My eventual fate doesn't make me happy. I don't know how much time I have, but I've got to make plans to get out of here.

Deciding to test what the stone can do, I walk about the room and lean my head against walls here and there. Now and then I catch a voice. Once I hear a guard say loudly, "You stupid fool! You almost dropped that rock on my foot!" Occasionally there are murmurs, but I can't distinguish words.

Then I recall how the stone enabled me to smooth parts of the walls of my tower room so I could draw on them, and how my hand sank into stone. Could I wear away enough of a wall to make an opening? I didn't want to try anything like that in the tower because someone was always coming in, but here I'm thinking no one is likely to disturb me for some time.

I examine the walls, consider the most useful place to break through. The only section where I have some idea of thickness is the wall holding the doors. All the others could be arms-length deep as well as being underground. If I can make even small holes near the hinges or the lock, I may be able to open the door. I choose to try the lock. First, I grasp the black stone tightly in both hands until it's almost too hot to hold. Then I set it down and place both hands on the wall surrounding the lock. Slowly, slowly my palms sink in. I press as hard as I can but make only a thin indentation. I sigh and lean down to pick up the stone to warm my hands again. The stone has sunk into the floor twice its own thickness, I can barely distinguish its rainbow shine. Quickly I pry it out so as not to lose it, hold it tightly again until it heats and then press the stone itself against the wall. It sinks through and strikes the metal of the lock. A few more applications and the door creaks open.

I lean out. No one in the hall. I could walk out of here right now. But then what? Even if I could somehow connect with Rowan or Samel and find out where they are, it would be difficult for me on foot to evade the soldiers, Varonne, and Julina. I close the door again and stare at the hole in the wall. As soon as someone comes to check on me, they will wonder what I've done and how. Was this stupid or what? Why didn't I think things through? Having this power is good and hopefully will be useful when the others come, but I've used it too soon.

Thoughtfully, I stare at the wall, holding the stone in one hand. I have destroyed part of a wall. What if I can use the stone to make, to rebuild? I hold it in my hands again, but this time when it heats, I place my hands beside the hole and smooth them over it, thinking of that part of the wall as thick clay that I can mold and stretch. I feel ripples of movement under my fingers. Close my eyes and imagine the wall whole, as it was. Raise my hands and open my eyes. It's rough, but the wall is intact over the lock.

I turn to study the dungeon cell. The room is large enough that I can choose a dim corner to experiment on for my next attempt at making a hole. First, though I'll have a nap. This magical work makes me tired.

Chapter XXIII

Atsu

I'm floating in warm turquoise liquid, my body stretching and undulating, long and sinuous. I sense fish and water plants nearby, sand not far below. My head breaks the surface and I spew droplets everywhere.

"Having fun?" someone says with a bubbling chuckle.

A woman's head with greenish brown hair rises; the head is connected to the long neck of a green and white scaled dragon. I recognize my mother who bends her neck as if bowing. Churning water hides the rest of her, but I know that she is longer than a house and as thick as two massive tree trunks.

"You can hold the shape of both human and dragon at the same time?" I ask.

"There is much you do not know how to do yet, my son," she responds. "I've come to teach you a few things. You'll need them in your upcoming struggle."

"I'm in the mountains, not in the sea. Is this a dream?"

"Call it a dream or vision if you like. Time and distance do not have the same barriers for dragons as they do for humans."

"If time and distance are so permeable, why didn't you take advantage of that and visit me after you left me in the orphanage? And why suddenly come to help me now?"

"Safety," she growls and water surges round my head.

"That's what the soldier Onoku told me, Oh Pearl Princess. You wanted to keep me safe from some battle or war. And yet you and my father, the Obsidian Dragon, have all kinds of powers. Could you not use them to visit your son?"

"It is not the time nor the place for this. You need to put aside your anger and childish disappointments. If you and your friends wish to win against the sorceress, you must do certain things to waken all your powers, to keep you and others safe."

She stops speaking and her green eyes regard me calmly. The waters around us have quieted and lie smooth as a turquoise mirror. I want to keep arguing with her; after all I do have legitimate grievances. Still, she's right that I want to help my friends and I don't think there's much time to learn anything new.

"Very well," I mumble grudgingly. "What do I do?"

"You must dive to the bottom of the sea and find the giant clam with the blue interior. Once you get there, you must shrink yourself and slip between the shells. If all goes well, you will awaken more powers and return here. I'll wait for you."

"And if all doesn't go well?" I ask.

"Then you won't return."

But if this is merely a dream or vision, I will wake up, right? I can't leave Rowan alone."

"Confidence!" she roars. "Don't think of failure, think of success. Now go!"

Before I can even begin to shape a response in my mind, I'm diving. Deep, deep, deeper. I thought sand was not far below me, but obviously I was wrong. Water presses against my body on all sides. Shrink, she said. I've never tried to be different sizes, never imagined that I could be, but this pressure is compressing me. I let it happen, discover, after a while, that I feel no bigger than a minnow. A large white fish waves its tail above and I dart away before it can open its mouth. And then I see it – a huge encrusted hinged shell with wavy edges. It's partially open, like a mouth stained with the juice of blueberries, and ready to engulf me. Panic grips me, but it's too late. I'm sucked in, lost in cushions of purple blue. It occurs to me that the clam is only gigantic because I'm miniscule.

Am I floating in waves or clouds? Suddenly my body is as large as a ship that surges beside me, and then I'm small as a butterfly fluttering in the sun. Many places flash before my eyes – waterfalls and lakes, rivers and streams, wide seas and oceans. I enter each of these places one after the other, feel their sources, follow their courses, understand what moves them, what holds them back. Rain gusts around me and I am rain; water trickles down a rock crevice and I am the power of that water to crack rock. I'm tossed and turned, squeezed and stretched.

"Who are you?" a voice whispers from out of a purple mist.

It takes me an aeon to remember. I had a name, but before that I was, "A dragon."

"Even a dragon has a name."

"Ah."

"Ah is not a name for a dragon."

"I had a human name – Atsu."

"You need a dragon name, a name of power. Close your eyes and let go, let your thoughts roam, open your mind to me."

The purple mist is all around, inside and outside me. Images of my life float freely: the great gong in the monastery where I lived as a child, the river where I thought my friend Watami drowned, riding across grasslands, the school in Vatnborg, Meewani and Pukan giving their real names, Rowan helping me hold back the flood at Aquila. My father is the Obsidian Dragon, my mother, the Pearl Princess. I am not black or mostly white. My colours are green and blue, the shades of the sea with hint of white spume here and there.

A long sigh, like a gust of wind blows most of the purple mist away. "It's too soon," the great clam says. "I can't give you a dragon name yet. You must prove yourself."

"Couldn't I be the Green and Blue Dragon? Or some name like that?"

"Hmm. That seems too dull. I sense that if you do well, in the future you may become a great daimyo, with much power. Green and blue is like the sea but also like the turquoise gemstone. Strong and powerful, it helps to clear the mind and assists with protection."

The great clam is silent and the waters around us lie still. Time has no meaning, no beginning or end. Who am I? Perhaps I'll stay like this forever and Rowan won't know what happened. But that can't be. I struggle to swim away, but all I do is churn the waters into turquoise foam.

"Calm yourself. Tell me what you want." the clam says.

"To help my friends," I answer.

"What are you willing to give up in order to do this?"

"Whatever I need to."

"Even your life?"

I float in a purple sea for aeons pondering this question. I don't want to give up my life here and now. On the other hand, if it meant saving Rowan's life I would die if there was no other way. And I can't stay here forever, even if time isn't the same for dragons as for others.

"I see your mind. Go, then."

Blueberry-coloured clouds toss and flip me. I tumble and quiver. Struggle to find equilibrium. There's some place I need to be. A direction to go.

"Return up here," she said.

I am spewed into foaming blue-green. "You are the Turquoise Tempest," a voice whispers. "Keep that secret for now."

My head breaks into air; water cascades down my cheeks, past my huge jaws. I open my mouth to speak and my lips shrink to human size.

"Adequate," my mother says. "Dragons aren't formed in a day." She is in the shape of a small woman sitting on a large rock where waves meet sand.

I'm lying in the shallows coughing. "How long was I gone?" I sputter.

"Long enough. Now get up, come sit by me and pay attention. I have a few more things to tell you."

Laboriously, I do as she bids, my body as heavy as a waterlogged tree. I sink at her feet. She touches my cheek lightly, smooths a loose strand of hair out of my eyes. I feel a great sadness and regret. It's hers as well as mine – all the days we missed spending together, shared laughter, shared tears, meals and games, caresses and scoldings. We are weighed down by it as the waters pressed on me under the sea. We stay so for a minute, an hour, days. And then, like water flowing downhill, a flood receding, the past pours off us and sinks away. There is debris to clear away, but the sun blazes down and we lift our heads.

"The sources of all your dragon knowledge and abilities lie within you," she says touching my chest. My heart thumps. "Some of your abilities still sleep, others are barely awake, and one or two are nearly full fledged. It will take time and work to assume your complete heritage. Believe in yourself. Know that you can find ways to meet the challenges before you."

"Will you be there to help? Can I call on you if I need to?"

"You can call. I can't guarantee that I will be available to answer. I have many responsibilities and so does your father. I have confidence in you."

"Mother," I say.

She smiles. And then she is gone.

I'm lying beside the coals of our fire under a tree near the great river. Rowan sleeps nearby.

Chapter XXIV

Rowan

The night forest is alive with chittering, rustling, a screech or two, the hoot of an owl, and the rattling of leaves in a breeze. I'm walking as quietly as I can so as not to disturb the nocturnal life. Near the edge of a clearing where the moon shines brightly down, I stop to take a breath. At the other end of the open space, just where trees start again, I see a bulky shape, tall as a person, but with a large curved lumpy back. My heart stutters and I hold my breath in expectation of a monster being revealed by the moon. But it's only a peddler after all, perhaps the one mother's cousin Thea met when she wandered in the woods looking for love. I open my mouth to speak, but the peddler has turned and disappeared among the trees.

Clouds slide over the moon and the earth shifts along with the light. I'm standing at the base of a hill looking up at a dancing figure. I've seen that dancer before, more than once, but never been able to come close enough to tell if it's a man or a woman. This time I notice something I never have before – a lumpy pack hunched on the ground, a weight discarded.

The silver circlet of ivy leaves on my left wrist blazes as a beam of moonshine strikes it. My eyes are dazzled so that I can't see, but I hear the tramp of feet, the sound of drums and other music. It's a parade down a cobblestone street – a few soldiers on foot and horseback, musicians, jugglers, and clowns. Near the middle of the group a woman festooned with flowers, scarves and bells, dances. Rings sparkle on her fingers and bare toes. She catches my eyes and smiles broadly. I can't help grinning back, and as she passes, she tosses me what I think at first is a red rose, but when I catch it, I see that it's a bunch of rowan berries. My head jerks up to look at her again, but she's gone.

I'm sitting in a dim room listening to Julina talking. "I was able to trace the silversmith, the one who made the bracelets. His neighbours in the town where he used to live said he'd always been an honest man. He left a few years ago, but no one knew where he went."

Would it help if I could find the silversmith? The peddler? The dancer? Perhaps I should have been looking for any or all of them. Perhaps that's why I'm wandering. Magically transported by the bracelets?

Grandmother Wisdom, of the Grasslands people, told me that great love was in my bracelet, but also heartache. My parents had both those things in their lives, and so have Samel and I. Hrashak tried to get the bracelets to conquer the city of Aquila. Julina has gone to tremendous manipulations to get them for her own purposes, whatever those are. How do I know that we're wrong in trying to keep the bracelets from her? An owl hoots again and I'm standing at the edge of a forest at twilight. A huge white owl soars over my head. Could it be Grandmother Wisdom watching over me, the way she promised?

Then I'm in the tower room of the castle again with Father and Samel; we stand inside a rotating silver sphere. Hrashak and Varonne strive against us, attacking our sphere with sword and knife. Hrashak mutters words that I can't understand. Some kind of incantation probably, and one of the strands of light disappears, another dims. Shadows rise around the old man. But many circles of light remain and continue to rotate as Samel beats the small drum that hangs at his belt. The rush of a harp comes in and I feel the presence of friends, reaching out to help. Walls vibrate; it's as if the tower itself has become a musical instrument. Varonne and the old man sway and stumble, shifting to keep their feet. The shadows around Hrashak grow and swell, looming over us. Currents surge and beat against each other, rise past my knees, shaking my stance.

"It's all illusion," Hrashak screams. "I'll master it and you, or I'll kill you all just the way I killed your mother!"

I sway with shock, then rage explodes inside my chest. There isn't room in my body to hold this fury; I feel it blaze out of my eyes, run down my arms. I draw silver fire from my own and Samel's bracelets to feed that rage. My brother raises a hand with the black stone between his fingers. I remember the image of a stone torch burning on a hilltop. I feel the necklace that Mother made for me long ago, heat around my neck. I tear the necklace off, scattering beads and the black feather from my raven, Morde; all the pieces burst into flame as they fly at Hrashak. I feel a piece of necklace still pressing against my hand. It's the dragon's tooth I found in the sand hills, curved and sharp. I send the tooth flying, straight as an arrow to Hrashak's heart.

I still see the man that I killed lying crumpled on the stone floor of the tower.

The long-haired dancer has stopped dancing and is walking down the hill toward me. She is carrying the peddler's pack. The moon is behind so that I can't see the face, but I must have been mistaken in what I saw, because it's a man walking toward me.

Halfway down the hill the dancer stops and speaks: "The silver ore used to form the bracelets came from a mine deep in the earth. It was smelted and formed in fire, with the help of water and air. So, you see, the bracelets contain the attributes of all four: earth, fire, water and air. And that makes for a great power indeed."

"How do you know this?" I ask. "And how dare anyone wield such a force?"

"You must not waver in your defence of the bracelets. You and your brother are meant to keep them for a while longer. When time changes, more will become clear."

"What else can you tell me? How do we defend ourselves against Julina and rescue Ali? I don't want to kill again. What will the bracelets make us do?"

"All of you together have knowledge and abilities if you use them well and together."

Images flash before my eyes: Samel and I escaping Hrashak's dungeon by using the bracelets. Atsu and I stopping the river from flooding over Aquila. Talking to my brother so many times by using our bracelets. Making heat with Ali and her stone. And yesterday when all of us worked together to stop the rainstorm and the flood that threatened Samel and Grandfather.

None of us have killed anyone since I destroyed Hrashak. Unless in that flood we stopped at Aquila, Julina's son and second husband drowned. But that wasn't our fault. We stopped the flood while they seemed to be causing it. Still, Julina might be angry about that. Is that what this has been all about? Does she want revenge?

I look for the dancer to ask this question, but he or she is nowhere to be found.

Mountains loom all around me. I'm standing on a narrow trail in front of a dark opening. Is the dancer inside the cave? Or is this the place where Hrashak found the secrets to his spell craft and magic? There's only one way to find out. I take one step and then another. The cave is very dark. I don't want to go in there alone.

"Samel?" I whisper. "Atsu?"

"What is it, Rowan?"

I'm lying beside the coals of a fire. Atsu kneels across from me. Three horses stand nearby. It's a cool morning by the great river.

"I'm awake, right?" I say.

"Yes. Did you dream?"

"A long, complicated dream."

"I dreamt about my mother," Atsu says.

"The Pearl Princess?"

"Hmm. What did you dream about?"

"A dancer, the bracelets, a cave. I think we're meant to find a cave before we go to the castle."

"Do you know the way? Do you know why?"

"No. But I'm hoping that we'll meet my brother and Grandfather today or tomorrow and then all of us can discuss our plans."

"We eat first," says Atsu, standing up.

Chapter XXV

Rendezvous

Wind soughs through pine trees at my back; sun bounces off the water in front of us bleaching out colours. We're sitting on logs by the river, our feet dangling in cool water, minnows playing around our toes. I smell rotting fish but can't see any nearby.

"Are you rested yet?" I ask. "We haven't ridden very far since our morning meal."

Grandfather raises his head from staring at the ripples spreading from his feet. "It's not about rest, Samel," he says impatiently. "Didn't I explain that already?"

"No, you didn't."

The old man sighs. "I don't always remember when I've said something and when I've merely thought it. Sorry."

It's my turn to be impatient. "Could you explain? Now? I'm anxious to get going and find my sister and her friend."

"Water," he says. "If you remember, I've done this before, told you about it. I can find connections because water flows everywhere. I've studied water for years like when I was in the cave and after I came out. We need good water to drink, for fish to live in so we can eat, to use for keeping clean, to water plants and animals. People often take all this for granted. I don't."

I wriggle, trying to find a more comfortable spot on the log. "Fine. What are you sensing here?"

"The river drew me. It seemed time to touch it, see what I could learn. The water is good here, and there are fish. The water that flows into this river comes from many places. I sense thin streams that hold darkness. This water could be connected to that old sorcerer's castle." I open my mouth to speak and the old man holds up a hand. "There are others close by. They'll find us soon."

"Rowan?"

"I don't know. I can't tell who it is, just a couple of people and three horses."

I pull my feet out of the water to dry on the bottoms of my baggy pants. "Well, we're not going to swim this river to reach the castle, so let's get going. We should be ready to meet them if it's Rowan or take evasive action if it's not." I pull on my lined boots and stand. "I can go up and get an eagle's view."

Grandfather doesn't move. "They'll be here soon enough. We should build a fire, make some tisane." He lifts his head to squint at the sky. "It's near enough to mid-day. We can get ready to share a meal."

"They're that close?" I sit again.

"Aren't you going to gather wood?"

"In a moment. Is there anything else you've sensed? That you've forgotten to tell me?"

He pulls his feet out of the river, dries them and puts on his own boots. "There's a cave," he says. "I don't know exactly where or how far, but there's water and it's calling to me."

"Not a cave again! We're here to save Ali."

"I know that. Still, why don't we build a fire here on the beach? I'll just sit while you gather wood. Oh, and could you bring me some blankets?"

Luckily, there wasn't much rain here recently because I find enough dry branches to get a small fire going. After that I bring larger pieces and pile them near the fire. Grandfather has moved to the sand, sitting on a folded blanket, and leaning against another draped over a log. The horses happily munch handfuls of oats and crop grass. How do I know the horses are in a good mood? Ears pricked, a hind leg cocked, an occasional relaxed sigh. I rummage in our food sack and find the last of our dried meat and vegetables, which I put into a pot with water. I guess we should have brought more food. If we weren't meeting Rowan and Atsu, we'd be in trouble. Unless they're short of food, too. Another pot of water is heating for tisane. I go back to the packs and rummage for a while, searching for any food packets I might have missed before. Near the bottom of one bag, I find a length of fishing line and some hooks. I take this to the old man.

"You can make yourself useful," I say. "Use your knowledge of water to catch us a few fish if you think there's no danger from the dark streams you mentioned."

"I thought you said you didn't have any fishing paraphernalia."

"Thankfully, I was wrong. Someone must have put this in for us."

He takes the line and hunches slowly to his feet. "The dark streams are very minute and come from a distance. They'll be diluted and are not a danger to us here."

I watch his tottering steps to a spot near a rock where the river swirls. Should I go and help so he doesn't fall in? He settles himself on the rock.

"I'm fine," he calls. "Just find me a branch I can use as a pole."

By the time I get Grandfather organized the stew is simmering. Time to stir. The other pot is boiling, and I add tisane leaves to the water. Between the blazing sun and the fire, I'm sweating. I pull off my coat and roll up the sleeves of my tunic.

"Got one!" the old man shouts. He unhooks a glittering fish, baits the hook with something I can't see, and tosses it back into the water.

I guess I'd better find a pan for frying. Before rummaging once again I walk a little way south down river road, hoping to catch a glimpse of riders. Nothing except a speck high in the sky. An eagle? I pull the feather out of my belt pouch and touch it to the bracelet on my left wrist.

Blue currents of wind swirl about me. I catch one of them and glide, rising up and up. Below lies a tiny world dotted with plants, a thin ribbon of water and a few creatures in motion. A hare darts out of a bush and into a hole. I circle, waiting for it to emerge. Tilt my wings, slip down a stream of air, lower. Two riders tow an additional horse. Not far away by the river, an old man and a younger one move about. There's a fish lying on the ground. Perhaps I can grab it before they notice.

"Samel! I've caught another!"

I'm standing in the middle of the road looking at a tiny dust cloud in the distance to the south. It's Rowan and Atsu, I'm sure of it. Grandfather calls again, so I turn and hurry back to him. He's got three fish laid out on the sand and is pulling another out of the water.

"One for each of us," he says. "I'll stop now."

"Well done," I say. "I'll clean them. But maybe you could catch another fish for the eagle up there."

Grandfather stares at me for a moment, then shrugs and rebaits his line. Soon he has another fish, which he tosses onto the bank. We back away, and I look up to see the speck of eagle growing larger. It barely touches down to grab the fish, then wings away.

Rowan and Atsu arrive, dusty and smiling just as the fish are nearly finished frying. Grandfather has already eaten one small bowl of stew and drunk two cups of tisane. He grins as the others arrive and our horses neigh in welcome. My sister nearly leaps from her horse to grab me in a squeezing hug.

"At last!" she says. "I thought we'd never find you." She stands back and gestures. "This is my friend, Atsu."

The dark-haired, moon-faced young man holds out a hand. We shake.

"Meet Grandfather," I say. "Actually, he's Thea and our mother's grandfather and his real name is Wintan, but he likes to be called Grandfather Frog or just plain Grandfather."

"I caught the fish," the old man says.

"Pleased to meet you," Rowan and Atsu say together.

"There's stew and tisane," I say, "and the fish is just ready."

"I really need to wash," my sister says.

"Me too," Atsu adds. "A quick scrub in the river."

Over the meal we catch up on everything that's been happening. Grandfather doesn't say much. His head nods now and then and I think he may be dozing.

"So, we should make plans," I say. "Figure out the best way to approach the castle."

Everyone is silent, and I'm about to ask if anyone has a suggestion when Grandfather raises his head and says, "A cave. That's what we need to find first."

I sigh and am about to chide him when I notice Rowan's expression. Her mouth opens and her eyes widen. Atsu leans forward gazing intently at the old man. It seems to me that the young man's face has turned rather green. It must be the reflection of the trees nearby.

"Samel thinks I'm wrong," Grandfather adds, "but I know I'm not."

"I think it's time to put out some protections," Atsu says. "Before we make any definite plans. Julina could be listening right now."

We all fall silent and look at each other. Atsu is the first to move. He lifts a water skin from around his neck and opens it, pouring a little into one cupped hand. Then he hands the skin to Rowan and begins to blow on the water in his hand as he circles around us. Droplets scatter into the air; clouds of mist form and grow. Meanwhile, my sister has corked the waterskin and is twirling her bracelet. I feel a faint buzz in mine. The mist turns silver grey, and soon we are encased, hidden.

"Will this work?" I ask.

"We think it has before," Atsu says. "Now we can go ahead and make plans."

"At least we didn't sense Julina when we cast the mist before," Rowan adds, "though we don't know if she could see us within it or not."

I shrug. Nothing is for sure. We do the best we can.

"I don't think you're wrong either," my sister says, touching Grandfather's shoulder. "What makes you mention a cave?"

"He's obsessed with caves," I explain. "It's a long story. You agree with him?"

"I had a dream last night," Rowan says. "Visions of a dancer," she continues, "a mysterious figure that seemed one thing and then another. At the end I found myself standing in front of a cave, and I knew I was supposed to go in."

It's my turn to stare. "A dancer," I say. "I've had more than one vision of a dancer, but never of a cave. Except I recently read a story in the Leather Book about goats in a cave." I shake my head. "Do you think the cave you want is the one Hrashak found when he gained power?"

Rowan shrugs. "It could be. And I know we didn't like or trust that old man, but he did find power in a cave. You must want to go and get Ali as soon as possible, but how do we do that? Do we just ride straight into the castle? Julina could have her soldiers put us in the dungeon."

"I thought of sneaking up on them," I offer. "We can talk more about that a little later. What about this dancer? Who is he or she? Why are we having these visions? Can we trust them?"

"I don't know who the dancer is, but I felt I could trust him or her. I think it may be a real person. When I was in Vatnborg there was a woman who danced in a parade and threw me a bunch of rowan berries. That same woman showed up in my dream."

"And that means trust?"

Rowan grimaces at me. "In my dream the dancer also seemed to be the peddler that Thea met in the northern forest where Mother and I lived."

"The peddler who fathered her children?" I ask.

"Maybe. I don't know."

"I think we should get back to caves," Grandfather interjects.

"Wait." I hold up a hand. "The story in the Leather Book was about Amalthea who saved a child. Thea told me she was named for such a person."

Rowan frowns. "The Leather Book is old and strange. I don't think we should get distracted by it right now."

"There could be caves everywhere in the mountains," Atsu says. "How do we know we've found the right one?"

"I think I'll know," Rowan says.

"Water," Grandfather adds. "I think water will help us find the right cave. A long time ago, I lived in a cave for a while, and there was a pool. I think I can find that cave again by listening to and feeling water. I think we need to go a little further south and find a narrow trail leading west."

"Your cave and Hrashak's cave might be two different ones," I point out.

"It doesn't matter. Even if it's a third cave, I say we try it," Rowan says. "And while we're finding this cave, we can think more about how we approach Julina's castle. I like the idea of sneaking up on it."

"A rainstorm," Atsu says. "We stopped a storm and a flood together, why couldn't we create one to hide our approach."

"It's an idea," I say slowly.

Grandfather shuffles to his feet. "Why are we dawdling then? Let's get moving."

"Just before we do," Rowan says, "I want to try to send a message to our father. Let him know that we've met and that we're all right."

"Won't that upset him? I mean you using the bracelet. He didn't like it when I used mine. And how will he get the message since he doesn't have a bracelet?"

"I told him before we left Aquila that I'd do this, and he was fine about it. All I can do is try."

"Do you want my help?" I ask. "Two bracelets better than one?"

Rowan shakes her head. "I think I can do it."

She withdraws a little, sits under a tree. The rest of us finish clearing the site and packing the horses. We don't watch her, not wanting to break her concentration. After a while, she joins us again.

"I talked to him briefly. He was home, about to eat. Said greetings to all of us and be careful."

"Let's go, then," Grandfather says.

Chapter XXVI

Ali

Someone keeps whispering in my ear. I wish they'd stop and let me sleep. It's probably Ivoire trying to annoy me so that I'll get up and go to the market with her. Well, she's out of luck; I'm going to keep my eyes closed and pretend to be deep in dreams.

"I thought you could see them."

See what? This is not Ivoire's voice. When I open my eyes, I'm in the dungeon, of course. Have the soldiers put someone else in here with me?

"Most of the time. I know they've all met by the river, but they've put up barriers against me so that I can't tell what they're planning."

"You could send them another message and tell them you'll hurt the girl if they don't come to you immediately."

"Thank you for your advice, Varonne." The voice sounds sarcastic. There's a pause. "Now could you please go check to make sure the guards are on high alert?"

I'm sitting up by this time, leaning against the stone wall of the dungeon. The walls still sparkle and give enough light that I can discern all the arrangements. I'd been dreaming that I was at home. If only Ivoire had been whispering to annoy me, I'd grab and tickle her until she broke into giggles. And then I'd hug my sister so hard. No, no time for tears.

I need to think about what I've heard. Samel and the others have met, and they must be close. Julina is frustrated because she can't hear their plans; they've figured out ways to block her. I've got to be ready for whatever they decide to do – walk in openly, sneak in, do something entirely surprising. Should I try to contact Samel? Or will their protections block me, too? Worse, Julina might be able to sense me and find out what's going on. Best not to try for now. I've not figured out ways to block Julina.

I slept last night near the water pail and the food box, so it's easy to have my limited breakfast. The bread is like a chunk of wood, the cheese almost too hard to break, and the dried apples even drier. I soak a few of the apples in water. When will they bring me more food? Perhaps I should ration what I eat.

The gloom has sunk my spirits. If only I could figure out which wall is an outside one, make a hole there. Grasping the piece of rainbow obsidian in one hand I circle my prison, touching the walls gently. At one spot opposite the door, I think I feel a tingle in my fingers. So, stretching up as far as I can, holding the stone in my fingertips, I touch it to the wall, close my eyes and think of the outdoors, sun light on cobblestones, wind blowing across castle walls.

My fingertips graze the stones of the wall, sense its hardness, granules packed tightly, formed long ago after a fire mountain exploded and spewed molten rock. That rock hardened, was buried in earth, dug up and cut to fit the walls of this dungeon. Granite. Is it just my overactive imagination or can I truly sense the makeup of these stones?

"We are kin to your stone," a chorus of faint whispers tells me.

Did I hear those words, or imagine them? I feel the obsidian stone slipping, open my eyes and see it slide up the wall to where the ceiling meets it. Amazingly, the stone sticks there. I watch it intently. Is it sinking in? I really hope it's going to make an opening, but then I might lose it for good if it falls to the outside or stays stuck up there.

"Wait," comes the whisper.

My stone gleams turquoise, orange, red and purple; the whole room swirls with rainbow colours. I'm thinking as hard as I can of a hole growing in the wall. Nothing appears to be happening.

Then, the floor under my feet trembles – an earthquake? Suddenly, there's complete darkness as if a door has closed. After a few moments, a tiny ray of brightness slants down. Very gradually it grows bigger until it's the size of a gold coin, and it continues to grow until it's like a small pale plate – sunshine penetrating my prison.

"Enough," I whisper, leaning against the stone wall, which feels warm.

With a faint clatter, the rainbow stone drops down onto the floor. I can see exactly where it landed, can see my cell much more clearly now. Quickly, I lean down to pick up the stone. My head whirls and I have to sit.

I cradle the piece of obsidian. "You clever thing!" I touch the wall. "Thank you."

There's a faint murmur, but I can't make out any words. Gradually my head stops spinning. I get up slowly and move over to sit on the blankets. Take out a bit of bread and cheese to soak and nibble because I'm hungry again. The room is about twice the size of the tower room and with the extra light, I see rusty chains hanging here and there from the walls. I shudder as I imagine what those chains may have been used for.

My speculations are interrupted by faint hissing. I scan the room. Could there be a snake down here? A whole nest of them like one of our neighbours in Aquila found in a hole beneath their kitchen. I see nothing moving. Lean my head against the wall in relief.

"SSS. Damn! The scrying is not working, and neither is my seeing glass. I've got to send out a spy or two, but I don't trust any of those soldiers to find their own boots on a dark night. It'll have to be Varonne. The girl has her faults, but she's not stupid."

Several small thumps and then one loud one, like a door being slammed. Julina, again, making plans. Can I warn Samel and the others? Now is the best time, when Julina's off talking to her daughter. She'll be concentrating on that, not paying attention to much else.

I stare into the rainbow swirls of the stone; they draw me in until colours fill my mind. The turquoise strand undulates like a tiny stream moving through a landscape ablaze with sunshine. It widens, broadens into a river. Beside it moves a mist. I hear the clip clop of horses, and faint voices, but I can't get through the fog. I take several deep breaths and think of Samel's face, try to see it in my mind – his smile, so infectious. From the river, a bar of orange rises joined by red and purple, colours of a rainbow reaching into the sky, twisting toward the mist, diving down into it and pulling me with it.

A troop of horses and riders: four riders, six horses. One of the riders has red hair; it's Samel. I call his name, but my voice is too faint. I see his head turn, his gold flecked eyes so like an Aquilan eagle's stare through the mist, through distance, into stone. He is inside the stone and so am I.

"Ali?" Samel whispers.

"A warning," I say as loudly as I dare, here in my dungeon room. "Julina is sending a spy to look for you."

"A spy from Julina," Samel repeats.

"It'll likely be Varonne. Take care," I say, as the rainbow begins to fade, the river to recede.

"Thank you," comes faintly.

The piece of obsidian lies cold and dull coloured in my hand. And I feel as if I've climbed all the stairs in the castle. I'd better eat again and then a nap. I hope that Samel and the others will be safe. And that Julina didn't sense what I just did.

Chapter XXVII

The Cave

"Varonne?" Rowan asks as they gather the reins of their horses and prepare to ride on. "That's who will come looking for us. That's what Ali said?"

"Julina's daughter," Samel adds for the others' benefit. "She was a mercenary soldier."

"Which means she's got skills," Atsu says. "We'll have to be on the watch for her."

"Won't the fog you've cast around us keep her away?" Grandfather asks.

"No. Anyone who comes close will spy the moving patch of mist and realize something's up. All it will take is persistence and she'll be able to penetrate the mist and find us. She might even hide and be able to listen to us talk. I don't really know how much concealment the mist offers if someone comes close."

"Maybe we need more fog," Grandfather says. "Spreading from us into the mountains and along the river. If it covers enough area, it will take a lot of time for her to find us."

"I don't think I have the strength and ability to create that much weather." In his mind, Atsu hears his mother say, "Confidence!"

"Can't the rest of us help?" Samel asks. "Rowan and I could try using the bracelets to give you strength. I can make wind to spread the fog."

"We still have to be able to find our way," Rowan says. "It's already hard enough. I don't want to blunder past a turn-off to the cave."

"Or step off a cliff because we can't see the edge," Grandfather adds.

"I think we've got a little time," Samel says. "Even if Varonne started riding right away, she won't get to us for a while."

"Take a look, Samel," Grandfather says. "Use your eagle feather and find out how far the castle is, try to spy the cave or at least a forking of the trail, and keep your eyes open for any sign of Varonne."

"Are you thinking we'll hide in the cave?" Samel says.

Grandfather shrugs and nods at the same time.

"Eagle feather?" Rowan asks. "What's that about?"

Samel explains. They all agree it's a good idea and pull the horses to the side of the road. Samel takes out the feather.

The exhilaration of gliding on currents of wind grabs him as always. The eagle dips and circles, dives and rises, screams in exultation. Does the bird feel the boy's excitement? Each giving to each? Samel remembers that he's supposed to be surveying the landscape.

The river glimmers blue, reflecting sky. Beside the water, a patch of mist hovers, not all that large. Grandfather's idea about making it larger is a good one. To the west, the mountains rise – ridges, peaks and valleys. At this height he can't see any specific caves, but in the distant northwest a small, crenellated structure hunches between two peaks. He estimates that the castle is less than a morning's flight away, at top speed. Samel doesn't understand how he knows this or even how fast an eagle can fly. Has he picked up an eagle's senses? Anyway, it's enough to take back to the others. But wait, he's got to try and find a branch to the trail. The eagle descends and circles until Samel spies a faint path not far south of where they are now.

"Thank you," Samel whispers. He's about to wish for the eagle to turn when he catches movement out of the corner of the eagle's right eye. "Wait."

The eagle circles again and Samel sees a hump of rock shifting on the side of a nearby mountain. Is there about to be a landslide? Perhaps he should wait and see so it's direction. The rocks shiver, then rise and move downslope.

"Rockfolk!" Samel whispers. "I don't know what to do about this."

"Well?" Grandfather asks when Samel blinks and puts the feather away. "What did you see?"

"No caves, but there's a fork to this trail not far. And Julina's castle looks to be less than a half day away by fastest eagle flight."

"What's that in speed and how does it compare to a horse?" Atsu asks.

"In mountains, I'd say that would take a horse at least four times as long, probably more," Grandfather says.

"How do you know?" Rowan asks. "Both you and Samel."

"I just sensed it," Samel says. "When I'm flying or soaring a part of me catches the thoughts of eagles."

"You never left here, though, so how does it work? Does your mind enter that of an eagle?" Atsu asks.

"I think so," Samel says.

Grandfather clears his throat loudly. "I'm old, have lived a long time, learned many things," he says. "Do you want me to explain the numbers to you? An eagle can fly about four times as fast as a horse can trot. On mountain trails it would likely take a horse even longer."

"I saw something else," Samel says. "Rockfolk moving near the other trail."

"Rockfolk?" Rowan asks. "I vaguely remember someone mentioning them."

"Legends and stories," Grandfather says. "Creatures made of stone that mostly sleep in caves, but if something warms them like a nearby fire or the sun, they may wake and move."

Atsu holds up a hand. "I think we encountered one on a camping trip with the children from the Vatnborg school. We moved to a cave because of a rainstorm."

"And a pile of rocks near the back of the cave came together into a creature with two arms, two legs and a head that touched the ceiling of the cave," Rowan says. "I remember one of the teachers talking about that."

"Everyone ran out," Atsu says. "I caused a gush of water that sealed the cave."

"So, they're dangerous?" Rowan says. "We should avoid it?"

"We encountered one at a distance once," Samel says. "Grandfather, two guards from Schönspitze and I. It didn't bother us, though."

"We didn't stop to find out what it would do," Atsu says. "The children were scared."

"If we proceed carefully, we should be all right," Grandfather adds.

"Let's get moving, then," Samel says. "The fork is close. There's a tall rock that marks the place."

When they reach it, the new trail looks narrow and unused, barely distinguishable. Samel and Grandfather guide their horses toward the tall rock. Rowan and Atsu hold back.

"Do you see anything moving?" Rowan asks, scanning the terrain.

"How do we know this is the right way?" Atsu asks. "You said you didn't see any caves."

"Yes," Rowan adds, "We don't want to wander off and get lost in the mountains and encounter who knows what."

"I see nothing moving except an eagle high above," Samel says. "Besides, it's the only trail I saw."

"I sense water ahead," Grandfather says, "deep inside a mountain. It beckons me."

Rowan and Atsu exchange a look.

Samel notices. "Skeptical? Grandfather and I haven't gotten lost yet. If the rest of you are determined to find this cave, I'd say listen to Grandfather."

"Atsu, you have an affinity for water," Grandfather says. "Stretch your senses, see what you can feel."

The young man looks at each of them in turn, as if seeking confirmation. Grandfather gives a short nod. Rowan shrugs. Samel merely smiles.

"Fine, I'll try."

Atsu closes his eyes and thinks of water. The river is nearby, and he can see it in his mind's eye: a long undulating creature that reminds him of his mother. But the river isn't a dragon. He turns his thoughts toward the mountains, senses tiny streams, rushing waterfalls, chilly springs, quiet ponds, a large lake, but none of these is underground. He's about to give up and open his eyes when a damp tendril reaches for him. It's cold and stretched thin, leads behind a mountain and down a crack. He can't follow it further, but it tugs at him.

"I've found something," Atsu says, opening his eyes. "It does come from inside a mountain, but that's all I can find out."

"It's enough," Grandfather says. "We go?"

"Can't Samel take another look through the eagle's eyes?" Rowan asks. "Just to be sure there's nothing wandering about close by?"

Samel sighs. "Fine."

The wind ruffles primary feathers out on the wing tips. The secondaries shift and shiver, tilting as needed and the tail feathers do their part. Samel thinks of staying here with the eagle, avoiding all the argument below and the possible trouble ahead. It's peaceful. In the distance the crenelated tower rises, dark against pale sky. Ali is there. He can't abandon her. Nothing moves below except a small animal. The eagle is about to dive.

"It's fine, no Rockfolk," Samel says to the others. "We go."

"What about making more fog?" Rowan asks. "Now would be the time, if we want to conceal our whereabouts."

Atsu nods, and sighs. "All right, I'll try."

He blows water into the air from his waterskin, using up nearly half of it. As the droplets scatter, he closes his eyes and thinks of mist over a river near which he once lived, remembers valleys thick with fog. As he is doing this, he is aware without direct vision, of whirling brightness to either side, sparkles that thicken and broaden the mist that has gathered above him. Three minds or is it four, imagine fog spreading ahead of them and to all sides. Atsu breathes in dampness, breathes it out again.

"We have to leave an area clear in front of us, so we can see where we're going," Rowan says.

Atsu opens his eyes to see tendrils of mist floating away, leaving a short area clear ahead, like a tunnel. Grandfather and Samel lead the way. Rowan nudges her horse to follow the old man and her brother. Atsu brings up the rear.

The horses pick their way in single file, slowly and carefully between fist-sized stones, past twisted tree roots, across patches of gravel, and along narrow ledges. The track winds up and down, sometimes almost disappearing, but Grandfather leads them onward without hesitation.

Atsu feels the damp strand, like a finger hooked into his mind, pulling gently. Now and then he thinks that he can smell damp stone, hear the slap of water against rock, but there's nothing to see. His skin prickles. The fingers of his right hand drag the reins over to his left so he can scratch, almost expecting to see scales instead of skin. His horse stumbles, and he quickly straightens the reins.

"I think we should take a break," Rowan says. "We've been riding since early this morning, and it must be almost midday. Time for food."

Just then a gust of wind surges across their path. They all feel a pressure in their heads, and then the sky darkens. The horses slow.

"We're close enough to feel Hrashak's castle," Rowan says slowly. "Can we keep going?"

"I don't feel anything," Atsu says. "What's it like?"

"Weight and darkness," Samel says with difficulty. "Will it get worse?"

Grandfather makes sounds like a frog croaking and then his words come clear. "There are four of us and we all have power. Use it!"

Atsu looks around at his companions. The other three are hunched over their horses, which have now stopped. His own horse, too. He nudges it hard with his knees and it takes a few steps then stops again. This must not delay them! He feels anger rise and then a vibration in his legs. It moves upward through his body – he's about to change to dragon shape, and that would spook the horses. Although it would be a way to get them going, it's not the best way. He dismounts, concentrates on staying human, and pulling his horse by the reins, gathers the reigns of the others as well. The wind continues to blow, scattering the fog. As he moves them forward and around a bend, the sun reveals a valley surrounded by rows of snow dusted peaks, marching into blue-hazed distance. The other three sit up and look around.

"What just happened?" Rowan asks. "Was that Julina?"

"Maybe," Samel says. "But if so, she didn't stay long. And it is nice to see the sun again."

"Look, there's a good stopping place just ahead," Grandfather's voice croaks. "I'd like to rest and eat."

"I wasn't affected," Atsu says. He mounts again.

The trail is wide enough for them all to ride abreast. Grandfather makes for three evergreen trees and a mossy dip with a stream trickling at the side. They sit on rocks and eat cold food, not wanting to waste time building a fire.

"Do you think Varonne is close?" Rowan asks.

"You and I could use the bracelets to try and sense her," Samel says.

"Or you could fly up again," his sister says.

"Reluctant to try the bracelets?" Samel asks. "I thought you'd got over that."

"I'm just wary of using them so close to Julina, especially if she's responsible for the mist blowing away."

"We'll have to employ them to fight her eventually," Samel says.

"I think you should use them now," Grandfather says. "To help Atsu smother these mountains in mist again. Once that's done, I have a few more things to say."

For most of the journey, Samel thinks, the old man was content to ride and doze and eat. Now he's their leader, face alert, eyes shiny, posture upright. Could it really be that the water in the cave is drawing him and giving him energy at the same time? If so, it's no wonder he wanted to find the cave.

Following Grandfather's suggestion, Samel, touches the silver circlet on his left wrist. Then he looks at his sister. She's staring at her bracelet, though she has made no move to touch it. Still, he feels a tingle up his left arm and down his fingers. Acting on impulse, Samel reaches across and grabs Atsu's hand. A sudden breeze lifts Atsu's shoulder length hair, and their clasped hands quiver.

"Are you trying to let go?" Samel asks. "I thought if we held hands the magic would be more powerful, like it was when we stopped the storm."

Atsu shakes his head. "You star … startled me," he stutters. "I wasn't ready. We didn't do it this way earlier."

"Sorry. It just felt like the right thing to do. Are you ready now? I think this will work. Rowan? Will you join us?"

But it's Grandfather Frog who links hands on Samel's other side. Samel expects the old man's hand to feel dry and wrinkled, but instead it's smooth and plump, a little damp.

"Rowan," the old man says. "Come. We're ready for you."

"I'm not sure," she says. "When the bracelets take over it scares me."

"It'll be all right," Samel says. "You'll see."

"I want to try something different," Atsu says. "Dip some water into a pan from the stream and set in here in the centre while we all stand around it."

It's this need that finally gets Rowan moving. She sets the full pan down and slowly takes Atsu's free hand, and Grandfather's. She looks toward Atsu. "You don't want to be touching the water?"

"No, it's fine. I'm going to blow on this water, and I want all of you to do the same. And while you're doing it, think of the densest, largest mass of fog that you can."

"Covering us, and several leagues around us," Grandfather adds.

Rowan's bracelet blazes suddenly and Samel's answers. Rowan's fingers feel like pins and needles, and she wants to pull away and shake them out, but Atsu and Grandfather hold her too tightly. A spray of water leaps from the pan and spreads above them, slowly thickening. The pins and needles in Rowan's hands fade and warmth takes their place, spreading up her arms and filling her whole body. She feels the fire inside her, as she did once before. It's terrifying. Who will she kill this time?

"It's all right," Samel whispers, "we share this power, and we keep each other safe."

Atsu's hand squeezes hers in reassurance and Rowan feels the cooling of summer rain on parched fields, and early morning fog over a lake. As the fog around them rises and extends in all directions, it gradually turns silver grey. Rowan becomes calmer, and soon hands release.

"I feel sure that we'll reach the cave by nightfall," Grandfather says. "I didn't want to say that earlier when we were out in the open."

"So, you think we're protected from Julina and Varonne?" Rowan asks.

"As best we can," the old man says. "All of us together wield enough power to thwart that woman."

"I think we should get moving," Samel says. "I keep thinking of Ali in Julina's power."

By the time they get back on their horses it's hard to see more than an arm's length in any direction. Grandfather, however, is not daunted and he again takes the lead. The horses' hooves are muffled by the fog and no one speaks. They move like ghosts through the mountains, still not being able to see more than a short distance ahead. The silver fog gradually darkens as the sun dips into the west.

"Don't you think we could let the fog thin now?" Atsu asks. "It's getting so dark we'd be difficult to see even without fog."

"Just a little longer," Grandfather says. "We're close. Can't you feel it?"

Now that the old man has mentioned it, Atsu can smell damp stone everywhere. That could just be the fog, though. A sudden picture enters his mind – a dark pool reflecting sparkles. Rowan lags to let Atsu catch up.

"I wish we could have arrived here in daylight," she says.

"Even if we find the cave tonight, we don't have to enter it until morning," Atsu says, grabbing for her hand.

She reaches across and touches his fingers, then draws back. "I've been feeling as if our original purpose got changed. Do you think that's Julina's doing? What if it's her plan to draw us aside, get us out of the way while she does whatever she wants."

"Remember I've never met her," Atsu says. "You're more likely to know what she might do than I."

"I've had this feeling before, with the bracelets. That we're pieces in someone's game, and we're being nudged and moved according to someone else's plans."

"And you think that's Julina?"

"I'm not sure. That dream I had, of a dancer on a hill. It haunts me."

"Could the dancer be Julina?"

"I didn't see the face. Don't even know if it was a woman or a man."

"We're here!" Grandfather calls.

At that moment, the fog blows away and a full moon shows them a sandy half circular area with a dead tree at one end. Straight in front of them rises a rough wall of rock with a dark triangular slash at its base. Surprisingly spry after all the riding, Grandfather is off his horse and at the cave mouth before anyone else has even started to dismount.

"Stop!" Samel shouts. "Don't go in yet. We need to be together, and we need torches."

"And we need to wait until morning," Rowan adds as she slides off her horse.

"Just stepping inside," Grandfather croaks and he disappears.

Instantly a shimmer outlines the cave mouth and Grandfather silhouetted in its midst. He's still as a statue. Rowan, Samel and Atsu are all off their horses now, but hesitate because of the light and Grandfather's motionlessness.

"Is it Varonne?" Atsu whispers. "Did she beat us here."

"Can't be," Rowan says. "How would she know where we were going?"

"She and Julina might have been listening when we didn't realize it," Samel says. "But it doesn't matter. Whoever or whatever's in there, we have to help Grandfather."

They look at each other. No one speaks. What else can they do? The three of them move forward.

Chapter XXVIII

Time Dancer

The golden radiance inside the cavern starts their eyes watering, blurring sight. Atsu is the first to blink away tears, and he discerns a tall form with long hair and flowing clothes. The figure shifts and twists within the light, which flickers like a candle flame in a breeze. Hands and arms undulate, feet stamp and slide, but make no sound. Atsu is tempted to reach out and grab, hold this person immobile long enough to tell if it's real, a man or a woman. Though it may not be sensible if this is just a vision; he's afraid of being burnt by the brightness.

To one side of the figure stands Grandfather, hands hanging loosely at his sides. He says nothing. His eyes are closed, his face calm, and he smiles.

Rowan gasps and grabs Atsu's hand. "The dancer on the hill," she whispers.

"Yes!" Samel says more loudly. "Are you real or another vision?"

The figure stills. Now they can see raven hair with silver streaks, night-dark skin and rainbow-coloured robes. "My name is Rasa. Some call me the Time Dancer."

"You brought us here, didn't you?" Rowan says, her voice stronger and louder now. "Why?"

"And what's a time dancer?" Samel asks.

"I am the peddler who fathers your cousin Thea's sons in the northern forest. I am the solider who stops you, Rowan, one evening in Timberton when you are disguised as a beggarwoman. I am the dancer in the parade in Vatnborg who throws you the rowan berries. And yes, Samel, I am the dancer in your dreams and visions. I am also the woman in the alehouse in Schönspitze."

"You're a shape shifter," Atsu says, feeling more comfortable now that he's been able to pin something down.

"I have the ability to be different people through time. Call me a shape shifter if you wish."

"Can you also be a goat?" Rowan asks.

Rasa smiles. "You're thinking of the twins. No, that's Thea's own legacy."

"You knew you had children and you ignored them," Samel says. "Why?"

"Is this the moment?" Rowan interrupts. "We have more important things to discuss."

Rasa's head shakes. "More than one of you have experienced absent parents. There are always reasons for why people behave as they do, though others may not know or understand them."

Grandfather stirs. "We didn't come here for useless words. Rather, for things to do with water and time, with hidden powers of the earth and air. Secrets to life and death. If you are truly a dancer in time, perhaps you can help us with those."

"You may have come for that, Grandfather," Samel says, 'but I came in hopes of help with rescuing Ali. Yes, Rowan, we need to get going on that."

"I have skill with the shifting and bending of time. Don't worry about urgency for the moment, Samel, there will be time enough and to spare. I brought you here because there are things you all need to know."

A clamour of voices, each one vying to be heard. "Why? … Ali. … Secrets. … Time … What?"

Rasa holds up a commanding hand and the noise stops. "Settle your horses for the night. Bring in food and bedding. I'll start a fire for hot food and tisane. Then I'll tell you a tale."

"We're being tracked," Samel says. "By a woman."

"Julina's daughter, Varonne. I know. But don't worry, she won't find you until later tomorrow. She's slightly lost. And if you wish, you can avoid her altogether."

Grumbling and mumbling, the group nevertheless does as Rasa suggests. When they are settled around the fire, the Time Dancer begins to speak.

"Once there were two boys who lived in the mountains. They were friends, perhaps cousins, close as brothers. And like brothers, sometimes they disagreed, at times they quarrelled, but mostly they got along, and they looked out for each other, defended each other, and got into scrapes together. They explored the mountains, hiking, climbing, and camping."

"Wait a minute," Samel says, leaning forward. "I know this story. I read it in the Leather Book."

"Much appears in that book that is relevant to this time, to the past, and perhaps to the future," Rasa says. "Listen and wait. Not all of you know this story, and even you, Samel, don't know it in its entirety."

Samel settles and Rasa continues.

"As they grew older the young men wandered farther afield and one day, they discovered a cave. To begin with they were wary – dangerous animals could live in caves – so they watched for a few days, but the cave seemed uninhabited. They didn't realize at first that there was another entrance.

"Finally, after they grew tired of watching without seeing any activity, they took courage and entered the cave. They found a fire pit, wood, furs, cooking pots and implements. No dust lay on anything; the place didn't look abandoned. The firepit was clear of ashes, wood neatly stacked, furs folded, cooking pots and implements clean.

"One of the young men wanted to leave immediately. 'This is someone's home,' he said. 'We're intruding.'

"The other shook his head. 'No one's here now. We haven't seen anyone in all the time we've been watching. Maybe whoever lived here has left. Or they could be hurt. We should try to find them. Look, there's another opening, more chambers maybe.'

"They explored further. One of them noticed several niches carved in the rock walls of the second chamber. Most were empty, but one held a pendant with a carved wooden 'R.' In another, they found a small scroll. The boldest picked it up and partially unrolled it. A glitter of silver dust rose into the air.

"The other said, 'What if it's magic? It could be dangerous. Best put it back.'

"His friend refused and peered at the writing. 'I can't read this.' Neither could the other young man.

"A voice stopped them. 'What are you doing here?'

"They turned and found a girl – raven hair shading in places to silver, midnight blue eyes, alabaster skin. Both young men instantly fell in love."

"Was that you?" Atsu asks. "In a different guise?"

"And this was the cave," Grandfather adds. "I think this was my cave, too. Or at least part of it, perhaps an extension. It feels right."

Rasa laughs. "Such impatience. Caves can be many things, depending on who enters or inhabits them. And, of course, there are uncounted caves in various mountain ranges. Can you not wait for the tale to continue? But perhaps hunger distracts you. Here is hot stew; help yourselves. And while your mouths are full, I can continue without interruption."

They reach for bowls and spoons, ladle stew, pour tisane. Each person rearranges blankets to make comfortable seats on the cave floor, leaning against a wall or a rock. Rasa waits patiently, smiling, until they are ready to listen again.

"The young men who fell in love with the same woman were a silversmith and Hrashak's uncle. Oh yes, Rowan, don't try to eat and talk at the same time. Chew carefully. All will become clear.

"Each of the young men wanted to do something to prove himself worthy of the young woman. She had slipped away from them, but each thought if he could impress her, she would return. Or he would haunt the cave until he saw her again, found more clues about who she was and where she might have gone. Many years passed. Hrashak's uncle decided to look for her in the city of Aquila, based on a scroll that he found with a map that had the city underlined. He died before he could reach the city, falling off a mountain during his journey, or perhaps he did reach the city and fell foul of an unscrupulous trader. The past can have many possibilities, depending on who is remembering." Rasa smiled and put a finger to her lips as Samel opened his mouth to speak.

"The silversmith searched for the young woman for many years and didn't find her, though in the cave he discovered a vein of silver. He smelted that silver and kept a lump of it for remembrance as he wandered the land, setting up a forge now and then, staying for a time, then moving on. When he carried the silver with him, he prospered and was safe. If he left it behind in his saddlebags or in a room at an inn, he lost at cards, or was robbed in an alley. Once he fell down a set of stairs and sprained an ankle. Gradually he determined that the silver held magic. From then on, he carried it in a pouch at his belt.

"He also searched out stories about metals that held magical power. In ale houses and hostelries, at campfires and caravans he heard about weapons, cauldrons, and many other things that supposedly conferred special abilities on the user. And once in a while he heard stories of sorcery involving twins or pairs of objects. This intrigued him, and he thought that perhaps instead of being rivals, he and his friend should have tried to work together. Alas, it was too late for that.

"Through his work as an itinerant smith, he gathered enough coin to set up a small forge in a mountain village. He thought about his lump of silver and what he could create – he would have to mix some other metals with it, for a pure silver object would be too soft to hold its shape. He experimented with small amounts and finally arrived at a combination that seemed right to him. He could plate the outside of whatever he made with the unique silver for additional shine. However, he didn't have enough for a weapon or cauldron. What should he make?

"One day a young couple came to his forge and asked for a pair of silver bracelets to mark their love. Pairs again, the silversmith thought. Perhaps this was what he should fashion with the rare silver. But not for the couple. Before making bracelets out of ordinary silver, he designed a special set that could focus power and create great magic. Yes, Rowan and Samel, these were the silver bracelets you now wear. The silversmith imagined using these with the woman he loved when he found her. They would combine their skills, seize any lands they wished, make a place all their own, gain whatever wealth they wanted. He imagined sharing a stately residence with her, servants, horses and other stock, jewels and costly clothing.

"When the magical bracelets were finished, he also created the set of ordinary ones for your parents. Unfortunately for him, and as Samel and Rowan have discovered, the magical bracelets have volition of their own and they moved on from him. He didn't know how it happened but woke one morning to find that he'd sold the wrong ones.

"It was then, as he lamented his loss, that the silversmith met the love of his life again. He discovered that she was a time dancer, could be a man or a woman and wanted to be referred to as heshe. His love was enraged about the silver he'd stolen from the cave. Furious that he'd made and lost the magical bracelets, heshe punished the silversmith's arrogance by turning him into a raven and sending him to hunt for the bracelets.

"Morde," Rowan whispers. "Morde? He's the silversmith? And was with me all that time? Where is he now?"

"He found you and your mother after your father had left. A geas was set on Morde to guard the two of you until the other bracelet could be discovered, but he failed, and your mother drowned."

"Is that all you could do?" Samel asks. "You're such a great spell master that you can turn a man into a raven, and you can't protect a woman or turn a pair of bracelets back into the ore they were made from? All this upheaval could have been prevented!"

"Was the silver yours?" Rowan asks. "Is that why you wanted it back?"

"The lode of metal in the cave held remnants of ancient magic," Rasa continues. "I've come across such things now and then, a legacy from the ancients who inhabited this land aeons ago, when dragons flew here. I sensed that the power of the ancients could be dangerous as well as beneficial, and I wanted to find out more. I didn't know then how to find more of the silver Morde stole or how to best use it. And the turning of a man into a raven was complicated."

"There are still dragons," Atsu says.

"Yes, I know about you and your parents," Rasa responds. "But you were not born here. The last dragons from this land died out long since."

"What happened to them?" Atsu asks.

"I'm not certain. Fragments of writing that I've found suggest that there were wars of power, but I haven't been able to reach the end time of those dragons no matter how much I try."

"So how does all this tie in with rescuing Ali?" Samel asks impatiently.

"I've seen various pasts and futures. In some, the bracelets are used for evil, in others they are lost, in still others they are used for good. Lines of possibility and power cross and break, wander here and there. It's difficult to know the exact right things to do, but I've determined that for now the bracelets must not fall into Julina's hands, and I need your help to stop her. I am not all powerful, have my limitations."

"Why don't we just give you the bracelets?" Rowan says, tugging at her belt pouch. "By your own admission, they should never have been forged. And I've not been totally happy using them." She pulls out her bracelet and holds it toward Rasa. The bracelet glimmers in the firelight and a few sparks fall from it onto the cave floor.

Rasa stands and backs away. "Didn't you listen when I said they have their own volition? They choose where they want to go and what they want to do. I can't take them, at least not now. It could be perilous, not only for me, but for the world."

"Why worry?" Atsu asks. "Maybe they don't want to go to Julina. You said there are various possibilities."

Rasa grimaces. "I don't always see future clearly; it can be just possibilities. Sometimes I'm transported there, other times the future is totally obscure to me."

"We kept the bracelets away from Hrashak," Samel says. "Why not Julina?"

"We can't take chances," Rasa says. "Julina should not gain more power. She's dangerous for this land. You've seen that already – floods, fire, a kidnapping. What other destruction might she cause? And she has enticed others to her side who will do her bidding."

"Then what do we do now?" Samel asks. "I want to get Ali home as soon as we can."

"Will you help us?" Rowan asks. "All of us together should be able to defeat Julina and rescue Ali."

"I have other responsibilities," Rasa says. "I've taken time away from them to be with you now. But one of the things I've discovered is that the bracelets have power as a pair because they were made from the same lump of silver. Now, not counting Grandfather for the moment, but including Ali there are four of you, two pairs. That could be even more powerful."

"But we have only two bracelets," Samel points out.

As if heshe hasn't heard this comment, Rasa says, "As well, according to the ancients, there are four forces of creation: fire, water, air and earth. Do any of you recognize these in yourselves?"

They look at each other. Grandfather speaks first. "Samel is air, of course: his ability to summon wind and fly with eagles."

When Rasa smiles and nods, Rowan says boldly, "Then Atsu is water. In his land dragons have affinity with water, and he can control rain, mist, rivers."

"But I had help with all that most of the time," Atsu protests.

"Exactly," Rasa says. "As you've already discovered, you are all more powerful when you join with each other."

"Fire is Rowan," Samel says softly. "She can start and wield fires."

"No!" Rowan says, before her brother can continue. "I don't want to be …"

"The Queen of Fire?" Rasa says gently. "Like Julina? You and she are not alike. Both you and Samel have abilities; the bracelets enhance them. You need to accept your abilities. I suspect the proximity of the bracelets has also affected Atsu and Ali. All of you have been learning how to control your powers, which is good and will help you in the coming task. Believe in yourselves."

"Earth," says Samel softly. "If we don't count Grandfather, who I think, has an affinity with water, too, then Ali's the only one left."

"You sound a tad doubtful," Rasa says. "When you gave Ali that piece of obsidian that you got from the castle dungeon – the stones of which, by the way, also hold remnants of ancient power – you were giving her a piece of earth. And while all of you have been travelling, she's been learning to use her own power. Surely you've realized that."

Samel grins widely. "Ha! Julina didn't know what she was doing when she kidnapped Ali, did she?"

"Certainly, she underestimated all of you. Perhaps she's been blinded by ambition and confidence in her own powers."

"What other advice do you have for us?" Rowan asks, hunching over her knees. "If you're not going with us to the castle, how do we plan this rescue?"

"No plan survives first clash with the enemy," Rasa says.

Rowan sits up straight. "That sounds like something Onoku would say."

"He's a soldier, mercenary, and wise teacher from my land," Atsu explains.

"It's a saying I came across in another time," Rasa says. "Meaning that you have to be flexible. Know your strengths. Don't be afraid to use them. And work together."

"That's it?" Rowan says.

"I have faith in you," Rasa nods. "You've proven yourselves in so many ways already."

Samel yawns. "It's been a long day. Can we sleep now? In the morning we can ride for the castle."

"What about me," Grandfather says. "It sounds as if I'm not one of the four. Can I go off to explore this cave?"

"What do you want to do?" Rasa asks.

"I'm not sure."

"Of course, you're with us, Grandfather," Samel says. "Without you we wouldn't have found this cave."

Rowan yawns. "I can't keep my eyes open much longer."

Blankets are unrolled, the fire banked.

"Time Dancer," Atsu says.

"Hmm?"

"Where do you come from? How did you get to be what you are?"

"Ah, that is much too long a tale for tonight. What I will say is that I was fostered in a cave by a shapeshifting goat. Supposedly my father was a wizard who wanted to kill me, so I had to be hidden until he died. Later I discovered strange powers."

"Amalthea!" Samel exclaims. "I read a story about that in the Leather Book."

"As I hinted before," Rasa says softly, "that is a special, magical book. You are lucky to have it. Now, it's time to sleep."

Sighs and mutters gradually fade away. A few snores begin. The horses shift, then still. Outside the cave mouth it's dark and stars glitter. A cloud moves across the moon.

A while later, Rowan opens her eyes, wondering how long she's been asleep. She stares out, trying to come to grips with everything Rasa told them. A white shape soars across the darkness and disappears. Was that an owl?

"Grandmother?" Rowan whispers and sits up.

A faint and distant hoot. The others in the cave are asleep, and Rasa is nowhere to be seen. All seems quiet and safe. How do the Grasslands People fit into all this? Rasa didn't mention them. Rowan remembers the damaged tents she saw the last time she visited there. And what her friend, Juniper, said about attacks on the camp and on lone riders. Could Julina be responsible for all that as well? She yawns, lies back down and closes her eyes. Too much to think about now.

Chapter XXIX

The Pool

Having spent so much time with Grandfather – riding, sleeping in the same tent – I'm attuned to him, aware when he stirs, coughs, sits up. I don't say anything, just watch what he's doing. There's sufficient moonlight and a subdued glow from the fire so that I can see well enough. I could ask him if he needs something but he's probably just going to the cave mouth to relieve himself. All of us stayed dressed, wrapped in our blankets, so the old man should be warm enough. But he turns toward the other end of the cave. I consider calling out; something stops me.

Only Rowan and Atsu still lie asleep. Rasa, the Time Dancer, is no longer here. Has Grandfather heard or seen her walk deeper into the cave? Is he following to see what she or he's up to? I want to know as well, don't entirely trust her. If heshe's been watching us and others all this time, he must have reasons, and who knows if those reasons are to our advantage or the opposite? We need to take everything she says and think about it, decide if we want her advice or not. I'm actually glad she or he's not coming to the castle with us.

Moonlight and firelight don't penetrate the narrow aperture at the back of the chamber where we've been sleeping. How is Grandfather seeing where to go? Maybe he's not awake at all and is sleepwalking. I need to catch up to him so that he doesn't trip over a protrusion or fall into a hole. I touch the bracelet and call up enough brightness to find my way. It's not a good thing to wake sleepwalkers I've heard. Don't know if its true, so decide to be cautious. I follow Grandfather quietly as my bracelet casts light beyond the old man's feet.

We're moving along a tunnel that's like a hallway. I get glimpses of niches here and there along the sides. A pottery urn sits in one, a bit of cloth crumpled in another, then a rusty dagger. Most of the niches are empty. I remember the story Rasa told of the two young men who came to the cave. Here? They found furs, cooking pots, other implements, a scroll, and a pendant with a carved letter 'R.' Rasa didn't say that these belonged to her, but that's what I think. Except the woman in the story had alabaster white skin not midnight black. Still Rasa can be whoever he she wants, and it wouldn't surprise me to learn that heshe lived here for a time, maybe still does. It could be the same cave that Hrashak found, where he got additional powers. Those thoughts make my skin prickle. What if spells and unknown powers still linger here?

Grandfather stops so suddenly that I nearly run into him. Peering around his shoulder, I find that we're standing at the entrance to a vast cavern. I hear the lap of water but can't see any because Grandfather is in my way. What is he waiting or looking for?

His shoulders relax as a huge sigh whooshes out of him and then the old man walks slowly forward. I follow. A pool of water is revealed. It covers the far end of this cavern and is the colour of black obsidian. Above the water and reflected in it hang long pieces of stone, like hardened candle drippings. Grandfather moves to the edge of the pool and sits cross-legged on the ground. I breathe a sigh of relief, having worried for a moment that he was going to jump in. I'm too far away to have stopped him, but I might have been able to pull him out if he didn't sink right away. He begins to hum. His eyes are closed, so I still don't know if he's awake or asleep.

As I sit beside the old man, his humming grows louder. He doesn't react otherwise to me sitting there. His voice echoes and reverberates around the cavern, vibrating the stone under us. My bracelet blazes; as if in answer, brightness flashes from the walls – crystals of white, purple, green glow all around. The hairs of my head stir, and out of the corner of my left eye, I see that Grandfather's white hair floats in an aureole around his head.

"Tangled in a dream," Grandfather whispers. "No cold, no hunger, no thirst, no old age. Better than the dream of aches and pains, weariness, and frustration with the world and people."

Chills crawl up my back. This talk is too much like what he said before, when Thea and I first arrived in Schönspitze. He was telling us about the time he fell into a lake and ended up in a cave. This cave? Who knows where this pool of black water comes from? I glance at it briefly and my eyes are riveted. It's no longer black but clear, and there are images scudding across its surface.

"Light in darkness," Grandfather whispers. "Images of many places."

I ignore him and lean forward to see the visions in the water. Scrolls unrolling, words inked on parchment and leather, a green frog nearly hidden by green grass. An old man wrapped in skins stumbles down a hillside, a leather bound book lies on a table, a great fire blazes and a man hunches over a forge. Fire mountains rise, belch smoke and red liquid rock. Wild cattle stampede as hunters on horses follow them. A quiet encampment of tents erupts in shouts as fire and smoke billow; arrows fly. On a distant mountain a castle stands dark against a morning sky; lightning flashes into a tower and stones begin to fall. A long-haired dancer cavorts on a hill, and a girl sits under a fig tree in a garden.

"Ali!"

Grandfather jerks and turns; his eyes open and he looks at me for the first time since we left our blankets. His eyebrows draw together as if he's not sure who I am. One of his hands reaches out and touches my bracelet.

"It's not good to gaze into the pool for a long time," the old man says. "You can lose yourself."

"You said that to me once before in a different place, but isn't that what you were doing here, just now? If it's not good for me, it can't be good for you either."

"I'm an old man. I've lived a long time. Died and come alive again. I can venture things the young cannot. And besides, my eyes were closed."

"But you still connected to the water even if your eyes weren't open, I could tell. I bet you saw the pictures in the water just as clearly as I did, even with your eyes shut. Was it the past or the future or both that we were shown?"

"Many worlds, many possibilities," Grandfather murmurs. "What you saw isn't necessarily what I saw."

"We need you," I say. "You can't lose yourself in these visions now. You said that you weren't sure if you were one of us, but you have to help us rescue Ali. Isn't that why you came on this journey?"

I gaze into his eyes and know the answer without him saying a word. He was pulled by whatever magic lies in this cave. Attracted by the powers of water. It doesn't matter whether this is the same cave or the same pool he found before. It's the magic that has drawn him. Coming with me to help rescue my friend was just an excuse. I sensed that but didn't want to accept it.

"I'm tired," he says.

"Come back and sleep then. It's not morning yet."

"Other people wanted things of me, just as you do now. I've lived a long life. More than one in many ways. Had a wife, children, grandchildren. Worked as a burgrave, maintained a house, businesses." His chest rises and falls as he takes in a great breath and lets it out. "Comes a time when one wants to let go of the things of the world – pain, worries, frustrations. When one wants quiet and peace, rest. You'll understand that some day."

"You can't leave us now!"

He grasps my left knee, squeezes, lets go. "Samel, I'm so glad that I got to know you, to meet your sister, to see Thea again and meet her sons. I would trade none of that for anything. Tell them all that I love them. I'll be with you all in whatever way I can. And remember, I believe in the four of you. You have the strength and courage to succeed."

And then, before I can say or do anything, the old man leans forward and slips into the water. Even though I've been fearing this, I'm momentarily stunned and unable to move. That's long enough for Grandfather to disappear.

"No!"

I reach out a hand, bend down, touch the water. A burst of force, like a stroke of lightning, knocks me backward. I hit a wall of the cave, lie there, stunned.

"Samel?"

Vague shapes hover above me. Then my eyes clear. It's my sister and Atsu standing there. I'd like to tell them what just happened, but I can barely breathe. My back aches, and I feel tears prickling my eyes.

"What are you doing here?" Rowan asks. "And where are Grandfather and Rasa?"

I shake my head, then stop as pain shoots across my forehead. Atsu comes to kneel beside me. He helps me sit.

"You've got blood on your tunic," Atsu says. I feel his hands on my back. "Scrapes, it looks like. What happened?"

"Grandfather," I whisper. "He jumped."

Rowan is beside me now as well. "Jumped?" She glances at the pool. "Into the water?"

"Yes," I rasp.

"But why?" Rowan asks.

Atsu is already at the pool's edge, his body shimmering blue-green and his shape shifting into the form of the dragon that I saw during the rainstorm and flood. He leans forward, but not far enough to fall.

"You won't be able to get into the pool," I say. "Some power knocked me back when I tried to save Grandfather."

The huge, feathered head turns to me and a gold eye gleams. The massive mouth opens, showing teeth. Then the dragon turns and slips easily into the pool, leaving barely a ripple.

"No!" I gasp. "Not him, too."

"Don't worry," Rowan says. "Atsu will find Grandfather."

"But what if the pool is enchanted? Grandfather seemed entranced by it."

"Don't forget that Atsu has power over water. I'm sure he'll be safe."

My sister's voice sounds a little doubtful, though, and I wish I hadn't said what I did. I should have tried to stop Atsu, but what if there's a chance he can bring Grandfather back? Both of us move closer to the pool. My back stings and I'd like to take off my tunic because it sticks and rubs, but that can come later. Right now, I need to watch the water.

I touch the silver circlet on my wrist and catch Rowan's eyes. She nods and fingers her bracelet, too. A sheen of silver spreads across the water. Nothing else happens for a few moments. Then, in the centre of the pool, water begins to spiral, forming a deep cone. Atsu's dragon head appears in the middle of the whirlpool, and he rises. Soon he's crawling out, turning back into a young man, shaking water out of his hair, and looking sad.

"I couldn't find him. The pool is very deep and there are various outlets with currents coming in and going out. He could have been swept away or swum somewhere. I had no idea which way to go so I came back. But if you want,

I can keep looking."

"What do you think, Samel?" Rowan asks.

It's tempting to say 'yes, go and find him' but there's Ali to rescue. Besides, Atsu might search for a long time and find nothing. I shake my head and turn away from the pool.

"I'm sorry," my sister says. "I wish we'd woken in time and could have helped you stop him."

"It probably wouldn't have made any difference," I say. "I think the whole reason he came on this journey was to find this pool. You haven't heard the story of what happened to him before, but he found a cave and a pool. Said he thought of dying and was reborn."

"Maybe…?" Atsu starts.

I shake my head. "He's an old man, years older now than he was the first time. How could he survive a dive like that?"

"Rasa might help," Rowan says. "Where is heshe anyway? I didn't see her last night after the rest of you fell asleep, either."

"I have no idea. Rasa wasn't in the cave when Grandfather got up."

"Heshe did say we would have to go on to the castle without him," Atsu says. "We should make plans."

"But first we've got to fix Samel's back," Rowan says.

She and Atsu help me back down the passage to the outer cave. The pale light of sunrise washes the rock walls. Our horses are moving restlessly. My stomach growls.

"I'll look after Samel," Rowan says. "Atsu, can you stir up the fire and start our morning meal?"

"I'll feed and water the horses first," he says.

Chapter XXX

Plans

So," Atsu says as he hands around bowls of gruel, "shall we let Varonne find us and lead us to the castle? Or shall we try to avoid her and surprise Julina?"

Rowan sets her bowl down. "Either way, we'll end up at the castle. It seems to me if we try to elude Varonne, she may find and ambush us anyway. That could cause its own problems. And I'm worried about that darkness and heaviness we encountered again. If we're with Varonne that might not happen."

"I want to get to Ali as soon as possible," Samel says, "but I also want to be cautious. We can easily find out where Varonne is but why not maintain our independence from her? And Atsu was able to get us out of the darkness yesterday."

"I'm sure I can get us through any darkness, but what about the rest of it?" Atsu asks. "We should have more plans, a strategy about what we're going to do once we get to the castle."

"Samel, you could use your eagle feather to go up and see where Varonne is so we can go to meet her or avoid her," Rowan says. "Though I agree we should talk about what else to do. Recall what we know and discuss what Julina may have waiting for us. We've learned some things from Ali. Samel, can you find out more? Like how many other people are in the castle, weapons, anything Ali has seen or overheard."

"Yes, I'll try and contact Ali to let her know we are coming so she can be ready," Samel says. "I'll ask her what else she knows. Keep my gruel warm. I'm going into the passage. I think it will be easier to concentrate if I'm by myself."

Samel walks far enough away that a little light still penetrates, then sits and touches his bracelet. Grandfather's face the way it looked just before he slipped into the pool comes to mind, and his throat tightens. He shakes the memory away. Think about that later. He rubs tears from his eyes, then closes them to concentrate on Ali. Pictures her long brown hair hanging over her shoulders, a smile brightening her face. Perhaps she'll be sitting on her cot in the tower room.

"Samel?" She's there, leaning forward, a dark stone wall behind her. It's almost as if she's in the cavern with him. Ali squints as if she can't see him clearly. "Where are you?"

"I'm in a cave with Rowan and Atsu. Never mind all that now. I need to tell you something, but first can we try to put a bubble of protection around you and me?"

"All right."

Samel focuses on the bracelet, imagining the silver bubble that it cast before. As the bubble grows, it has a swirl of darkness as well as rainbow colours. Soon he and Ali seem to be floating and encased in a bright sphere.

"This is different," Samel says.

"Must be the piece of obsidian. It's taken on the colours of the rainbow. Hopefully we're safe from Julina overhearing or seeing us." Ali grins broadly.

"I guess you have things to tell and there's things I need to ask you. But there's too little time. The important thing for you to know right now is that we're close. We haven't decided whether we're going to let Varonne catch us and lead us into the castle or not."

"If you go with Varonne, Julina will make you prisoners. Why do that?"

Samel touches the bracelet so that its light flares and the sphere around them becomes more opaque. "We're going to use the power of the bracelets and Atsu's power over water to join with whatever power the stone has given you. And it seems to be quite a lot. Rasa thinks we'll defeat Julina."

"Who's Rasa?"

"Time Dancer. Never mind, it's too complicated. Are you still in the dungeon?"

"Yes, but I'm sure I can get out." Ali waves her hands. "I've already melted a small hole in the rock wall to bring in light. I can destroy parts of walls and rebuild them."

"That's useful. No one noticed?"

"The soldier who brings my food only comes in the evening, so I don't think he's aware. I made it up high and he doesn't look much farther than his own feet. Or else he was never down here before and didn't know the hole shouldn't be there."

"Any idea how many soldiers Julina has?"

"I overheard there's half a dozen. I think all of them are followers, not doers. If Julina hasn't given them direct orders, they don't pay attention. Julina complains about the trouble they cause, but I think it's her own fault. She doesn't seem to trust other people very much, not even her own daughter. There are a few servants, too, I think, but I don't know how many."

"And you haven't escaped yet because …"

"I didn't know where you were," Ali snaps. "Didn't want to end up wandering through the mountains until Julina or Varonne found me again."

"Makes sense. Any idea what Julina is really after?"

"Not sure. Doesn't seem happy with anyone. I don't know whether she wants to stay here or go out and conquer other places."

"What else can you tell me about Julina and the situation at the castle? We want to be prepared."

"Well, Julina senses when you use your bracelets, though she can't see through the mists you've made. She's told Varonne that her scrying glass doesn't work that well to see what you and the others are doing. She also doesn't seem to sense the magic of the piece of obsidian you gave me."

"That's all good. Anything else?"

"Her mind control. She's attempted more than once to enter my head, to find out things, to get me to tell her things. It's hard when she does that, she's strong. But I've managed to hold her off partially for short periods of time. I'm not sure what would happen if she pushed at my mind for longer or what would happen if she had several people to try and control."

"Hmm. I remember she tried something like that with me when I travelled with Grandfather earlier and she started a fire in the mountains. We'll remember that."

"Good. I can't wait to see you!"

"All right. We'll be there as soon as we can, probably later today. I'll try to send a message when we're close."

"Samel?"

"What?"

"Be careful. Don't get overconfident."

And then, before he can respond to that, Ali has disappeared and the bubble fades. Samel stretches his cramped back and legs and hurries back to eat his lukewarm gruel.

"Couldn't you have kept it hotter?" he says.

Rowan frowns. "We can't dawdle here all day. I told Atsu to douse the fire."

"Did you learn anything useful from Ali?" Atsu asks.

Samel recounts the conversation. The other two don't interrupt, nor do they say anything when he's finished. They should be coming up with ideas and a plan for how to act when they find Varonne, and what to do when they confront Julina.

"I miss Grandfather," Samel says.

Rowan frowns. "What brought that on? I'm sorry, but we still have things to do, can't think about what happened, what we can't change."

Samel turns from his sister to look at a mountain. "It just came over me again that he's gone when I saw his horse standing there."

"We don't know for certain that Grandfather is dead," Atsu says, putting the last of their possessions except Samel's bowl and spoon into the bags on one of the pack horses.

"He had good ideas," Samel says. "I wish I could have asked him what we should do next and when we get to the castle."

"Um, it sounds as if the castle isn't that well defended," Atsu says. "I think we should concentrate on defending ourselves against Julina specifically."

"I wish we didn't have all these horses to deal with," Rowan says. "They distract me. Keeping them all together with only three of us won't be easy."

Samel swallows a last spoonful of gruel. "We'll need a horse for Ali, and we can use both pack horses for supplies on our way home. Now let's get outside so I can use the eagle feather to try and get a glimpse of Varonne."

Samel stretches his body in blue sky among white clouds. Sun warms wings, feathers tilt in the ruffling wind. The temptation to soar on circling currents is strong, to fly high and fast and get away from his troubles. A scream of joy erupts from an open beak. Faintly, a voice calls; he tries to ignore it, but it's persistent. Finally, he glances down, notices a tiny group of horses and humans. And he's there, too, as well as up here. He doesn't know how it works but remembers that he's supposed to be looking for a particular person – a woman in black leather armour.

The eagle banks and circles, peering at rocks, crags and trees below. The bird seems to know what his human companion wants and mostly does it, except when eagle needs take precedence. A narrow trail winds from the cave toward a distant castle. That's where the people want to go. Half-way between the cave and the castle a lone figure in black armour urges on a horse. It doesn't look as if there are any side trails. If they plan to avoid Varonne they'd have to find a place to hide and that would be difficult with all the horses. It seems as if one decision has been made for them. Time to leave the sky and return to his body.

"Thanks again, eagle," he whispers.

"Samel!" Rowan exclaims as he puts the feather away. "You were a long time! Did you see Varonne?"

"She's in that direction, about halfway to the castle, heading toward us. Not long until we meet. There's really no place we can hide from her."

Atsu shivers. "This is it then. We're really doing this."

"You're having second thoughts?" Rowan says.

"Not exactly. I'm nervous, wondering if I'll be able to do what's needed."

"We don't have to do anything except ride for a while," Rowan says.

Atsu takes a deep breath and lets it out. "I've been thinking – we've all got our strengths. What if each of us does one thing when we first confront Julina? Say that I turn into a dragon and call up water to flood wherever we are. Samel could summon a wind, maybe strong enough to blow some of the soldiers away. Rowan could you start a fire? If we can distract Julina, encircle her with our powers, maybe that will give Ali enough time to escape the dungeon and join us. Then the four of us together can get away."

Rowan shivers. "We did something like that when I killed Hrashak."

"Don't have second thoughts now," Samel snaps as he swings onto his horse. "You did what you had to do then, and we'll do what we have to now. I think your ideas are good, Atsu. Let's get going."

Samel shoots a glance at the sky where a distant speck circles. He sighs, and nudges Izmeer down the trail towards Varonne and the castle. The other two follow.

Chapter XXXI

Interlude

Samel leads Grandfather's horse while Atsu takes charge of the two pack horses and Rowan follows last. They keep the horses to a slow walk, none of them in a hurry to meet Varonne, even though they've agreed that's the course they'll take. Now and then Samel briefly touches the eagle feather to get a quick view of how close Julina's daughter is. He's starting to get dizzy from the changes in perspective. Near a scrawny clump of trees by a shallow stream, Samel pulls Izmeer and Grandfather's horse to a halt.

"What's the matter?" Rowan says.

"I need a drink of water and the horses do, too."

"Varonne is close, isn't she?" Atsu says. "And you're nervous." He shrugs. "So am I. But remember, Rasa said we could do this."

Samel attempts a grin but doesn't succeed. "But heshe's not here. Left us to our fate. And Grandfather's gone, too." He swings off Izmeer, hiding his face.

"I keep remembering the last time we were in that castle," Rowan says, shivering.

"That should make you feel confident," Atsu says. "You escaped."

"And killed a man."

"Rowan, I know you're not a killer. You did what you had to, then. You saved your father and brother. Now you, along with the rest of us, will do what's necessary. We'll protect each other and get Ali out of there."

"Sounds easy when you say it. But it won't be!" Rowan flings at him. "I'm not dragon spawn!"

"What's that supposed to mean?" Atsu asks.

"Ali's perfectly capable of getting out of there herself," Samel interrupts. He turns to his sister and Atsu. "We could just let her know that we're close, and she'll get out and come join us."

"You really think that's possible?" Rowan asks. She slides off Lady, starts to lead the horse toward the stream.

Samel follows, leading Izmeer. "She told me she can melt stone."

"It's not just about Ali's escape," a voice says. They all turn to see a pale-skinned dark-haired man, wearing a rainbow-coloured tunic and black trousers, standing on the trail behind them.

"Rasa?" Rowan says tentatively.

The man nods.

"Where did you come from?" Samel asks.

"Here and there. That's not important. You need to collaborate, not argue amongst each other. Remember what I said about Julina. She's after the bracelets, and she won't stop coming after them, even if Ali escapes. She will find ways to chase you down. Think of what she might do with the bracelets' power – the potential devastation – wind, floods, fire, earthquakes. I need all of you to work together to finally defeat Julina."

"It's a lot to expect of us," Samel murmurs.

"I still don't understand why you can't defeat her yourself," Rowan says.

"As I told you before, I have other responsibilities, and I do have limitations. If you all cooperate, I'm sure you'll be able to stop her."

"Even if you can't help us directly, you're watching over us, aren't you?" Atsu asks. "Why else would you know to come now?"

Rasa shakes his/her head. "I can't tell you more. You should hurry if you want to drink and eat. Varonne isn't far away."

The horses tug them toward the stream. Atsu turns back to speak, but Rasa is gone again. He shrugs, following the others toward the water.

Rowan scans the area. "How does heshe disappear so quickly? Maybe he wasn't really here, just a vision."

"Who knows?" Atsu says. "Heshe won't tell us."

"I don't trust him or her," Samel says, "so I'm glad not to have Rasa with us. Remember how you thought Julina was helping you find me and Papa, Rowan? And now see what she's doing."

"Yes, you're right," Rowan says. "Who can we trust?"

"Each other, of course," Atsu says. "We're in this together after all."

"Should we still go ahead and meet Varonne?" Rowan asks. "Rasa said we had the choice, that Varonne was lost, and we could avoid her if we wanted to."

"And then what?" Samel scratches his head. "We're going to the castle anyway, so why not go with her? I don't exactly trust Rasa's motives. And besides, when I look around from up in the sky, I can't see any place for us to hide."

"If we don't go with Varonne, how do we approach Julina?" Atsu asks. "Or will we try to sneak up on the castle and get Ali to escape to us?"

"I like that idea," Rowan says.

"But Julina could follow and find us," Samel argues. "I think we have to try to defeat her no matter how nervous we are about it. And it seems to me the best way to do that is to pretend that we've been taken by Varonne."

Rowan rubs her arms, looks around and frowns. "I keep thinking someone's watching us. Samel, can you see where Varonne is now?"

Samel sighs. "I'll take one more look with the eagle's feather, but that's it. It's making me too dizzy. And Rowan, could you try to contact Ali while I do? Just let her know we're close." He doesn't wait for his sister to respond.

Looking down again through the eyes of an eagle, Samel sees Varonne sitting on a stump on the edge of a valley not far away. She munches bread and cheese, drinks from a flask. Samel considers sending the eagle down to give her a scare but decides that wouldn't be helpful. And he notices that she has a bow and a quiver of arrows nearby. What if she decided to shoot the eagle?

He comes back to his body to see Rowan perched on a rock with her eyes closed. Atsu is pulling dried meat from saddle bags. All the horses have their noses in the water.

Rowan opens her eyes.

"Did you see her?" Samel asks.

"Yes, just long enough to tell her we were close. She said she's ready."

"Want some of this meat?" Atsu asks.

Rowan takes a couple of pieces.

Samel shakes his head. "I'm going to fill my waterskin and have a long drink."

As Samel bends toward the water one of the horses snorts and rears away from the stream. Samel grabs for the dangling reins, captures them, and puts out a hand to soothe the animal, which he now realizes is Rowan's horse, Lady. The horse quiets and then jerks its head at the sound of a muted horn and a vibrating bass string. Samel turns his head. On the bank of the stream sits a green frog, the size of a small dog; its body swells and deflates with the sound. Familiar-looking eyes stare unblinkingly at Samel.

"Grandfather?" Samel whispers, letting go of the horse. He kneels. "Is it you? Can you change back?"

The frog continues to sing the single note, the permanent curve of mouth imitating a smile. Maybe it's a real smile. Samel puts out a finger to stroke the damp head. The frog doesn't leap away, rather swishes his feet through the water.

Atsu crouches beside Samel. "I didn't know Grandfather for long, but I think you're right. There's a sense of the old man about this frog."

"I don't think he can change back," Samel says. "Or he doesn't want to. He's left age and worries behind. It's hard. I miss him."

"Are you sure you're not just imagining what you'd like to see?" Rowan asks from behind them.

Samel shakes his head. "It is Grandfather. You didn't know him for long, didn't get to find out what it was like to have a grandfather."

"He seemed like a rather confused old man to me," Rowan says. "I don't think he could really have helped us."

"I get flashes of rain, flood, a cave and a stream," Atsu says. "I think he's telling us what he can about who he is."

"I wonder if we could take him with us," Samel says.

"Carry him on one of the horses?" Rowan asks. "I don't think they'd like it. They're all standing over there by the tree. And what if the frog fell? Splat, green mush."

Samel turns to berate his sister for her insensitivity; after all Grandfather Frog is right there. A large splash distracts him. The frog has hopped back into the stream and disappeared. Samel bends closer to the water but sees no sign of the frog. He rinses his fingers in the stream to remove the slime and stands.

"Happy now?" Samel says. "He might have stayed longer if you hadn't said that."

"I have a feeling he didn't want to come with us," Atsu says. "But maybe, like the Time Dancer, he'll find a way to stay near."

"What about Varonne?" Rowan says.

"Atsu and I are ready to go ahead and meet her," Samel says. "It's you who are having doubts about it."

"I didn't exactly mean that," Atsu says. "Though I do think we may as well meet her. Isn't that what we decided a while ago? From what you've told me, she's not that bad. Samel, you agreed with what I said earlier about each doing something to distract Julina when we arrive at the castle. Have you changed your mind?"

Samel stares into the distance, then shakes himself and meets Atsu's eyes. "It's a reasonable plan.

Rowan sighs. "Fine. Let's go ahead and meet Varonne."

Chapter XXXII

Traverse

Around a bend in the trail, they encounter Varonne riding. "Halt," she says.

Before anyone else can say a word or move further, Varonne has her bow armed and pointed at them. Samel's bracelet flares briefly where his sleeve has rumpled; Varonne shifts her bow to him alone.

"Don't try anything. I'm fast with this."

"No one's going to try anything, Varonne, so just stay calm," Rowan says. Out of the corner of her eye she catches a glimpse of a blue green shimmer. She turns toward Atsu and glares at him. "Not now!"

"Sorry, couldn't help the instant reaction," Atsu murmurs.

A brief scatter of rain dampens their heads. Atsu shrugs when Rowan frowns at him. Varonne misses the byplay.

But she doesn't lower her bow.

"There's supposed to be four of you. Where's the old man?"

"Gone," Samel says. "He fell into a pool."

"Drowned?"

No one answers. Varonne shrugs. "All right then. One less to worry about." She gestures with her bow toward Samel, who is at the head of the group. "I want you to ride single file past me at a walk. Keep moving. I'll be watching for anything weird, so no tricks."

"We're just riding to the castle the way your mother asked us to," Samel says. "Is my friend Ali all right? Have you seen her lately?"

"No talking," Varonne growls. "Move!"

Rowan nudges her horse to follow behind her brother, who is tugging one of the pack horses. Atsu brings up the rear, leading the other pack horses. He twists his head to smile at Varonne. She scowls at him but doesn't speak.

A cold wind ruffles the manes of the horses, but the sun warms the riders' faces. Snow covers most of the mountain peaks and lies on the slopes of many. As his eyes scan the mountains, Samel notices movement. Another Rockfolk! Could one be following them? And is that good or bad for them or for Julina?

It's a good thing Ali hasn't tried to escape the castle. Too many hazards. Without help she'd have a hard time with the cold, no way to carry water, lack of food. He doesn't know how good she is at living off the land. It's not something they've ever needed to discuss in all the years he's known her. There's probably a lot he doesn't know about her. Hopefully, all will go well, and they'll have time to talk about many things in the future.

Is the Time Dancer sparing a few thoughts for Ali in the castle dungeon? As Samel thinks this, he has a flash of Rasa on a distant mountain top, rainbow-coloured clothes swirling. Is there an actual hint of a rainbow in the distance over a mountain peak? Even though it's the wrong season? Samel blinks and the rainbow is gone.

"We're coming, Ali," Samel says in his head. *"Be careful. Don't take any unnecessary risks."* The circlet on his left wrist warms slightly, but it's covered now by his sleeve, so Varonne can't see any flashes.

Faintly, he hears Ali's voice, *"I'm fine. Ready. Be careful."*

Samel hears Rowan clear her throat. His head swivels, and he shakes it to remind her not to talk. She gives a tiny nod. *"I heard,"* she whispers in his mind. *"Did you see the Dancer?"*

"Face front!" Varonne yells from the back.

"This is new," Samel responds to his sister in the same way. *"Do you think Atsu can hear us, too?"*

"I don't think so."

"Too bad. Maybe the Dancer helped us just then to connect with Ali."

"Could we pick up the pace?" Atsu calls back to Varonne. "It's cold out here."

"No!" she yells back. "I don't want anyone getting too far ahead. We stick together."

They pass through a narrow valley with a stream in it. Samel speculates on whether Grandfather might be following but doesn't see any sign of a frog or any other creature in the water. He glances at the sky, spies the dark speck high above that could be an eagle. Has Varonne noticed? She's probably too busy watching all the horses and riders. Samel grins to himself. She might be good with weapons, but she has no idea of all that they bring with them. As they ride along the stream, a whisp of mist rises from the water; it gathers and increases, swirling around behind them.

Atsu trots alongside Rowan. "Speed up," he says quietly. "Varonne can't see us now."

"But she'll hear our hoofbeats."

Atsu shrugs and rides up to Samel. "Let's show her it won't be all that easy to control us!"

They gallop out of the valley to the yells of Varonne behind them. When they reach a narrowing of the trail they slow, and the mist dissipates. An arrow swishes over their heads as Varonne catches up.

"Don't ride away from me again!" she yells. "I'll find you anyway."

Not if we don't want you to, Atsu thinks. We still have some control.

None of the others responds out loud, but they continue to ride slowly along the trail that winds up and down and around mountains. The sun moves past midday. Will Varonne let them stop to feed and water the horses? The trail widens and they pass a few stunted trees.

"I'm hungry," Samel sends to his sister.

"You can last a while longer, can't you? Let's not make her angry by asking."

"I wish she'd let us ride faster. I really want to get to the castle, to see Ali. But we should eat, keep up our strength."

"I've got nuts and dates in my belt pouch."

Samel fumbles at his own belt.

"Hey!" Varonne rides up beside him. "What are you doing?"

"Just getting out some dried fruit to munch on. Since you aren't letting us stop to eat." He shows her a handful of dried apples.

The woman raises her hands, one palm up, the other still holding the bow. "Fine," she says and falls back.

Her hand gesture has suddenly brought a picture of his father to Samel's mind. The movement is like one Papa uses sometimes, except without the bow and arrow. Papa must be worried because it's been a while since Rowan contacted him. Papa used to be so against the use of the bracelets, but that has changed. He seems to have learned to appreciate that they can talk to each other.

Faintly from above sounds the shriek of an eagle. They all, even Varonne, raise their heads. Varonne quickly goes back to watching the other riders, but Rowan has managed to catch Samel's eye and nod. They know at least one eagle is with them. Beaks and talons could come to their aid if they need them, and large, powerful wings.

Excitement and fear crackle inside Rowan, like a fire catching dry wood. It warms but could also burn her or anyone else who gets too close. She remembers Hrashak. Does Varonne think of him, too? After all she was there when Rowan killed her father. The other woman must have felt anger, resentment, perhaps wanted revenge. She could still feel some of that; it would be natural. Best to keep a close eye on Varonne. Thankfully, the sense of Samel in her mind remains a warm comfort. And now, annoyingly, Ali is there again.

"I'm out of the dungeon and they don't know it. Am hiding. I know you're close."

Rowan is nearly unhorsed by the surge of joy from Samel. *"Control yourself!"*

A strong gust of wind chills her. Grey clouds have massed in the sky, hiding the sun. A handful of snow hits

Rowan's face. She shakes it away. Could this be Julina trying to cause them as much discomfort as possible to weak-
en their defenses before they arrive at the castle? She touches her bracelet and instantly her body warms. Maybe Julina
will be aware of that, but Rowan doesn't care. She'd rather
be warm. Samel has also used his bracelet, she can tell.

There's a tickle at the back of her neck. The touch of
something warm, like a finger, but slightly damp. The
snow stops hitting her, blows to both sides. Atsu using his
powers? She doesn't turn but feels his smile adding to the
warmth given by the silver wristlet. He's in her head, too?

"Yes, I can hear you think!"

Before she can respond, Rowan feels the heaviness
again and the day turns dark as twilight. They've reached
another one of those areas where everything slows and hope
fades. Does Varonne feel it too or is she immune? But this
time the effect doesn't last for long. And then Rowan sees
the crenellations of the tallest tower of the castle emerging
from behind the peaks to her left.

Chapter XXXIII

Ali

No one has come to check on me in the dungeon, so I have plenty of time after warning Samel and the others about Varonne. Julina and her minions will likely be busy getting ready to receive their visitors, so I start an escape in earnest. The stone around the lock melts as easily as before and soon I stand in the lantern-lit passage outside my cell. As I move slowly toward the dungeon entrance, I listen carefully but hear nothing except skittering, and catch sight of a couple of rat tails as the rodents scramble out of my way; I'm glad I didn't encounter them more closely! When I arrive at the barred gate, the lock there presents no problem either.

Now what? I sit on the bottom of the staircase that leads up to the rest of the castle considering my options. If I wander too far, I'll likely run into someone, and I'd prefer to avoid that. Should I find a place to hide in the castle or attempt to get right outside? The problem is, I know very little about the exterior of the castle and the land surrounding it. I've had glimpses of a courtyard, of the front gate, of the mountainous landscape. But I have no idea if there are good places to hide beyond the castle. Also, I might miss Samel and the others when they arrive if I'm outside. Within the castle I could run into other people, but it's large enough that I can likely find empty rooms to stay in safely. It would help me make up my mind if I had some idea if anyone is close to me. I lean against the wall; maybe I'll be able to hear something useful again.

At first, there's nothing. Then a faint scrabbling that reminds me of the rats. Next, the ring of a horse's hooves against cobblestones; I've heard it often enough outside our house in Aquila to recognize it – Varonne, perhaps, leaving to intercept Samel and the others. The thump of a gate closing, heavy footsteps. What if some of those footsteps are coming towards me?

I jump up and look around. Notice a narrow wooden door. It opens easily on a small storeroom filled with shelves, ceramic jugs, cloth bags, wooden bins – a pantry. Before I close the door on myself, I grab a bundle of candles and dash out to light one from a lantern.

The floor is cold for sitting, so I upend an empty bin and perch there, melt a bit of candle and stick it down. The half-full bin beside me holds potatoes. My stomach rumbles. I used to like eating raw potatoes when was young, though cook always said too many would make me sick. These still have dirt stuck to them. I rub it off one and crunch, peel and all. Not bad. One of the jugs holds apple cider. I haven't a cup, but my hand works fine. A dry loaf tastes better after being soaked in cider that I pour into a large shard from a broken bowl. When my hunger is partly satisfied, I listen with my ear against the wooden door. Nothing. I peek out. No one.

I decide to try the stairs, stopping now and then to lean my head against the wall. No sounds, except an odd sort of crunching, like when you walk across gravel. Stones rubbing against each other? I hope that's not a sign the walls are unstable. That's all I need.

At the second landing I reach another corridor and can see doors leading off in both directions. It might be best if I could hide in a room with a window so I can see what's going on, make a plan for when Samel and the others arrive.

I'd love to get out of the castle entirely and meet them, avoiding Varonne and Julina altogether, but as I told myself earlier, that's not practical. If I didn't find the others right away, without a coat, no food, I'd not survive long.

The first two rooms I find are totally empty. The next holds heaps of musty smelling draperies and clothes. I spend a while in that one rooting through the piles and find a too large wool tunic, which I pull over my head, wrinkling my nose at the smell. It's warm, though. I also pick out a leather belt, which cinches the tunic nicely at my waist. This room has only a narrow slit of a window and all I can see from it is a turret of the castle.

Two more rooms hold broken furniture. The last room is the best yet. It's empty, but two windows look out on the courtyard, including one edge of the main gate. I seem to be on the main floor of the castle, but not in the part where Julina uses rooms. When Samel and the others arrive, I want to be able to join them quickly, which means I have to explore further to find doors to the outside, hoping no one catches me. While I'm peering out of the window, a guard crosses the courtyard to a well. He lets down a pail, brings it up again full of water. I'm suddenly very thirsty. Maybe I'll find water later.

"We're coming, Ali," Samel's voice comes in my head. *"Be careful. Don't take any unnecessary risks."*

I answer in a whisper, "I'm fine. Ready. Be careful."

I leave the room, thinking that I'll have to head back to the landing and go up one floor, hoping to find a different stairway that will lead me the way I want to go. Then I notice a tapestry hanging on the wall at the end of this hall. It could be a dead end, but sometimes tapestries conceal doors. I listen again, hear nothing, move forward.

My instinct was good. A wooden door hides behind the tapestry, but it's locked. I take the obsidian stone out of its pouch, touch it to the stone wall beside the door frame, move it around, concentrate, think of melting stone. Soon, I have a hole big enough to reach an arm through and try the handle from the other side. But before I do, I listen and then I put an eye to the hole. I can't see or hear anyone, though I catch glimpses of more stone walls beyond the door, and stairs going down. Quickly I reach through and tug, but the door doesn't open.

The smell of onions cooking and meat roasting wafts through the hole. My stomach rumbles loudly. I hold my breath and pull my stomach in. Listen. A faint murmur of voices. From the kitchen perhaps? I've got to get through. The door and frame are solidly set into the stone wall. Maybe I can make the hole big enough to crawl through. So far, I haven't done anything like that, but why not try? It might take a while, though; best make sure the tapestry is totally covering me while I work.

I close my eyes and press the piece of obsidian against the stone wall of the castle. It's dim behind the tapestry, but a little light comes through my eyelids. I think of the mountain where this stone might have originated. It may have come from one of the ancient fire mountains deep in the wilderness beyond this castle. The stone warms in my hands. I've heard the tales about when the world was much younger, and the four elements, fire, water, air and earth struggled with each other to see who would rule. In the stories each of these elements was represented by a great sorceress or wizard. The Water Dragon sent floods over everything. Sky Father called up thunder and lightning, hurricanes and tornados, whirling water, trees, rocks and beings away. Earth Mother rattled the land with quakes and shook down mountains, opening deep cracks. The Fire Queen pulled fire from various places – from lightning strikes to burn forests, and from deep within the earth to melt stone. At first, these sorcerers used their abilities individually against each other. It took ages for them to realize that the powers could destroy the very lands they were trying so hard to rule.

The only way forward was for them to cooperate. They used their powers to shape the world together, to create mountains and plains, rivers, and clouds in the sky, a place for many creatures to live. Each of the mages did their parts to sculpt our land.

I want only to melt a hole big enough to let me through this wall. Did that ancient Earth Mother hold this very stone, pull it out of the fire at risk to herself? Did the Fire Queen help her? Rowan is like that queen because, as Samel told me, she can sometimes make fire using her bracelet. I regret not getting to know Samel's sister better; I might have been able to learn useful things from her. Hopefully, we'll have more chances to do that. Time to concentrate. I take deep breaths and let them out slowly, concentrating on the stone. Perhaps some of the ancient powers of fire and earth reside in it.

Through my fingers I sense the denseness of stone, the solidity of walls. I hear that faint crunching again, only this time it sounds more like someone murmuring. While keeping a hold on the stone, I lean my ear against the wall.

"Mumble, crunch, mumble, sigh, heavy."

Concentrating even harder, I realize suddenly that the light that came through my eyelids before is gone. I open my eyes to darkness, feel coolness and damp. Weight presses against me from all sides, but gently. Still, my mouth goes dry and my body starts to shake. I have no idea where I am or how to get out.

"We are here, we are stone," a deep voice whispers. "You are one with us."

I try to speak but can't. Somehow, I've been swallowed by the wall. I have to get out!

"Don't be afraid."

There's a bit more pressure, as if I'm being lightly squeezed and then I'm lying on the floor between the dusty tapestry and the stone wall. And yet I smell the interconnectedness of stone, taste sand and dirt, hear the creaking of walls and floors. In a way that I don't understand, I'm part of the castle now, can see how each stone was laid on another, held together by the cunning of masons to form a foundation, walls and turrets. There are places where a nudge or two could bring parts of the edifice crashing down. And others where walls stand strong. I know that wind and water wear away stone, earth can shake and crack. Do I have some of that power? I feel a tremor under my feet.

"No!" I breathe. "Not yet." Perhaps never.

I sit up. The hole in the wall is large enough for me to step through, the edges smooth, as if melted. Quickly I put the piece of obsidian back in its pouch. Cautiously, I peek out. No one. I nearly fall flat on my face as I crawl through the hole; my legs shake and my arms tremble. Now I really need to eat.

By the time I manage to get down the stairs to reach a wooden door that stands ajar, the murmur of human voices has stopped. I move my head gradually around the edge of the door and find that I was right about the kitchen: two large tables, a fireplace, shelves. Piles of food and various good smells entice me forward. I can't see anyone, though a fire burns and a cauldron hangs over it. A couple of other doors stand open. Quickly I grab a wooden trencher, load it with scraps of cooked meat, a bit of cooked onion, a couple of slices of warm bread, a carrot, an apple, and a small berry tart. Then I rush out back the way I came. I almost close the door to the kitchen firmly behind me, then decide to leave it as I found it. When the servants return to the kitchen I hope they'll think one of the soldiers came and took the food.

Shutting myself in the room with the best window view, I relax finally. Before I begin to stuff myself, I'd better let Samel and the others know that I'm loose. I take out the stone and hold it in my hands. Concentrate until I can see Samel in my mind – his red hair, his gold flecked eyes. It didn't take long to find him. They must be very near the castle.

"I'm out of the dungeon and they don't know it," I whisper. "Am hiding. I know you're close."And then the vision is gone.

The smell of food overwhelms me. I finish every scrap on the trencher, lick my fingers and am tempted to lick the trencher, too. Decide not to in case it leaves splinters in my tongue.

Yawn so widely that my jaws ache. How long has it been since I slept? Surely it will be a while before Varonne and the others arrive. I get up and peer out of one of the windows. Two guards stand at the gate. One of them yawns. I do the same and nearly fall over. All looks quiet. I make sure the door to the room is secure, then curl up on the stone floor under the window.

For a long time it's very quiet. Now and then I think I hear distant hoofbeats or the murmur of voices, but I feel no urge to move. Am I awake or asleep? I'm not sure, but I'm too tired to try to find out, my eyelids are too heavy to open. The stones beneath my body are warm and pliant, comfortable. Who needs blankets? I smile to myself, then frown. There's something I should be thinking about. What is it?

Chapter XXXIV

Confrontation

A pair of double wooden gates braced with strips of met-al creak and shudder as they slowly swing open onto a cobblestone courtyard. Riders Samel, Atsu, Rowan and the two pack horses clump together, blocking the entrance.

"Hey," Varonne yells from behind them, "move in!"

At the same time, a voice from inside shouts, "Varonne? Are you there? Did you see them?"

"I brought them!" Varonne yells. She pushes forward and slaps the rumps of two horses one after another to get them to shift. One is a pack horse, the other Samel's horse, Izmeer. The pack horse surges forward, pulling the lead out of Samel's hand, and squeezing through into the castle yard. Izmeer kicks backward, hitting the legs of Varonne's horse and knocking it to its knees. Varonne scrambles off. The other pack horse spooks and jerks away from Atsu, running down the trail away from the castle. Rowan and Atsu's horses stamp and whinny.

"By the triangle!" Julina, dressed in a long red robe, stands in a clear space by the gates, arms raised to the sky. "Varonne, I might have known you'd jumble things. I didn't ask you to bring them, just to spy on them. And it's taken you long enough. Get them in here!"

Atsu quiets his horse first and nudges it forward straight at Julina. She lowers her arms and moves out of the way slowly, scowling. A small black cloud appears above Julina's head and rain gushes down, soaking her from head to foot.

Julina points one hand at Atsu, the other up at the cloud and mumbles several words. The rain stops and the cloud dissipates. Atsu hunches low on his horse as if he's been knocked askew. Julina grins at him. "That's all you've got?"

Rowan moves forward on Lady and raises her left arm so that the sleeve of her tunic slips down, and her bracelet is exposed. It flashes silver in the sunlight, sending small arrows of fire hurtling toward Julina. The woman shakes her head, black hair with its reddish streak streaming out, growing long and thick, making a shield against which the fire arrows fizzle. Julina brushes back her hair, thrusts her hands toward Rowan, muttering words. A burst of invisible power nearly knocks Rowan off her horse.

Next comes Samel, bringing a small tornado with him, whirling his arms. Everyone's clothes billow and snap like sails on a ship. Julina's hair whips around her head and neck, tightening like a noose. She bends, grasps something at the front of her tunic, straightens and throws her hair back with a gesture. Then she raises both hands and brings them down slowly. The wind dies.

The soldiers stand immobile and silent while all this happens, frightened by the magic whizzing about the courtyard, and hesitant to move in case they are hit by spells. Julina ignores them, absorbed in her battle with the young people. Varonne still hovers outside the castle gates, blocked by the horses. Then Julina laughs loudly and everyone shifts and shakes a little.

But the three on horseback have recovered somewhat and move ahead, partially surrounding Julina against one side of the courtyard. They are hesitant to try anything else just yet, needing more time to gather strength, and so just sit quietly on their horses. Varonne, staying well away from all the horses, limps in. A couple of soldiers step forward to close the gates. Meanwhile, Julina ascends several steps of a stone staircase leading to the top of the castle wall. From there she looks down on all of them, smiling slightly. The soldiers cluster in front of the gate.

Then Julina frowns. "Where's the old man?"

"Drowned," Varonne says, as she bumps into a low heap of stones, then hobbles to a nearby bench and sinks onto it.

"What? How did you let that happen?"

"It was before I found them."

Julina scowls, then lets her face smooth. "Let's begin again. I'll pretend you didn't each try to attack me. Welcome to my castle. I can offer food and drink as well as washing facilities. You must all be tired and hungry. Dismount and let us provide for you."

Samel sneers, "Hah! We're not here to visit. We've come to get Ali."

Atsu nods agreement. Rowan is not looking at Julina, but rather at a familiar dark-haired young man standing by a stone well near the back of the courtyard. She doesn't know if he's been there ever since they entered or just appeared. He's wearing a black tunic with red thread embroidery. His hands are cupped around a pendant that hangs from his neck. Ash-coloured light shines through his fingers as he mutters words Rowan can't hear.

"Jernan!" Julina calls, "Desist! Now is not the time."

The young man lets go of the pendant, which swings against his tunic – a dark triangle. Rowan remembers how he used that pendant to bring a massive wave down the river at Aquila. She and Atsu stopped him then; she'd thought he and his father had been swept away. Quickly she scans the courtyard but doesn't see Jernan's father anywhere. Perhaps he's not involved this time.

Rowan dismounts, prepared to do what she can if Jernan tries anything. "Not the time for another flood?" Rowan asks. "What do you want, Julina, why did you call us here?"

"Let Ali go," Samel says, as he, too, gets down from his horse. He feels more ready to use the bracelet when he has solid ground under his feet. "She's nothing to you."

Atsu dismounts as well. At a gesture from Julina, one of the soldiers from the gate comes forward and moves the horses to a side alcove. The three ignore this, focused on Julina, hoping to be prepared for whatever she is about to do next.

"None of you are stupid," Julina says, "although at times you act like it. I want the bracelets, of course."

"Conquer Aquila like Hrashak planned?" Samel taunts. "The Lord and Militia will never let you do that."

Julina smiles. "What would I want with that degenerate city?" she asks. "They didn't appreciate me when I lived there, and I don't expect they've changed. A city of men who wanted to control me in one way or another. I'm tired of people who try to manipulate me." Her voice rises. "I want power to make a life in a place where no one can tell me what to do. I'm better than all of them, than all of you. I have visions of things that none of you have dreamt of."

"Like what?" Rowan asks.

Julina takes a deep breath and stares at each of them one by one, as she lets the breath out slowly. Immediately they feel the pressure of her in their minds, can't speak or move. Jernan stands as immovable as the rest, and so do the soldiers by the gate. Rowan notices that a cluster of ravens are perched on the stone wall of the castle above Julina. When did they arrive? At the moment, they too, are unmoving.

"A land where I rule," Julina continues, "where people work to achieve my vision." She turns toward Atsu. "Perhaps I'll bring dragons back to this land." Toward Rowan and Samel. "Or maybe I'll bring back the dead." She nods. "You're astounded? I'm in the prime of life and have so much more to do. Who knows what powers I can summon with the bracelets? I've worked long and hard already, subtly, gathering power slowly, but I've had enough of deliberation and caution." She waves her arms. "This castle will be my base and my influence will spread from here. Perhaps I will build a city of my own." She points at Rowan and Samel. "I need those bracelets to solidify my strength here before anyone else realizes what I'm doing and tries to stop me. Of course, even if someone tried to stop me, they wouldn't succeed, but I don't want to waste time on skirmishes. I have more important things to do like visiting places where ancient spell craft lingers. As a weaver gathers wool and works with it, I will card and spin orders of power, unifying them into a shining fabric." Julina claps her hands sharply and they all jump, released from immobility. "Give me the bracelets now! Or I'll send my soldiers to get your friend out of the dungeon and bring her here. If you don't obey, you'll see her blood spilled on these stones."

An eagle's scream and the hoot of an owl jerk Samel and Rowan's attention away from Julina and loosen her hold on them. "No!" they shout together.

Julina looks up, searching the sky. Samel and Rowan do the same. Samel sees the dark speck circling far above. Rowan notices a second long-winged silhouette in the sky. She remembers the hoot earlier. The shape and wing spread of the second is wrong for an eagle, more like an owl. Julina doesn't seem to see either of the birds, because she turns to the soldiers still standing by the gates; she nods at them, and they put their backs to the entrance and draw their swords. Rowan is certain that Grandmother Wisdom is in the sky in owl shape, lending strength. It gives her confidence.

Julina looks back at the group before her. "So, you'll not make it easy for yourselves by handing over what I want? Fine." She turns to the soldiers. "Two of you go to the dungeon now! Bring the prisoner."

***

"Hey," someone yells, "move in."

Another voice shouts, "Varonne? Are you there?"

I jump up and cautiously look out of the window. They're all gathered in the courtyard by the gate: Samel, Rowan, Atsu, Varonne, a few soldiers, and a dark-haired young man standing by a stone well. He looks familiar, but

I can't see him very well at that distance and among all the others.

"By the triangle!" Julina, stands in a clear space raising her arms to the sky. "Varonne, I might have known you'd jumble things. And it's taken you long enough. Get them in here!" She scans the courtyard.

I duck down so Julina can't see me. I should have been out of this room before now, have to find a way to get closer to the others. I'm not sure that there's much I can do to help from here. And I am determined to help, though I haven't figured out exactly how yet.

Back in the hall, I head for the hole behind the tapestry. Crawl through and listen for a while. There's no sound from the kitchen, but a lot of noise from the courtyard – voices raised in argument. I guess if they're still talking it means no one has been attacked. At least I hope not. Slowly and carefully, I make my way down the stairs until I reach the wooden door which is firmly closed. I put my ear against it. Hear nothing. I ease up the latch, pull forward. The door creaks slightly and I stop, but there are no voices from inside the kitchen.

"I have visions of things that none of you have dreamt of," Julina's voice is loud. I hope she's still in the courtyard.

Then as I move my head to look through the crack in the door, a paralysis grabs and holds me. It can't be anyone but Julina. Does she know I'm here? Or is it just spillover from what she's doing to the others?

Though I can't move, I can still think and feel. My feet stand on a stone floor, one hand rests against a stone wall. Once again, I sense my way into the structure of this castle. Grey, pink, red, black and white surround me with warmth. The stones of this castle have come from ancient fire mountains – granite pressed into shape under the earth and dug up long afterwards. That's why my piece of obsidian joins with them so easily. And of course, Samel pried it out of the dungeon here.

Granite is me and I am it, shifting through walls, listening to creaks and pings, feeling the weight, the power of stone. I have no idea how long I wander, sensing crystals, bits of grit. Is there a vein of silver, shining in the dark? Other metals, pockets of water? How can I use this new knowledge to help my friends? Will stone serve me if I ask?

An eagle screams.

Faintly, I hear Julina's voice, "Go to the dungeon now! Bring the prisoner."

***

Two soldiers march away. Meanwhile, Jernan moves closer to the well and starts his spell muttering again. Rowan can see his pendant more clearly now – an iron triangle with two slanted lines through it. Out of the corner of her eye, Rowan catches motion from Julina. As Rowan turns back to Julina, she notices that the woman is pulling a similar pendant from inside her robes.

Nervously, Rowan looks around for Varonne. Will Varonne, Julina and Jernan unite to attack? Rowan touches her bracelet surreptitiously. It's only slightly warm; did she use most of its power when she tried to hit Julina with fire arrows? She lets go of it. Varonne, sitting on the bench, is massaging an ankle. The bow and quiver of arrows lies on the ground nearby and Varonne's sword is sheathed.

Samel feels the eagle in his mind, talons and beak. The great bird is ready to dive if necessary. Julina glances quickly at Samel as if she senses something but after a moment, she turns to her daughter.

"Varonne," Julina calls "bring your weapons to the ready and don't let these people attack me again."

Varonne shakes her head. "I'm tired, Mother. I've had enough, have done enough. First Father, now you. You both wanted to use me, but neither of you cared what I want or appreciated what I did. My ankle hurts and I'm resting."

"Varonne!" Julina shouts, stamping her way down the stairs to the courtyard. "Obey me now!" She makes a fist of one hand and fumbles for her pendant with the other.

Under cover of the squabble, Rowan and Samel grasp their bracelets at the same moment. Silver light flares around them. Julina immediately leaps back onto the stairway and clutches her pendant. Iron-coloured light flares from two directions – round Julina and Jernan.

A soldier stands beside an open inner door. He clears this throat loudly. Everyone turns to look at him.

"Madam," he says, "the prisoner is not in the dungeon."

"What do you mean?" Julina shrieks. She raises her arms and dust and pebbles swirl around the courtyard.

"Escaped!" the soldier yells, then runs inside and slams the door. The whirl of dust and pebbles hits the door and falls to the cobblestones.

Samel and Rowan concentrate on the bracelets and surround themselves and Atsu with bubbles of silver light. Dirt and stones can't hit them. They grin at each other. This is better. Is this all Julina can do?

Julina points her hands toward them, flexing and spreading all her fingers. Spears of darkness lance toward the bubbles but can't penetrate. The three young people feel fingers scrabbling at their minds, like a cat scratching at a door to get in. They resist; it's a small cat so far. Nothing changes for a few moments as power surges back and forth, each side struggling against the other. More dust and debris swirls about the courtyard.

Jernan shouts and Julina's voice joins in, "By the triangle, matter and mind and mystery, water rise and conquer silver!"

Distracted, Rowan turns to look at Jernan. She though him handsome and interesting once but no longer. The silver bubbles thin and weaken around them.

"Rowan!" Samel shouts, "Pay attention!"

A curl of darkness wraps itself around Rowan's throat, tightens. She struggles for breath. Water begins to trickle over the edge of the well.

"Rowan!" Atsu calls. "You can do this! Concentrate. I'll help you."

"Me too!" Samel shouts.

An eagle screams. An owl hoots.

The noose around Rowan's neck loosens a little. Gradually, she regains control, brightening her part of the bubble. The darkness fades, disintegrating. But by now water is gushing from the well. It pours over the courtyard.

"Are you all right?" Atsu asks.

Rowan nods.

Atsu laughs and shimmers blue-green, a faint shape of dragon hovering around him. His roar is the sound of a rushing torrent. It drives the water away from the three in the silver bubble. The water surges and rises, forming waves that lap and tug at Jernan's knees. Jernan has to hang onto the edge of the well to keep from being swept away. Varonne grips the bench as water pushes it against the wall. Julina climbs further up the stairs, first shaking her head and then smiling broadly.

She waves her arms, flinging them up to the sky, and lightning flashes, thunder cracks. Dark grey clouds mass overhead. Atsu watches, dismayed; she too can command water. How can he fight her? The shimmer of blue green dragon disappears as his concentration falters. Samel notices that the eagle has disappeared, and Rowan can't see the owl. Some of the flood in the courtyard swirls around Atsu's feet. Samel and Rowan realize that a single silver bubble now covers only them.

"Hang on, Atsu!" Rowan shouts. "We'll get you under the bubble again."

"Working on it!" Samel yells, biting his lips and clasping his bracelet hard.

Atsu roars again, though not as loudly as before, still he manages to send spheres of water spinning up and away. A huge one drenches Julina, a slightly smaller one splashes Jernan, and a tiny one dampens Varonne. The soldiers have all run away. Julina shakes herself free of water, screams unintelligible words and reaching high, grasps flashes of fire from the sky, some in each hand. She hurls fire toward Atsu.

No wonder I couldn't harm her with fire, Rowan thinks, discouraged.

But Atsu is not giving up. He remembers the predictions of the Great Clam. And his mother's words, "Believe in yourself." He is part dragon. His father is the Obsidian Dragon and his mother, the Pearl Princess. Their blood flows in his body. They have studied rivers and lakes; he can stop rainfall. He closes his eyes and breathes in water vapour, exhales it. Water foams and soars, forming a bubble of protection around him. The lightning fizzles out against it. The well is deep Atsu senses, connected to an under-ground river; he can meld with that river, but can he control it? Perhaps he doesn't yet have that power. Water continues to rush over the cobblestones. It surges against the silver shield around Samel and Rowan but can't touch them. It does build up around all of them, continuing to rise. Will it eventually break through and sweep them away? Julina has moved higher and now stands safely on top of the castle wall. Varonne has climbed up to sit on a wide window ledge. Jernan, on the other hand, is having difficulty maintaining his balance. Neither Julina nor Varonne pay him any attention.

Rowan begins to feel sorry for Jernan, the young man whose mother uses him but doesn't protect him, and whose sister ignores him.

Then a small crack opens in the cobblestones near Jernan. Water gurgles down, beginning to drain from the courtyard. Atsu frowns; he didn't do that. The hole expands, and Jernan's hold on the well is loosed; he is sucked down with the flood. Julina yells incoherently, waves fists and stamps her feet. Thunder crashes again, and rain pours down.

***

It's time for me to get out into the courtyard, do what I can. Slowly, oh so slowly, stone loosens its grip on me. Becomes liquid so that I can swim upward and outward.

I stand in the middle of the kitchen, which is empty. All this working with stone seems to sap energy and I'm famished. There's still food lying about, so I grab an apple and crunch it, then chew a hunk of cheese. I finish a slice of bread.

Silver light flares, then grey. I move toward a window, but before I can get there, a voice says, "Madam, the prisoner is not in the dungeon."

"What do you mean?" Julina shrieks.

I hear pebbles rattling against stone.

"Escaped!" the soldier yells; then a door slams very close to me.

I walk toward one of the other doors in the kitchen. Perhaps this one leads into the courtyard. As I stand at the door, trying to decide what to do next, thunder cracks, but there's no sound of rain. A roar of a huge animal. Could that be Atsu? Has he turned into a dragon? I hurry back to the window. Water swirls in the courtyard. Samel and Rowan are surrounded by a silver bubble and protected. A gigantic blue-green dragon undulates to one side, its mouth wide open. But the water is rising. I sense it has something to do with the young man standing by the well. Is this Julina's son, Jernan? Can I do something to help stop the water?

The cobblestones of the courtyard are granite, too. I grasp my own stone in my hands and think of all the stones of this castle being connected, kin to my stone. As I stare at the floor of the courtyard I think of a hole and the cracking of stone. Under my feet the floor shivers.

"Not here," I say. "Out there. Please."

A small split in the cobblestones near the well grows larger. Water is sucked down. The floor shudders again and outside the hole expands. Jernan loses his footing, is sucked away with the flood. I gasp, not having expected that. Julina yells incoherently, waves her arms and stamps her feet. Thunder crashes again, and rain pours down. Water still swirls about the courtyard.

I feel the pressure of Julina's mind, but it's directed at Samel, Rowan and Atsu, not me. I can feel them pushing back, straining against Julina, unable to move her out of their minds.

***

Once again, Rowan, Samel and Atsu all feel the weight of Julina's mind attacking theirs. It's a black wind laced with lightning. They push back, strain against Julina's storm. They can't budge it, can't push Julina away. She is anchored to this castle by a power they don't comprehend.

Perhaps the power is from deep caves or water, Samel thinks. Grandfather would know about things like that. Why did the old man leave? They could use extra help now.

"Grandfather," he whispers, "where are you?"

Within their thinning bubbles of protection Samel, Rowan and Atsu sway in the wind amid flashes of power and spell craft directed against them. How much longer can they hold out?

Samel wonders where Ali is. Maybe she can escape and get help. But she's never met the Time Dancer and doesn't know Grandfather so what help could she find?

Then Samel notices a faint flicker of green in the middle of the courtyard. It glimmers and grows into a translucent image of a large frog. The frog opens its mouth and swallows the rain, sucks in the dark clouds. The water on the ground swirls around the frog, seeming to sink into its skin.

Julina shouts, "No!" She lowers her arms and stamps her feet. The ground trembles. Julina points her hands at the frog and mutters.

"Grandfather," Samel says, loudly. "Thank you." But the frog has disappeared, and a storm still rages.

***

From the window I see a faint flicker of green in the middle of the courtyard. A huge translucent frog sits there. The frog opens its mouth and swallows the rain, sucks in the dark clouds, then disappears.

It's time for me to get out there. I run and open the door that I think leads outside, find myself in a short hallway with one door to the right, another to the left. The latter should lead me outside. I hesitate for a few breaths, gather my courage. Can I do this?

I hear Julina shouting, "No!"

At that moment I feel the stones under my feet tremble again. Voices whisper in my mind – all the stones of the castle are with me. The ground shudders with their power.

I take a deep breath, raise the latch, push against the door.

***

Sun beats down, sweat pours off everyone. Someone groans. The silver bubble is much thinner now, as is the water bubble around Atsu. The three of them can move, but Julina still pushes at their minds, though her power feels weaker; she too has been tired by the struggle. How long can they all fight without giving in to exhaustion? Who will hold out the longest?

"Why didn't Grandfather stay longer?" Samel whispers.

"We could really use Rasa now," Rowan adds.

"I wonder if Ali is safe?" Atsu mutters.

A creaking noise turns all their heads. The small door to the inside of the castle where the solider left, opens.

Ali steps out. "Nice to see all of you," she calls, grinning.

Chapter XXXV

Retribution

Julina screams wordlessly. Then, as Samel, Rowan, Atsu and Ali converge on her, Julina lifts her hands, holding the iron triangle. She mutters words under her breath and a transparent, ashy pyramid flashes into the air around her. As she starts up the nearest steps to the wall, probably to get above them again, ravens swoop down, open beaks screaming, clawed feet reaching for her. The ravens can't penetrate the protection of the pyramid, but they keep flapping about, obscuring her sight.

Rowan hears a whisper in her mind, "You are the Queen of Fire." At first, she wants to shout, "No, I'm not!" Then she reconsiders: fight fire with fire and create protective space between. She's seen people do that in the northern forest where she once lived with her mother. Fight with whatever skills and gifts you have. Is that her mother's voice? There is Ali to rescue and perhaps a land to save from an evil woman. Pulling her bracelet off and holding it between her and Julina, Rowan yells, "I am the Queen of Fire!" Flames appear in mid-air, larger ones this time. They rise, crackling, and lean towards Julina, singeing the edges of her triangle. Smoke billows. The ravens rise.

Samel, remembering how the eagles helped him during the fire in the mountains, shouts, "Eagles, bring me the wind of your great wings!"

A gale races from all directions, driving smoke away while fanning the flames, whirling up grit and shards of stone, flapping clothes, knocking Varonne off her perch on the window ledge. She huddles at the base of that wall. The doors to the courtyard creak and vibrate, a small gap appears between them. Rowan, fearing the flames will get out of her control, pictures the fire dying and lowers her hands. The flames respond to her wishes.

Julina's defensive pyramid is blown to tatters by Samel's gale and it turns to grey smoke. The ravens dive down, tear at Julina's clothes. Again, the young people feel Julina pressing against their minds, trying to get control, but the ravens distract her. Wind lashes Julina's hair into her eyes.

Atsu roars again, a wordless howl. Water spills out of the well and surges toward the stairs. Julina steps further back and up, trying to get away from the water. She strikes at the birds and they tumble away, gaining control as they leave.

Julina has almost reached the top of the wall when Ali raises the rainbow-coloured piece of obsidian. "Stones are my sisters," she shouts, "my family! This castle is built on rock and of stone! We can change it as we wish."

The ground shakes, a few cobblestones crack, and parts of a wall disintegrate. Next the steps in front of Julina smooth out so fast that she slides down and lies in a wet and bedraggled heap on the cobblestones. A heap of stones rises with legs and arms, a head. It's short, like a small child. It stamps one of its feet and the ground shakes again, a few stones fall from a wall, just missing Julina. Other stones sink below the woman until she is held tightly in a cold embrace.

"Rockfolk!" Samel whispers. "But I thought they were taller."

Abruptly, the wind dies, the water sinks away or dries up. The Rockfolk shrinks back into a heap of stone. All is unusually quiet. Julina opens her mouth, but no words come. The others can't speak either. Wondering what has caused this, they look around.

In the middle of the courtyard, a whirl of rainbow colour appears. The motion becomes a smear of brightness that gradually fades to early evening light. The Time Dancer poses, arms akimbo, half alabaster skin, half midnight dark, long bi-coloured hair flowing to his/her waist. Heshe is clothed in a rainbow tunic glittering with light.

"You've done excellently well," heshe says, and smiles at Rowan, Atsu, Samel, and Ali. The smile loosens all their tongues.

"Who are you?" Julina demands, struggling in her stone box, but unable to get out. "What is your purpose here? This is my castle."

"I am retribution. I know all that you have done from the beginning. The people you harmed, the ones you killed, the children abandoned, the merchants cheated, the incitements to quarrels and attacks. I haven't time to go into details. This is not your castle any longer and you'll not get the things you want. Except for one."

Julina yells, "You know nothing!"

The Time Dancer holds up a hand and Julina becomes silent again.

Varonne gets to her feet. Turning to her, the Time Dancer says, "You, on the other hand, might claim innocence, say that you were used by your father and mother." She stops as if expecting Varonne to reply, but the woman says nothing. A slight nod from the Time Dancer. "You are a grown woman and had choices. One would have been not to aid them, to stay away from evil and go your own way. Actions have consequences. You will share your mother's fate."

Varonne opens her mouth but still doesn't speak. She shakes her head, sits and goes back to massaging her ankle.

"Who is this person?" Ali asks.

"All in good time," says the Time Dancer, holding up a hand. "Wait."

"Are you going to kill them?" Rowan asks.

The Time Dancer shakes her/his head, speaks to Rowan and Samel mind to mind. *"I want to bind both Julina and Varonne more permanently so they can't do any more damage. I need the power of the bracelets to do it. Are you willing to give the bracelets up if they will leave you?"*

"Maybe," from Rowan.

"I'm not sure," Samel responds.

"Will it help if I tell you that you won't lose all your abilities? The bracelets awakened gifts that were already in you, developed and strengthened them. Samel will still be a companion of eagles, able to fly with the great birds using the feather they gifted him. Atsu is still a child of dragons with all that

entails; even I don't comprehend those powers. Ali is a daughter of earth, has just begun to learn about sharing power with stone. And you, Rowan, will still be a queen of fire if you want to be. You can nurture and develop your abilities if you wish or let them lie, your choice. Now, are you both ready to let the bracelets move on to their next task?"

Rowan's and Samel's eyes meet. A shrug of one shoulder, a raised eyebrow. They've come a long way since being separated by and with their parents. Felt anger, sadness, fear, and joy. Have been seduced and amazed by the powers of the bracelets at times, feared them now and then, been puzzled by them. They've met new people, lost or left others. Learned a few things and realized how little they knew.

Rowan thinks of her mother who is gone and who she will always miss. But there's Thea to see again and the twins. Perhaps Atsu would come on a trip to Schönspitze some time. And there's her father who she wants to spend more time with, and the city of Aquila to know better.

Samel knows that he's grown up. He can take care of himself, but he'd like to live with Papa again for a while, and with his sister if she will stay. And there's so much he and Ali have to talk about.

Each of them glances at the wrist where a bracelet dangles. Silver leaves entwined, fragile-looking and also heavy. After a few more moments of thought, Rowan and Samel both nod.

"All right then," the Time Dancer says.

Rowan and Samel slip off the silver wristlets and hand them to the Time Dancer.

"What's happening?" asks Atsu.

"This is the Time Dancer," Samel says, turning to Ali. "Also called Rasa. Heshe helped us earlier. It's a long story.

Tell you later."

"The Time Dancer will use the bracelets to deal with Julina," Rowan says.

Julina screams, "I still have spell craft! You made a mistake ignoring me, giving me time to recover power." Her lips move in silent chant, until she can raise an arm. She points at Varonne, mumbles more words. Both women shimmer and shrink, becoming foxes. The fox that is Julina leaps out of the stone embrace to crouch on the cobble stones beside her daughter. They bare their teeth, begin to sidle toward the gate, which stands slightly open.

Quickly the Time Dancer tosses the bracelets in a graceful arc over the heads of the foxes. These settle around their necks, becoming silver ruffs of fur. The foxes' barking voices rise, becoming high and squealing.

"You fell into my trap," says the Time Dancer. "I knew you'd try something like this and was waiting. The bracelets will bind but not hurt you," heshe adds. "They are a part of you and will keep you in fox shape, unable to use any spell craft." Heshe points at the castle gates and they creak open more widely. The foxes race out.

"And now," Rasa says, "there's one more thing to do." Heshe points at the ravens that have once more settled on the castle wall. "Morde, come forth."

One raven alights on the ground at the Time Dancer's feet. Rasa gestures and the raven shifts, glitters, grows rapidly, and becomes a black-haired and bearded, swarthy, bent-backed man.

"You're free now."

"But not free to be with you," the man says, bending his head. "Isn't that right, Rasa?"

"No, you'll have to make a life for yourself. But avoid places of ancient power."

"I only dreamt of the power of silver and the moon to find my love." He looks at Samel and Rowan. "I did make the magical bracelets for Zarmine and Yarvan. The stories were wrong. It was no mistake. I hoped that when they put the wristlets on, they would be tempted to step into the light of the moon, and time would change." He turns back to the Time Dancer. "I wanted to open a gateway to the past and future so that I could go and find you, Rasa. But Zarmine and Yarvan didn't step through. And when you found me, you punished me for taking the silver, making the bracelets and losing them." He sighs. "I stayed with you and your mother, Rowan, hoping for another opportunity to unite the bracelets. I'm sorry that I wasn't able to guard your mother properly. I was afraid to go near Hrashak in case the old man's power would see me for what I really was. I feared that he would try to use me and my skills."

Rasa's head shakes. "It's over so let it go. You've done well in the end."

"Will the silver bracelets stay with the foxes, imprisoning them forever?" Morde asks.

"That's uncertain; I can see only that they will be held as foxes for a long time. The bracelets may disintegrate eventually or turn to someone else. The women may forget that they've ever been anything but foxes."

"There's one more thing I want to know, Rasa," Rowan says. "You've been more or less with us all this time. Manipulating? Protecting? What?"

"Observing," replies The Time Dancer with a slight smile. "You all fascinate me. I admire your courage and resilience. Now it's time for us to part. But before we do,

Ali there's one more task you can do as you leave."

"What's that?"

"With your power over stone, your connections to it, you can cause this castle to collapse."

Ali's eyes gleam and she grins. "The stones like that idea."

"Not until we've left though!" Samel insists.

Ali nods and moves beside her friend. "Thanks for coming to get me."

"Your family will be happy to see you," Samel says, tentatively reaching for her hand.

"And so will your Papa to see you and your sister." She smiles and clasps his fingers.

"Oho," Atsu says, and he steps closer to Rowan. "Will you come with me to visit my homeland?"

"And meet the Pearl Princess and the Obsidian Dragon in the flesh?"

Atsu nods.

"Probably. After I've gone back to see my father for a while. He'll be angry if I leave again too soon."

"The ravens, Thought and Memory, will see you all safely to Aquila," Morde, the man says. "And I think that you'll find the pack horse that ran out is not too far away. There are probably supplies of food in this castle you can take."

"What about you?" Rowan asks. "What will you do?"

"I might explore the mountains around, find a village. I'd like to have a forge again and make beautiful things for people."

"Just stay away from ancient places of power," Rowan says, looking around, but the Time Dancer is nowhere to be seen.

Morde nods. "Would you like to have a meal with me or even stay overnight?"

"No!" Ali exclaims. I've spent enough time in this castle."

"You could go to Schönspitze, Morde," Samel says. "They'd probably welcome a silversmith."

"Let's leave as soon as possible," Atsu says. "Pack whatever food is available."

"I can help with that," Ali says.

"We can find places to camp along the way," Samel adds.

An eagle screams above. An owl hoots. A scatter of rain dampens heads. The ground shakes briefly, then it's still.

Regine Haensel's first book in The Leather Book Tales series, *Queen of Fire,* was short-listed as one of three finalists in the 2015 Young Adult Category of the High Plains Book Awards. The second book in the series, *Child of Dragons,* was published in 2017, and the third book, *Companion of Eagles,* was published in 2020.

She also has two published books of short stories: *The Other Place* and *A Rain of Dragonflies.* Her short stories and non-fiction have appeared in magazines and anthologies and have been broadcast on CBC Radio in Saskatchewan. She has won several Saskatchewan Writers' Guild Short Manuscript Awards.

Regine was born in Germany and came to Canada in the 1950's. She has worked as a waitress, teacher, advertising copy writer, and arts administrator. She lives in Saskatoon, Saskatchewan, Canada where she gardens and walks along the river when she isn't writing. She is currently working on another book in The Leather Book Tales world: *Time Dancer.*

Connect with Regine:
Facebook – Regine Haensel writer
Twitter - @RegineHaensel
Blog – serimuse.blogspot.com